RIVER'S EDGE

A River Collins Mystery Thriller

KATE GABLE

Byrd Books

Be the first to know about my upcoming sales, new releases and exclusive giveaways!

Want a Free book? Sign up for my Newsletter!

Sign up for my newsletter:
https://www.subscribepage.com/kategableviplist

Join my Facebook Group:
https://www.facebook.com/groups/833851020557518

Bonus Points: Follow me on BookBub and Goodreads!

https://www.goodreads.com/author/show/21534224.
Kate_Gable

About Kate Gable

Kate Gable is a 3 time Silke Falchion award winner including Book of the Year. She loves a good mystery that is full of suspense. She grew up devouring psychological thrillers and crime novels as well as movies, tv shows and true crime.

Her favorite stories are the ones that are centered on families with lots of secrets and lies as well as many twists and turns. Her novels have elements of psychological suspense, thriller, mystery and romance.

Kate Gable lives near Palm Springs, CA with her husband, son, a dog and a cat. She has spent more than twenty years in Southern California and finds inspiration from its cities, canyons, deserts, and small mountain towns.

She graduated from University of Southern California with a Bachelor's degree in Mathematics. After pursuing graduate studies in mathematics, she switched gears and got her MA in Creative Writing and English from Western New Mexico University and her PhD in Education from Old Dominion University.

Writing has always been her passion and obsession. Kate is also a USA Today Bestselling author of romantic suspense under another pen name.

Write her here:
Kate@kategable.com
Check out her books here:
www.kategable.com

Sign up for my newsletter:
https://www.subscribepage.com/kategableviplist

Join my Facebook Group:
https://www.facebook.com/groups/833851020557518

Bonus Points: Follow me on BookBub and Goodreads!

https://www.bookbub.com/authors/kate-gable

https://www.goodreads.com/author/show/21534224.Kate_Gable

- amazon.com/Kate-Gable/e/B095XFCLL7
- facebook.com/KateGableAuthor
- bookbub.com/authors/kate-gable
- instagram.com/kategablebooks
- tiktok.com/@kategablebooks

Also by Kate Gable

FBI Agent River Collins Mystery Thriller
River's Edge (Book 1)
River's Shadow (Book 2)

Detective Kaitlyn Carr Psychological Mystery series
Girl Missing (Book 1)
Girl Lost (Book 2)
Girl Found (Book 3)
Girl Taken (Book 4)
Girl Forgotten (Book 5)
Gone Too Soon (Book 6)
Gone Forever (Book 7)
Whispers in the Sand (Book 8)

Girl Hidden (FREE Novella)

FBI Agent Alexis Forest Mystery Thriller

Forest of Silence
Forest of Shadows
Forest of Secrets
Forest of Lies
Forest of Obsession
Forest of Regrets
Forest of Deception

Detective Charlotte Pierce Psychological Mystery series
Last Breath
Nameless Girl
Missing Lives
Girl in the Lake

About River's Edge

FBI Agent River Collins knows firsthand the terror of being taken. Twenty years after escaping her own abductor, she still carries the scars—and he was never caught. Now, in the quiet college town of Charlottesville, Virginia, two mothers have vanished on their way to pick up their children from school, leaving behind empty cars and unanswered questions.

While her sister enjoys the picture-perfect life River could never achieve—marriage, children, a beautiful home—River throws herself into the investigation, recognizing patterns that only someone with her traumatic past could see. But as the case intensifies, so do her nightmares, forcing River to confront the darkness she's spent two decades trying to outrun.

With time running out for the missing women and her own past threatening to derail the investigation,

River must decide if facing her demons will be the key to solving the case—or her ultimate undoing.

Suspenseful and full of thrills, River's Edge is the first book in a new addicting FBI mystery series from bestselling and 3-time Silver Falchion award winning author Kate Gable.

1

River

There's a reason I prefer to wait until the office clears out a little before I start on paperwork, also known as the bane of my existence. Distractions, for one thing. As absorbed as I tend to get while I'm in the middle of a case, the paperwork side of things bores me to tears. The slightest distraction – someone passing in the hall, a phone ringing, soft laughter from the breakroom–and my subconscious jumps at the opportunity to think about something, anything, more interesting. Fewer distractions means I'm able to work faster.

At the moment, that's sort of impossible.

"I'm telling you." The sounds of a bag crinkling are almost enough to set my teeth on edge as Agent Daniel Brennon fishes for the last chocolate covered pretzels inside. The vending machines here at the field office are always good for a pick-me-up. Sometimes, my entire day's meals are purchased from them. Not exactly healthy, but they get the job done.

He gestures toward Agent Emma Bertanelli with a pretzel before popping it in his mouth. "It's fine for somebody without kids to set all these rules about organic foods and setting limits on TV time, but when you're on your third day in a row of minimal sleep and nothing else will make them stop fussing, all of that goes straight out the window."

She rolls her eyes, sighing while slumping a little in her chair. I wouldn't call this my office, per se, but it's large enough for me to keep extra furniture, which is a step up from some of the tiny, cheerless cubicles where new agents cut their teeth. "I know, I know," she sighs, running a hand through her black curls. I've always envied her hair, so thick and wild unlike my limp, mousy brown locks. "Nobody ever told me having a baby would make me question literally every choice I ever make." She pops a few pieces of candy into her mouth, grunting as she chews.

"Believe me," he tells her, nodding slowly. "By the time you hit number three, you're just glad everybody's alive and breathing at the end of the day. Everything else will work itself out."

Even though most of my attention is on my computer screen, I catch him looking my way from the corner of my eye. "I bet this kind of conversation has you champing at the bit to start a family."

"How could I not, when the two of you make it sound so much fun?" They understand my dry sense of humor and penchant for sarcasm after having been part of the same team for years. Though I wasn't really making a joke. When I try to imagine being responsible for a life other than my own, my mind pulls up nothing but question marks and thick fog. I can't picture it.

"Hopefully when your time comes," Emma points out, "you'll have a nice, contented baby who doesn't scream for you every second you're around." I look her way in time to catch her miserable frown. "Maybe you won't feel like the world's worst mother for not being around more than you are."

I get the feeling this is where I'm supposed to say something, so I offer, "I think most mothers feel that way, and sometimes babies can be especially clingy. I know my sister went through that with her kids." Was that enough? I hope so. I don't really know any further details – besides, I would like to get my paperwork done before it's time to start another workday in the morning.

Daniel crumples his bag and tosses it in my wastebasket before throwing his arms overhead and stretching. He's in good shape for a man in his early 40s, and can still run circles around some of our youngest agents. "Speaking of which, I better get moving. Claire has the twins at soccer practice and I promised I would grab dinner on the way home so it's waiting by the time they get there."

Emma stands next, tipping the candy bag into her mouth so she can finish the rest. "Yeah, I'd better get moving, too. So should you," she concludes with a pointed look in my direction.

"Oh? Who says?"

"I say."

"There you go, having a baby and treating everybody around you like they're your kid."

She takes that with nothing more than an arched eyebrow. Emma is the closest thing to a friend I have, though that isn't saying much. I'm no good at making friends and even worse at keeping them. "Somebody has to look after you," she reminds me. "Now that this case is wrapped, you deserve a little time to decompress."

"I'll be fine. I am more than capable of getting my work done and going home."

"If only that wasn't all you do."

I need to end this conversation before it gets heated. There isn't much in this world that gets under my skin as easily as people who think they understand me and know what I need. I don't comment on their lives or tell them what to do. Why is it so important that I have a social life? "You of all people know how exhausting this job is." Leaning back in my chair, I offer a shrug. "I don't even have a dog because I'm not sure I can be home for them."

"And yet somehow, I found a way to get married and start a family."

She means well. Stand down. It's not easy to cool the bubbling irritation her comments spark. Part of living in the world and being a part of it is learning to live with people who can't relate to me. I'm not going to make it their problem – especially not Emma, who has come through for me more times than I can count. Besides, some things can't be understood without personally going through them. People can express concern. They can be sorry, they can commiserate, but they can't understand.

"One more report, Mom." Somehow, I manage to

sound like I'm joking and even eke out a smile that leaves my jaw aching.

"I know that's the best I can hope for." She's shaking her head as she walks away, clearly disapproving.

My relief is real. Tension I was unaware of drains from my muscles now that I'm alone. My social battery is officially drained now, something I've tried to work on especially for the sake of my career. There are days when countless interviews are required, meaning I have to suck it up and interact with people, no matter how low my social battery happens to run. I've made progress, for sure, considering there were days when a simple conversation with the cashier at the grocery store was downright unthinkable.

My eyes are tired, burning by the time I've finished my report. Hours of sitting at my desk have left my back in knots. I push back from my desk and bend at the waist, stretching out the tight muscles before getting up and getting my things together.

There are plenty of floors at the field office that will be just as busy no matter what time of day, but it's quiet around me as I make my way past rows of desks, nodding to anyone who happens to look up and notice me. Special Agent Siwak told me a long time ago that my naturally standoffish personality can be mistaken for rudeness. Granted, I don't care very much either way whether anybody thinks I'm rude, but that seems to matter to some people. I'll play along if I have to.

As always, once the elevator door slides shut, I begin my preparation. In one hand, I hold a can of mace pulled from the inside pocket of my shoulder bag. The other hand is devoted to my keys, which I thread through my fingers before the doors slide open into the bleak, concrete parking garage.

I know there are people who would find it funny, an FBI agent looking over her shoulder everywhere she goes. I'm supposed to be able to protect myself, right? If I can't, who can? If there's one thing my work has taught me, though, it's the overlap between people who assume they can handle everything and people to whom tragedies occur.

Life taught me quite a bit about that, too.

After checking the Civic's interior as a matter of habit, I open the door and slide behind the wheel. Good thing I'm only a five-minute drive from the field office—my eyes are positively burning. Emma was right about one thing; I'm worn out after closing my last case. Agent Siwak questioned whether I could handle it, which of course left me more determined than ever to throw myself into the work. Tonight, there are a few less child traffickers out there in the world.

A few more nightmares plaguing me, but then that's nothing new. I once heard grief described as a song that's always playing, with only the volume changing from time to time. Trauma is like that, too. The nightmares will never completely vanish, but there are times when they lessen a little. Then there are times when they torture me every time I close my eyes. It will be a relief to get home, where if I can't sleep well I can at least be alone and recharge.

No such luck. I've barely backed out of my parking

space before my phone rings with an incoming call from Agent Siwak. My senses go on high alert before I answer.

"Hey, boss," I murmur. "I've barely been out of the building five minutes. Do you miss me that much?"

"Your presence does add a sparkle to the surroundings," he replies with a dry chuckle. "But no, this doesn't have to do with missing you. It has to do with a press conference the Charlottesville PD are about to hold regarding the disappearance of two young mothers who never picked their kids up from Shenandoah Elementary this afternoon."

Immediately an image comes together in my mind. Upper class women, probably homemakers, probably much too involved in their children's lives for this to be anything but an emergency. Women like my sister, whose entire life revolves around her home and her family. The sort of thing the media eats up with a spoon.

"I was about to head home to a microwave dinner, but I guess I can head to the sheriff's office, instead." I'm already on the way, turning right instead of left once I reach the bottom of the garage ramp.

"I knew I could count on you to be my eyes and ears down there. Just… be careful," he urges in a voice full of understanding and maybe a touch of apprehension. "You know how it is when the locals get a whiff of the Bureau sniffing around their territory."

"Don't worry," I assure him while making the short drive down dark, busy streets. Strange how the exhaustion that plagued me minutes ago is nowhere to be found now. "I'll use my natural charm."

His snort tells me he got the joke. "That's what worries me."

2

River

There's barely space to move my arms in this conference room.

Breathe. In, out. There's nothing inherently bad about being in a tightly crowded space. There is no threat here beyond being forced to smell the onions on the breath of some nearby reporter who needs to practice breathing through their nose. I'm safe.

I wasn't wrong about the media eating this up with a spoon. They're much too transparent. Practically salivating like hungry dogs while we wait for the chief to get started. There's a white screen set up behind a podium and a young uniformed cop fiddles around with a laptop in preparation. There's a lot of murmuring, soft questions, confusion over why this is taking so long to get started.

"Ladies and gentlemen, we're going live in three minutes." The announcement sends a wave of energy through the room, like ripples on an already churning sea. I get my notepad ready, pointedly ignoring the pressing in of bodies on all sides. Charlottesville is a quiet town. Things like this don't happen often here. All the more reason for everybody to jump on a story like this.

It's morbid, but I understand the reason for their eagerness, and it leaves me swallowing back a sense of mild disgust. There's a reason the word vulture is used so often when referring to journalists. They pick every bit of meat off a carcass before posting photos online for everyone to see.

A hush falls over the room when a man somewhere between his mid-fifties and early sixties steps up to the podium. He removes his hat, revealing a head of close-cropped gray hair. This is a man who's used to being stressed, strained, the lines on his face a virtual map of the cases he's seen, handled, maybe neglected to close.

His voice is low, gruff, when he begins. "Good evening. Thank you for joining us here for this announcement. We need to make the public aware of the disappearance of two Charlottesville residents at some point today. The timeline is still foggy, but we know for certain these two women dropped their children off at Shenandoah Elementary this morning, but neglected to pick them up at the usual time. Since then, both women have been out of reach of their loved ones, something which is highly unusual. We are currently tracking their credit card activity and security footage in the area in hopes of spotting them."

"Tamara Higgins." The image of a woman in her early forties appears on the screen behind Chief Mark Perkins' head. It looks like she was dressed up for some sort of event, considering her makeup and jewelry. Pretty, with bright blue eyes and hair somewhere between dirty blond and light brown. The camera's flash probably had something to do with that.

"And Beth Clyburn." The image changes, now revealing a petite brunette wearing what looks like workout gear, her hair in a high ponytail, AirPods in her ears. It looks like she just got back from a run and she's glowing, grinning for the photographer.

The captain continues. "This afternoon at approximately three o'clock, the principal of Shenandoah Elementary School placed a call to the spouses of the women in question when their children were not picked up from school and the women's phones went unanswered. Once their husbands were unable to reach them, a call was placed to the police department. Since then, the department has conducted a cursory search of the area and contacted family and friends of these women in hopes of tracking their location, but nothing came of our efforts. It was at that point this was considered an active disappearance."

Watching him, I scribble on my pad without looking at the page. It's something that drives Emma crazy whenever she has to check my notes. "How can you read this chicken scratch?" Like it's not enough for me to be able to read my writing.

Husbands? Other kids? Friendship, connection? It does seem strange for two unrelated women to go missing on the same day. I want to know how they knew each other, whether they were close. Could it be a case of women joining forces to leave unhappy situations? Anything could be possible at this point.

"Was there any evidence of a struggle found in either of the homes?" one of the reporters calls out.

The chief's bulldog expression doesn't change. "At this time, we are not going public with details out of an abundance of caution, but we will keep the public posted on any pertinent developments. In the meantime, we ask you all to keep your eyes out for any sign of these two women."

The image changes, now a split screen between the two photos. On the surface, they're very similar. Roughly the same age, pretty, healthy.

Once the conference is over and the room begins to empty, the chief is in my sights. I manage to hold back while he has a quiet conversation with a pair of plainclothes detectives, their badges hanging from lanyards around their necks the way mine does. I make a point of adjusting it now, making sure it's visible. If there's one thing local PD generally doesn't appreciate, it's the presence of the FBI. The way they see it, we're telling them they don't know how to do their jobs. Sadly, that can sometimes be the case.

"Captain Perkins?" I raise a hand to catch the man's attention as he peels away from the detectives.

Immediately, his steely eyes go narrow while the lines already bracketing his mouth deepen in a frown. "Can I help you?"

Be cordial. You can catch more flies with honey than with vinegar. The words run through my head as I force a brief, professional smile. "Agent River Collins, sent down from the field office."

He's unimpressed, folding his arms rather than shaking my hand. "We didn't request FBI presence here."

"You might want to take that up with my boss, then, since he sent me down. Special Agent Eric Siwak. I'll give you his number if you would like to call him directly." Easy, easy. Pump the brakes.

Captain Perkins' eyes harden, but it's clear he understands I'm not playing around. He's not going to get me to back down. "What is it I can help you with?" he grunts, sizing me up. Normally, I don't mind being a little on the short side—if anything, I enjoy proving people wrong when they assume I'm a pushover at only a few inches over five feet.

At times like this, though, I find myself standing up straighter, making myself look larger. "For starters, we'd like a little more information on the case. Specifics. I need to get in touch with the husbands, take a look at the homes."

"One thing at a time, Agent." He says it like it's a dirty word, something I should be ashamed of. I notice the looks being shot my way by the local officers who spot me following the chief from the conference room to a small, cluttered office down the hall. He didn't invite me to follow him, but I'm not about to hold my breath and wait.

"The clock is ticking," I remind him once he's behind his desk, heaving a sigh as he opens a folder which I assume holds any information he currently has. "The sooner we can hit the ground running, the better."

I watch, impatient as he heaves a pained sigh once again. "We already have cruisers on the streets, officers going door-to-door in the neighborhood. Nice neighborhood, everybody knows each other."

"So they live in the same neighborhood?"

"Their kids go to the same school, Agent Collins." The man turns sarcasm into an art form. "Yeah, they live in the same neighborhood. Opposite sides, though."

There's a faint ringing in my ears that always accompanies being spoken down to. "What are the spouses saying?"

"What do you think? They don't have the first idea where the wives could be, they've always been reliable, dependable. No problems at home, nothing to hint at any reason to pick up and walk away. The usual."

For these families, this is anything but usual. "Is there anything unusual here? What about the cars? Do we have eyes out for their vehicles?"

"Both vehicles were at their homes."

Interesting. "So there's no saying they ever left to pick up the kids today," I conclude. "They may have left the house, but it wasn't to go to the school."

"It could be," he agrees. "For now, that's the most we can share. The husbands insist their wives would never just, you know, walk out. They don't seem like the type, either," he admits, running a hand over his stubble covered jaw.

"No, they don't," I agree, staring over his shoulder at the wall behind him but seeing those two women, instead. Bright, sunny smiles. Probably the first to volunteer at school. If they're anything like my sister, they're highly involved in their homes, with their kids. "What are the ages of the children?" I ask as an afterthought.

He looks down at his file. "Tamara Higgins has a nine-year-old daughter and a seven-year-old son. Beth Clyburn has a pair of boys, nine and six."

"So it's not outside the realm of possibility that the two nine-year-olds were in the same class," I muse. "It could tie the women together."

"Plenty of things could tie the women together," he points out. "Now if you'll excuse me, I have a few phone calls to make."

I have been dismissed. Once again, I have to grind my teeth to keep my irritation in check. My emotions are running high, something I can't afford if I want to maintain any semblance of a professional relationship. I might need his help at some point down the line, so it won't do any good to alienate him.

With a tight, professional smile, I murmur, "Thank you for your time. I'll be in touch."

On my way through the door, I hear him grumble behind me. "I don't doubt it."

Pushing it aside, I head straight for the exit. I'm craving a breath of fresh air after being crammed in for so long with so many people. I need to clear my head.

I also need to cool down, to center myself. My hands are shaking as I tuck my notebook in my bag, ghosts of the past are crowding me the way those bodies did in the conference room. This time, there's no hope of getting away from them. I've carried them with me for more than half my life. They aren't going anywhere.

3

Tamara

The Day Of

"You have your gym clothes, right?" When Molly doesn't answer, I have to repeat myself, raising my voice to get her attention. "Moll? Gym clothes. Do you have them?"

"Yeah, I told you I do." She holds up her blue duffel bag with Shenandoah Elementary printed on the side. Disdain drips from her voice, making me cringe to think of the hormonal years ahead of us. Things are bad enough now.

"Excuse me," I tell her while pouring the rest of a smoothie into a travel cup, then leaving the blender carafe in the sink for when I get home. "Remind me again who left them at home last week?"

"That wasn't my fault." My daughter's light brown hair fans out behind her as she turns in a huff and marches to the front door. From where I'm standing in the kitchen, I can make out the way she folds her arms, her foot tapping on the floor. "And it looks like I'm the only one running on time."

"I'm coming!" Josh gives me an exasperated groan, rolling his eyes at his sister's antics. At seven, he's more level headed than she is. The girl is nine years old going on sixteen.

A happy morning sets the tone for the entire day. One of my mother's old adages runs through my head before I put on a smile and pretend my daughter's attitude doesn't sadden me the slightest bit. We were so close not so long ago. Now, her life revolves around the latest TikTok dances and whatever else her friends tell her is cool.

It wasn't so long ago I cared just as much about being liked, being cool, knowing about the latest trends. Childhood is hard enough without feeling like you're standing on the outside, looking in.

"Miss Clay asked if you were gonna help with the bake sale next week." Josh tosses his backpack into the minivan before climbing in. "I'm supposed to tell her today."

"Of course," I reply as a matter of habit. "Have her text me about it. Tell her I said whatever she needs."

"Did you sign the form for my field trip?" Molly asks from her seat, where she is already on her iPad. She's not allowed to bring it into school, which of course means she hovers over it like it's the most precious thing in the world in the final moments before drop-off.

"It's in the folder in your backpack," I tell her,

backing out of the driveway and rolling down the street. Their chatter mixes with the music coming through the speakers, and I allow myself to relax a little. We got out of the house on time and traffic is light.

There's no denying a brief but potent sense of relief once I send the kids off, waving goodbye from the driver's seat, watching them walk up the concrete pathway leading to the double doors. Molly finds a few friends further up and waves before dashing after them, while Josh's best friend Drake meets him on the steps.

I can breathe now. This part of my morning is complete.

Now there are errands to run. David's dry cleaning needs to be dropped off and the finished items picked up, then there's a stop at the post office to pick up stamps. I need to get out invitations for Josh's birthday party in a few weeks.

On the way home I grab a latte from Starbucks, chatting with a couple of moms from the neighborhood whose names I don't quite remember but whose faces are very familiar. David is so much better at remembering names than I am. Finally, the barista calls out their names when their order is finished, so at least I can remember for next time. There's nothing like the relief of avoiding an awkward social situation.

That's the thing about Charlottesville I've never quite gotten used to. It's a beautiful, safe place, somewhere I'm blessed to call home. Somewhere I feel secure raising my children.

All of that comes with a price. The feeling of always

being watched, judged. That behind the friendly smiles and friendly curiosity lies cold judgment.

David never fails to wave off my concerns on the rare occasions I share them with him. As far as he's concerned, I have nothing to worry about, nothing to complain about, nothing to second-guess myself over. "Those women look at you and wish they could be you," he tells me all the time. What he doesn't understand is how admiration can turn to envy at the drop of a hat, and how everything goes downhill from there.

Once I'm home and everything is tidied up after a typical rushed morning, I enjoy a sense of satisfaction in admiring my sparkling kitchen. There is a deep sense of pride in my home, and I enjoy it more easily in these quiet moments when there's nobody begging for my attention, nobody asking questions. I can set aside my calendar for a little while in favor of doing something for me, which I forget about more often than not anymore. I'm trying my best to stay consistent with my work – even if I do nothing with it, it's nice to have something for me.

As usual, stepping into the converted second-floor bedroom makes me smile. Just being in this room, surrounded by my supplies, reminds me of who I am. Not that there's anything wrong with being a wife and a mother. My family is my deepest source of fulfillment. I take pleasure in caring for the people I love.

But there's something to be said for sitting down in front of a blank canvas, pallet in hand, and creating something that didn't exist until I birthed it from my imagination. This is mine, only mine, the bright, bold colors bringing the canvas to life. Soft, classical music plays through a speaker hooked up to my phone, and before I know it, I'm lost in the process of creating something new. I'm not sure what it is yet. I only know it's bright, brilliant, that it holds nothing back. Sort of the way I wish I could be.

I used to be that way. What happened? What changed? Did I change? I told myself I wouldn't, that marrying a successful lawyer and devoting my energy and creativity to maintaining our home and raising our children wouldn't change who I was at my core. I told myself I would still have my own life, that I would tend to my own needs. I wonder how many women tell themselves the same thing, only to wind up where I am now.

Vivid shades of red, blue, and gold fill the canvas as I sink deeper into the creative process. As my brush glides over the canvas, my tangled thoughts untangle and smooth out. I have nothing to complain about, really. I live the kind of life many people dream of.

It's what those people don't understand that leaves me with this annoying feeling deep inside. How challenging it can be for a person who was already prone to anxiety. The sense of the bar being set a little higher all the time. Just when a person reaches what they told themselves was the pinnacle – the right car, the right clothes, the right body type even – there's some new hurdle to jump over. It never ends. How does anybody ever feel like they're good enough?

I pour it all out across the canvas, the brush moving without me thinking about it. This is how I work out my frustrations and settle my nerves. It doesn't matter if nobody else ever sees it. So long as I do, that's all I need.

I also need to hurry. My watch beeps, letting me know it's time to clean up if I'm going to make it to school in time to pick the kids up. Amazing the way the hours fly by when I'm deeply involved. I clean up quickly, clearing the paint off my pallet, cleaning the brushes, finally hanging my smock on a hook embedded in the wall beside my easel. I'm not finished yet, but I've come a long way.

I give the colorful canvas a smile before heading out, feeling more clear headed and sure of myself than I did before I started working. It always does the trick.

4

River

The Higgins house is impressive. That's the first word that comes to mind when I come to a stop at the curb and gaze across a gorgeous, emerald green lawn. The two-story brick structure is set far back at the end of a curved driveway which I would rather not drive up at the moment. It would feel too much like an invasion if I was the one sitting in that house, wondering where my wife or mother had disappeared to.

It's now seventeen hours after Tamara and Beth failed to pick up their kids yesterday afternoon, and local law enforcement still have no answers. On the surface, it looks like these women vanished off the face of the earth.

That's not possible. Nobody simply vanishes. Some things, I know from experience. It's possible that even after two entire years, a person can reappear as if from the dead.

I have to shake myself free of those thoughts before forcing myself out of the Civic. If I'm not careful, I'll drown in the memories. There's no time for that. Two women are still missing, and I know too well the feeling of waiting and hoping and praying somebody was looking for me. I can only imagine they're thinking the same thing, not to mention worried sick about their kids... and whether they'll get home to them.

As I walk up the wide driveway, I can't help but catalog everything I see. It's not only the lawn that's manicured within an inch of its life. Neatly trimmed rose bushes featuring lush blooms in red, pink, and white line the front of the house. Their fragrance reaches me around halfway up the driveway, and I wonder how much time and effort it takes to keep them looking so healthy and vibrant. Does Tamara do that herself? The lawn, I can imagine being outsourced, but the roses strike me as a labor of love.

There are no signs of the kids out here – no bikes, no sports equipment. This doesn't seem like the sort of house where the parents let their kids go wild outside. It makes me think back on my childhood home, the basketball hoop over the garage door, the ever-present bicycles leaning against the wall.

There's a basket on the front stoop with a big yellow bow attached to the handle. There are baked goods inside, protected from the elements by cellophane. I'm still studying the contents when I ring the doorbell. This sound chimes inside, and the absence of little voices and footsteps strikes me as a point of interest. Where are the kids?

The door opens and I'm greeted by a tall, good-looking man who appears to be in his mid-to-late forties.

There's a touch of silver at his temples, but the rest of his hair is a rich golden color. I can imagine it being neatly combed any other time, but now it's a little disheveled like he's been running his hands through it. That, plus the circles under his eyes hint at a man who's been through a lot in the past day.

"David Higgins?" He nods, wary. "My name is Agent River Collins. I was assigned by Special Agent Siwak down at the field office. I'm investigating your wife's disappearance."

He looks a little distracted, his fingers raking through his hair yet again. His eyes are a pale blue which stands out in sharp contrast to his bloodshot whites. "I've already talked to the police," he tells me. As if that puts an end to my visit.

This is not the response I was expecting. Not even close. "I understand," I tell him, speaking more carefully. If I were in his shoes, the first words out of my mouth would be a question as to whether anything new has been found out. But maybe that's just me. "I was hoping to get a little more information from you. Anything you might have missed last night. I'm sure it was a very trying, emotional time. The hope is, you've remembered something since then which might point us in the right direction."

"Do you have a badge or something?" he asks, his gaze sweeping the space behind me. What is he expecting? For somebody to jump out and yell boo?

"Of course." I unzip my plain black jacket and hold up the badge hanging from my lanyard. "Do you mind if we step inside? I could use a glass of water, if you wouldn't mind. And I'd hate to see this basket forgotten on the doorstep," I add, lifting it and handing it over. I'm afraid the man won't let me in if I don't flat-out ask. I would rather not conduct this interview on the front stoop.

His eyelids flutter before he releases something close to a chuckle. "Sorry. I'm not exactly thinking clearly. By all means." He steps back, opening the door wider, revealing a striking foyer featuring a winding staircase and an ornate iron chandelier. The first thing I notice is how absolutely pristine the house is. Alarmingly clean, even. There is not so much as a hint of the children anywhere except for photos on the walls and lined up along what looks like an antique credenza. Cute kids, bright and hopeful looking. How quickly hope can die. I hope that's not the case for them.

"The kitchen is this way." David leads me there, shuffling along in a pair of moccasins, dressed in gray sweatpants and a Vanderbilt t-shirt.

"Did you attend Vanderbilt?" I ask, glancing around, taking in my surroundings. The floors are clean enough to eat off of, and there isn't so much as a fingerprint on a window.

"I did," he tells me. There's an obvious note of pride in his voice. "Then Yale Law."

"That's impressive." Even more impressive is the kitchen to the left of the foyer, a room or roughly four times the size of my apartment with ceilings that must stretch at least fifteen feet overhead. Everything is top-of-the-line, down to the glass doored refrigerator with its built-in touchpad and a beautiful, navy blue stove and range hood.

"Is that a La Cornue?" I ask, nodding toward the shining stove.

"It sure is. Are you an admirer of the brand?" he asks before reaching into the refrigerator for a bottle of water which he opens for me.

"My sister has one," I explain, leaving out the part where I know it costs around twenty grand. Clearly, Mr. Higgins is doing well with that Yale degree.

He perches on a stool at the long, wide island positioned in front of the stove. "Tell me somebody has found something by now," he almost begs.

"I'm afraid not, which is why I'm looking for more information we can work with." I look around, confirming what I noticed from the start. "Where are the kids? Are they aware of what's going on?"

He shakes his head, frowning. "They're smart kids," he finally murmurs, sounding more than a little defeated. "I'm sure they know something's wrong. They're with my mom right now."

"I see. I'm sure that's for the best." Some people might argue spending time with their father would be better for them. Looking at him, though, it's clear he's a mess. Being here probably wouldn't do them any favors.

"I just don't know how this could have happened. I really don't. This is so unlike her." He scrubs a hand over his head before releasing a defeated sigh. "She wouldn't have left. No way. Not on her own."

"What makes you so certain of that?" I ask while

withdrawing my notepad and uncapping my pen, taking a stool across from him.

At first, he looks at me like I'm crazy. He then releases a breathless laugh that holds no humor. "I mean, look around. This house is her life. Our home. Our family. I've asked myself more times than I can count how she finds the time to get it all done and take care of herself."

"Does she?" I ask. "Take care of herself, I mean. Did she make that a priority?"

It's clear he wasn't expecting that question. In fact, he looks at me like I've lapsed into a foreign language. For a few long seconds, the only sound in the room is that of the clock on the wall ticking away. Finally, he releases a sigh, lifting his broad shoulders. "Honestly, I couldn't tell you. I want to say yes, but I also want to be honest. I can't honestly say."

A sudden ringing makes us both jump before he fumbles to pull his phone from his pocket. "Sorry. It's been ringing all day." He takes a look at the screen, frowns, then silences the call before leaving the device face down on the countertop.

"I'm sure there are plenty of people who care about your wife."

"I've gotten nonstop calls since the press conference last night. People I never heard of. I don't even know how they got my number," he confesses, sounding bewildered. "And this basket? That's the third so far." He reaches inside and pulls out a card which he quickly skims before setting it aside. I glance toward the refrigerator and now notice two cakes inside, along with three covered casserole dishes. I've never understood why people feel the need to provide food at a time like this. Who wants to eat when they're distraught?

Was that what my parents' refrigerator looked like in the early days?

Not the time. It takes effort to pull my thoughts back to the present moment. "This seems like a tight knit community," I observe.

"Definitely. That's one thing Tam always appreciated. The way everybody looks after everybody else. I can't tell you how many times I've come home from work and found her finishing off a batch of cookies for something or other. A bake sale, a birthday party, stuff like that."

"Does your wife have a lot of friends?"

Again, something alarmingly close to confusion washes over his chiseled face. "To tell you the truth, I'm not sure. She certainly knows everybody. She's on a first name basis with every mom in the kids' classes. We can't go out shopping without her running into somebody who recognizes her. She's practically a celebrity."

That isn't the same as having friends. I should know. "Well, she sounds like a very busy person, so I guess it would make sense. But there's a world of difference between having a bunch of acquaintances and having friends."

"You're right." He sounds bewildered. Can this be the first time he's given serious thought to his wife's life?

Why doesn't he know her better – if that's the problem at all? Is he this clueless, or is he trying to hide something? Why is he so vague about her life? He can't name a single friend of hers? I find it hard to believe she doesn't have any at all. Not everybody operates the way I do. Not everybody has a reason to.

"What does she do with her free time, if she has any?" Looking around, I add, "I can imagine taking care of the home and the family eats up a lot of time."

"What is this all about?" he blurts out, taking me by surprise. "How are these questions going to help anything? You're supposed to be looking for my wife, and all you can do is ask me who her friends are? Why do I feel like I'm being interrogated?"

The sudden flash of irritation makes me sit up straighter, the hair on the back of my neck rising. Time to switch gears. "Tell me, Mr. Higgins. Is there a reason I should interrogate you? Exactly where were you yesterday when your wife was supposed to pick up the kids from school?"

5

River

The question hit home, that much is obvious. Color rises in his cheeks and his nostrils flare while his well-sculpted mouth tightens into a thin line. "What kind of question is that?"

"Considering the antagonistic tone, sir, I would say it's the next natural question." When all he does is sputter, I clarify. "I've asked about your wife to get a sense of who she may have run into yesterday. Whether there's anyone who may be able to provide further insight into what she does during the day when your children are at school and you, presumably, are at work."

"Presumably? What, do you think I'm lying about that?"

"Not at all. I'm sorry if I misspoke, but I've given you the wrong idea. I'm only saying—"

"I get what you're saying." His phone rings again and he grits his teeth before flipping it over. His scowl fades before he mutters, "My mother. Give me a second."

Rather than leave the room, he answers here and now. "Mom? What's that? No, it's fine, they can both have a Pop Tart. Just one, though, not the whole sleeve. Josh said what?"

For the first time since I arrived, his expression softens. "Tell him I said it's okay. Screen time rules don't have to apply today. Okay. Keep me posted."

He ends the call, still wearing a fond smile. "Can you believe that? Seven years old, and he tells his grandma he's not allowed to watch TV because he's only supposed to have an hour of screen time a day. What kid is that devoted to following the rules when his mom and dad aren't around?"

"He sounds like a good kid," I offer, glad for the opportunity to take a break from questions. "My niece is six, and I'm pretty sure she would forgo sleep in favor of watching TV."

"It's Tamara," he explains before groaning softly. "I'm sorry. You haven't caught me at my best today. I don't know which end is up. I only want my wife to come home."

"That's all I'm trying to help you with." I'll be darned if I don't pursue the funny feeling he gave me just a minute ago, when he let the mask slip and revealed the anger underneath. "Can you tell me where you were yesterday?"

"Where else? I was at the office."

"You're a lawyer?"

"Right. I have an office downtown."

"And what time did you leave your office yesterday?" I ask, pen poised.

He glances up at the ceiling for a second like he's thinking about it before shrugging. "Six o'clock."

Immediately, a red flag the size of the state of Texas waves in my head. "Six? I thought the principal over at Shenandoah Elementary reached out to you around three o'clock to say your wife hadn't picked the kids up."

His head bobs slowly. "I called my mom and asked her to do it."

It's not so much what he says, but how he says it. Like it's obvious enough that I shouldn't have to ask. "You weren't concerned? The way you made it sound, this is unlike your wife. You weren't worried enough to leave work?"

He may as well roll his eyes. What must it be like to live with a man so prone to disdain? "It's not that simple. We're in the middle of a major case. I have a team to consider. It's bad enough I'm not there now – my inbox has been blowing up all day. The world doesn't stop for something like this."

What a prince. I can see how he swept his wife off her feet. "Did anything seem off yesterday morning, before you left for the office? Did Tamara strike you as being in a bad mood? Was she feeling ill, complaining of a headache or anything else out of the ordinary? I'm only trying to rule out the possibility that she had a medical emergency somewhere."

"We don't usually have a lot of time together in the morning. I'm getting ready for the office, she's getting the kids ready for school."

I am starting to get a clearer picture of family life around here, and I have to wonder how this woman has managed to pilot the ship on her own all this time. Some people think it's enough to simply provide money for their family – not that being the breadwinner is any small feat. But too often, the breadwinner thinks that's all they need to do.

"So you say you left the office at six. When you spoke to the kids, did they mention anything strange happening yesterday? Maybe a discussion she had with one of the other moms outside of school? A close call with another driver? Did she seem agitated?"

His deepening scowl tells me clearly he's sick of this line of questioning. "I told you. My mom picked up the kids."

Unreal. Doesn't he see how strange that is? "So you haven't seen them at all?"

"Agent Collins, what do you want from me?" He throws his hands into the air, scoffing. "No, it's better for the kids to think of this as a fun little adventure. Grandma picked them up from school and took them to her house for the night. They're having Pop Tarts for breakfast and watching cartoons on a school day. Do you think it would be better for me to traumatize them needlessly when there's no telling exactly what happened?"

"That's a good point. I understand." Why is he so confrontational? Defensive, twitchy. He keeps cracking his knuckles, clenching and unclenching his jaw. The man is a bundle of nerves, even more so than I would normally expect in this situation. "Is there anything you can tell me for certain in relation to your wife's movements yesterday?"

"She left the house around two-thirty. That's when she normally leaves to pick up the kids from school."

Right away, his certainty makes me curious. He's been so vague up until now, but all of a sudden he knows exactly when his wife left the house. "How do you know that for sure if you were at your office?" I ask.

"We have a Ring camera," he informs me with a sigh. "I receive an alert on my phone whenever there's activity outside."

"Oh. I see." Making a note of this, I add, "I imagine you'd be willing to provide that footage to the police."

"If and when anyone asks, sure."

Quite the attitude he has. It isn't helping him. "And how would you describe your marriage?"

When his eyes fly open wide, it's clear I jumped too far ahead in questioning. What's the point of dancing around, pretending this isn't what I want to know? It's a waste of time, and more than enough of that has already passed. "This is all routine questioning," I assure him as he processes his shock. Agent Siwak's head might explode if he hears I blurted it out like that.

"Is that what this is about? Is that why you're here?" This time, when his phone rings, he ignores it in favor of glaring at me. "I invite you into my house, and all you can do is question the integrity of my marriage? You think I had something to do with this, don't you?"

If there's one thing I excel at, it's presenting a blank stare when I'm challenged by an angry interview subject. It's a skill I had to pick up years ago, when nothing mattered more than staying quiet and still. There's a lot of fog and darkness when I try to remember those days

—when I dare to search my memory—but that much is sharp. "As I said, it's a routine line of questioning in a situation like this. It's nothing personal."

"Sure," he replies, barking out a humorless laugh. "It just so happens you asked me a bunch of questions about my wife that I doubt any husband could reasonably answer when they work the sort of hours I do, then you decide to paint me as the bad husband who made his wife miserable enough that she ran away ... at best."

"Respectfully, sir, that is not at all what I intended." Though now that he's already opened the door, I may as well go all the way through. "However, I do find it odd that your wife's disappearance wasn't enough to get you out of the office."

"I told you—"

"I remember what you told me. I made a note of it." My pen taps against the notepad, but my eyes never leave his. "It strikes me as odd, like I said. If my always reliable wife suddenly neglected to pick up the kids and nobody could reach them, I would leave work in a heartbeat if only to make sure the kids were all right. I would want to check the house, in case there was a reason for her to return."

"I told you, I only got a notification that she left the house. There was never a notification that she came back."

I'm glad he mentioned that. "You were so busy with work that you weren't able to leave even in the case of an emergency, but you noticed an alert from your Ring camera as soon as your wife left the house?"

His brows knit together, eyes darting over my face

before he cracks his knuckles again. "I'm not sure what you're insinuating."

"I'm only wondering whether you really did notice the alert when it first came through, or if you happened to be monitoring the activity on the camera."

"Are you asking whether I check up on her?" When I nod, he shakes his head. "The answer is no. Obviously, I went back and looked at the footage to see if there was any clue on when she left. That's how I know for sure what time it was." There's sweat beading at his temples and his voice is slightly higher pitched than it was when we first spoke. I'm sure his heart is racing, too.

With his palms against the countertop, he stands, glowering at me. "I love my wife. She and my children are my world. I spent half the night pacing the house, going over every word we've spoken to each other in the last few weeks, trying to come up with an answer. Every time the phone rings, my heart stops. Is it the police, telling me they found her? If they did, what condition was she in? This is devastating, Agent Collins. And I resent the way you're making it sound like I have anything to do with it, because I don't. Perhaps if you would stop wasting time, you would have found her by now."

He may as well be reading directly from a book I've become acquainted with throughout my career. It's called *Things A Guilty Person Says*.

It's clear this interview is over. "I'll be in touch," I promise, noting his height when I stand. He's a big man. Has he ever loomed over his wife? "I can see myself out."

"Please do. And the next time you reach out," he calls out behind me, "Make sure you have some news for me."

Yes. Those are definitely the words of a man who had nothing to do with his wife's sudden disappearance.

6

River

"That sounds pretty sketchy to me." My little sister shakes her head while she stirs a pot of spaghetti sauce before replacing the lid. "I would hope if anything like that happened to me, Chris would be going out of his mind, trying to remember anything he could that might help the authorities."

I probably shouldn't have shared anything about my conversation with Tamara Higgins' husband, but it's not like I walked in here flapping my gums, ready to gossip. I only wanted to know if Leslie thought it was strange for a husband in his position to have no answers about his wife's life. I wouldn't know what's normal in a marriage beyond what I've seen from others. Emma tells a lot of stories about the way she and her husband work to navigate parenthood, and about how they still try to get together for dates whenever possible. That's around as far as my knowledge goes.

My gaze travels over her stove, which aside from the

difference in color is exactly the same as the one in the Higgins house. I then admire the perfectly coordinated backsplash which picks up the sage green of the stove and the pale pink enameled cookware Leslie uses. Everything has been thought out to the very last detail. She's always been very deliberate, intentional with her choices. Like her choice to leave the career she worked so hard to earn in favor of raising her kids.

It's not that I can't understand her motives, and I don't judge her choice. If she's happy, I'm happy, even if I can't imagine my whole world revolving around errands and play dates.

The problem is, I have to wonder if she's happy.

The kitchen opens onto a large, brightly lit family room where my niece and nephew are currently deeply absorbed in a video. While gazing fondly at them, I notice something. "Did you rearrange the furniture in there?"

Leslie glances back over her shoulder, blowing a strand of mahogany colored hair off her forehead. "Oh, yeah. I wanted to freshen things up a little. I'm considering new furniture."

Turning back to her, I ask, "Didn't you only buy that furniture after Bennett was born?" My nephew is only three years old, for heaven's sake. And the furniture is in better condition than anything I have in my apartment, but that isn't saying much.

"What's your point?" she asks in a light, overly bright voice that instantly gets my instincts pinging.

"There's no point." Because there's no point in starting a fight when I'm sort of trapped here for dinner.

I forgot we made these plans—that's nothing new, even at the very beginning of a case. I tend to suffer from an inability to compartmentalize. When I'm working, there's little hope of getting me to focus on anything else.

"We'll be eating in a few minutes. Hey, Ava?" she calls out, and like magic my niece's curly, dark head pops up. "Can you let Daddy know dinner is almost ready?"

"Aunt River! Come sit with me!" Bennett pats the cushion beside him, and my heart melts a little. He is such a sweet little boy.

"I'm supposed to be helping Mommy set the table." Strange, but I can relate so much better to him than I can to most people. Maybe because he doesn't ask anything of me but my presence. He's too young to know better.

"I'll help!" The next thing I know he's hurrying across the room the way only a little kid can do, smiling from ear to ear.

"Thank goodness. I'm no good at setting a table by myself." His little face glows, and now I'm very glad I came over tonight. This was what I needed, even if I didn't know it. The chance to release all of my questions and memories for a little while. What a shame he can't help me get rid of my nightmares.

"Hey, Ben?" Leslie winks down at him once she places a big bowl of salad on the table. "Ask your Aunt River what she's doing Friday night."

"Do you need a sitter?" I ask, already going through my schedule in my head. I doubt I'd have the time, though I could try to make it if necessary. I hope the kids don't mind me going through case notes the entire time I'm here.

She shakes her head before turning back toward the stove, but she's not fast enough to avoid me noticing her sly little smile. She's got something up her sleeve.

"Leslie?" I ask while a sinking feeling takes hold. "What aren't you telling me?"

"Chris has this friend…"

"Oh, you are kidding me." My brother-in-law had better hope he takes his time getting down here for dinner. "You are not setting me up."

"For dinner!"

"I do not have the time, and that's not a lie. When are you going to learn?"

"And when are you going to loosen up a little? You act like I'm asking you to do something painful or harmful or something." She plops the bread basket on the table hard enough that a couple of rolls bounce right out and roll across the polished surface. "You need more than your job to keep you going. There is more to life than work."

It's a good thing Bennett is currently setting napkins at each plate, or I might have to remind my sister that not everybody is interested in giving up everything they ever worked for in favor of making spaghetti and redecorating their house for the second time since they moved in eight years ago. We don't all want to live in a fancy, gated community with a golf course and all the other amenities. My blood pressure is starting to rise, and my ears are beginning to ring. This isn't going to end well.

"I do not appreciate being put on the spot, Leslie," I grunt, teeth clenched.

"And I do not appreciate my good intentions earning me nothing but a bad attitude, Rebecca," she grunts back. If I didn't know better, I'd think we were back in our childhood bedroom, fighting over who gets to use our shared laptop. Glaring at each other from across the room, our arms folded.

"Rebecca?" Ava asks as she skips into the room, her brown pigtails bouncing. "Who's Rebecca?"

"Remember? I told you a long time ago. River is my nickname," I explain, shooting my sister a dirty look. It must be nice, being able to use her kids as a shield. "My real name is Rebecca."

"How come they call you River?" Bennett asks as I help him into his chair.

"That's a silly nickname!" Ava declares, giggling.

"One time, years ago," I explain while pouring iced tea, "Grandma and Grandpa took us on a camping trip. We used to go a lot, up to the Blue Ridge Mountains."

Leslie's frown softens. "Dad always wanted us to love the outdoors the way he did," she recalls.

"That's right," I agree, chuckling. "One time, we camped close to a beautiful river not long after heavy rains had fallen. There was a morning when Grandpa woke up and found me sitting out there all by myself. Just watching the water racing past. That was when he started calling me River, and everybody else did too, after a while."

I can help but reflect as we sit down to eat how silly, incidental things like that can impact a person's life forever. I've been known as River since I was seven years old, because I happened to be enthralled by the river we happened to camp near on that particular trip. Life is funny that way.

My brother-in-law joins us for the first time since I arrived, leaning down for a quick hug from me before kissing Leslie. I can't help noticing the look they share, one that's full of affection. There must be something irreparably broken in me, because the sight leaves me fighting back a grimace. What would it be like, feeling confident and comfortable enough to be that openly affectionate with somebody else? To let myself trust? Other people do it all the time. Why can't I?

I know very well why I can't. It's the same reason why there were two years in which my sister and I didn't share that bedroom. She slept there alone, while I slept somewhere else. Somewhere dark, cold, cramped. The room that haunts my nightmares.

"So…" Chris clears his throat after taking his seat. His black hair gleams in the light from the new pendant lamps hanging over the table. "From what I overheard, it doesn't sound like the idea of having dinner with my friend Lucas went over very well."

"Are you surprised?" Leslie asks him, wearing a wide, entirely fake smile. "This is River we're talking about."

"Rebecca!" the kids remind her in unison, making me chuckle in spite of the situation.

"Either way," she continues, "there is no getting through to her. She's determined to chain herself to her desk and work her life away, all alone."

"Ouch," I mutter while plating spaghetti. "Harsh.

And I'll have you know I was going to agree before you insulted me that way."

"You were not," she retorts, rolling her eyes before accepting the spaghetti bowl once I pass it over. "You're only saying that now to have the last word. I know you too well."

"Believe whatever you want." I lift a shoulder, then unfold the napkin on my lap.

They exchange a long, questioning look while I watch from beneath lowered lashes. No, I don't want to go on a date. I have no desire to put myself out there like that. But there's also the matter of making sure my sister doesn't have the last word. She wasn't wrong about that.

"Fine." Leslie's all smiles and sweetness as she plates her food. "Chris will give him the all-clear to call you tomorrow and make your plans."

"He's a good guy," Chris insists. "You'll get along great."

It's going to take a lot of recharging to get my social battery ready for this.

7

River

What day is it?

Squeezing my eyes shut, I try to think. I'm pretty sure they feed me twice a day when I think about the type of food I get. Usually oatmeal or cereal or eggs in the morning, a sandwich later on in the day. The last tray was my forty-seventh ... or was it the forty-eighth? Either way, it's been weeks. That much, I know. I guess it doesn't matter how many.

A tear rolls down my cheek and I brush it away, almost angry with myself for crying. How many tears have I shed? That's a question I can't answer.

There are more too. Why was I so stupid? When is somebody going to come for me? Do they even know I'm still alive, waiting for them? Did they already give up on me? Am I going to be here for the rest of my life? And how long will that be? Because I don't know how long a person can live this way before they die. The only light I ever see comes from whatever light is outside when a new tray is left for me, or when a tray is taken away. Other than that, a thin beam of light comes in underneath the door, but even then it's only sometimes.

That's it, and even then, the light is bright enough to blind me a little when the door is open. It's too bright after being in the dark all day, every day. I can never make out what's outside this room. Whether there's a way out.

It stinks in here. I can smell my body after so many days without a shower or clean clothes, but what's worse is the bedpan thing in the corner farthest away from where I sleep. They actually gave me a bedpan to use. Besides that, there's the cot I'm now sitting on, wedged into the corner with my knees pulled up to my chest. The ceiling is low enough in here that I can't stand up straight without hitting my head and it's only a few steps in any direction before I hit a wall. This has to be a smaller, closed-off part of somebody's basement. Even though I can't see what's outside the door, I know what I don't feel, fresh air. There's no breeze, or wind, or rain. Nothing.

A soft whimper stirs in my throat, but I bite my tongue hard to keep quiet. It's not that I think anybody would hear me. I don't even think there's anybody on the other side of the door right now. I can always hear their footsteps right before the lock clicks, but that's it. Maybe the door itself isn't all that thick.

Either way, that's not why I have to fight the urge to cry and even scream. I know if I let myself start, it'll be almost impossible to stop. I did a lot of crying those first hours after I was taken and brought here. It didn't help anything. I'm still here, forty-seven or forty-eight trays later. Nothing changed except for needing to blow my stuffed-up nose and not having anything to do it with.

When are they going to let me take a shower? It's like there's a film on my skin. I feel slimy and filthy. My hair is stringy, greasy, hanging around my face since I don't have anything to pull it back with. I'm glad there isn't a mirror for me to look into. It's bad enough feeling this way. If I had to see myself, I might not be able to make it through. That might be what breaks me.

I only wish I knew why. Why am I here? What do they want me for? Nobody has said a word. I don't even know if it's the same person who leaves and takes my trays or picks up my bedpan every few visits. I can never see them. They're never here long enough for my eyes to adjust. I guess that's on purpose, but how long can that last? How long will I last before I have to beg them to speak to me?

What if they want to sell me to somebody? I've seen movies, the kind of movies Mom and Dad don't like me watching. I know what happens to girls sometimes. Is that going to happen to me? Are they only keeping me alive until I'm sold off?

How much longer do I have before that happens?

That's why I can't think about it. Whenever I start asking questions like that, the panic starts to rise in me. Panic isn't going to help. It didn't help me before, when I first figured out I was in trouble. I started to panic when I should've been paying attention to where I was and where we were going. But I didn't, and now I wouldn't even know where to go if I got free. Where is home? How far away is it? I would probably only run around in circles and get more and more lost before somebody caught up with me. The idea makes tears fill my eyes before I can help it. I can't think about this now. It only makes everything worse.

What else is there to think about, though? How cold I am? A shiver runs through me and I bite back a whimper before pulling myself into a tighter ball. They couldn't even give me a blanket. Why can't I at least have a blanket? What did I do to deserve this?

Squeezing my eyes shut again, I shake my head. I keep telling myself not to give in when it feels like something is sitting on my chest. Only babies can let themselves cry and scream. If I'm going to get out of this—and I have to somehow—I need to be brave. And I need to be smart.

That means I can't keep wondering how Mom and Dad are getting through this. Do they think I'm dead? Stop thinking about it. I can't help it. I love them too much. I hate to think of them being afraid for me.

If they're so afraid, why hasn't anybody found you yet?

Gritting my teeth doesn't help to quiet that voice in my head. It's mean, it's cruel, it asks awful questions and makes me wonder if anybody really cares where I am. Aren't the police supposed to be able to find girls like me?

What if they never do? What if I walked out of my house one day and didn't know that was the last time I would ever see it? What if I really am sold off and sent someplace far away? Will anybody remember me? Will they think of me on my birthday? Remember what I sounded like, what my favorite food was, anything?

My arms are folded on top of my knees and now I

rest my forehead on them, trembling, fighting the emotion and failing. I want to go home. I want Mom and Dad. I want my house. I want my bed, and my sister, and my life.

I must fall asleep at some point, because the next thing I know, footsteps on the other side of the door have me wide awake with my heart racing. I guess it is time for a new tray – my stomach is growling, but then it does that a lot.

At first, it grossed me out, having to eat without washing my hands first. Already it doesn't bother me as much, because I'm too hungry for it to matter. Is this what's going to happen to me now? Everything about me is going to change so I can survive. How much more of myself am I going to lose?

The thought of having to lose any part of myself makes me have a funny reaction while the footsteps get louder. I'm trembling again, only this time it's not out of fear. It's the opposite. I'm angry, furious, with my blood pounding and ringing in my ears while I wait for the door to open. Who do they think they are? What did I ever do to them? How dare they make me live in this filthy place where I'm not even able to see the sun?

By the time the lock clicks, I'm shaking so hard the cot squeaks. The door swings open slowly, and as usual the light on the other side is so bright, it blinds me before I can get a good look at whoever is here now. That might be the worst part of all. I can't even look in the face of whoever is doing this.

They don't wait around – they're probably too grossed out by the smell. By now, I recognize the sound of my tray hitting the floor. I guess they don't feel like taking my bedpan yet, because right away that dark figure steps out of my prison and starts to close the door. My mouth opens and I take a breath, but it's like I forgot every word I know. My tongue doesn't want to move. I don't know for sure what I would say, anyway. Or whether it would make a difference.

When the footsteps fade out, I crawl off the cot and creep across the floor until my toe hits the edge of the tray. I must really be turning into an animal, because knowing there's food here makes me drop to my knees and grab the sandwich waiting for me. Ham and cheese. I never used to like ham, but now it's the most delicious thing I've ever eaten. I should take my time and chew it more slowly, but it's enough effort just to chew it at all instead of swallowing it down right away. I know they aren't feeding me enough. The filthy, baggy clothes I'm wearing fit a lot better when I first put them on.

What was I even thinking about that morning? Probably something I thought was important. When I was a different person. Back before I knew there was a version of me that would crawl across a filthy floor and eat a sandwich like I had never eaten in my whole life.

I can only do this for so long. Somebody has to find me.

Otherwise, I might break for good.

8

River

It occurs to me that working on a missing persons case might not be the best idea.

Relax. That was then, this is now. You are safe. I know that's true, but in the moment? When my memory forces me to relive anything about that terrible, awful time? I might as well be back there, twenty years ago, slowly coming to the realization that nothing in my life would ever be the same. The growing dread, the understanding this wasn't going to have a quick, happy ending.

The desperation. The loneliness. It stirs in me even now, sitting behind the wheel of my car after parking in the field office garage. Physically, I'm here, but mentally? Emotionally? I'm that little girl again, twelve years old, snatched off the street. Hoping the people in my life loved me enough to find me or that the people who took me were stupid enough to leave a clue.

The only way to get through this is to actually get through it, which means no hiding out in my car the morning after dinner with the family. Sometimes, I don't know what drives my sister harder, keeping up the appearance of being satisfied with her life, or any sort of guilt she might feel after what happened to me. Not that I've ever done anything to make her feel guilty—at least, I sure hope I didn't. I've never wanted her to feel that way and would hate to imagine if she did.

But whenever she sticks her nose in my business and decides I can't possibly be happy the way I am, I have to wonder. Does she feel like there's something to make up for? Why does she figure it has to be her who does it? Last I checked, I'm the older sister.

These are the questions running through my head by the time I step off the elevator, but I guess that's better than almost having a panic attack thanks to the fresh, raw memories of those early days in captivity. Once again, I have to remind myself to greet people as I make my way across the floor, heading for my desk. Even when I was little, before my life got derailed, I didn't understand why people had to be nosy and inquisitive. What did you do last night, how was your weekend, do you have any plans ... what's the point? And that was before life itself gave me plenty of reasons to steer clear of most social situations. More often than not, I don't have it in me to pretend. I'm better off on my own.

How wonderful, then, that I have a date tonight. Lucas insisted he couldn't wait to meet me after Chris talked me up. I can't even bring myself to think about it as I pull the laptop bag's strap over my head and place it on my chair before pulling out the computer and opening it on my desk. My personal life or lack thereof can wait.

I haven't yet taken off my jacket when I hear him. Special Agent Siwak has a lot of qualities I admire, but the one that's benefited me the most over the years we've spent working together is his even-tempered nature. He's patient with me when I push harder than I probably should. He's not the sort of boss who rants and raves and bullies people to get results. I don't do well with being bullied and I'm more likely to talk back than bite my tongue. I guess certain social skills were taken from me along with the two years of my life spent living as a prisoner.

That's a real shame today, because Siwak is in a bad mood by the sound of it. "What I want to know is, what does a guy have to do around here to get a solid lead? We have two missing women and not a single lead to go on!"

He's heading my way, his voice louder all the time. Emma and Daniel are probably with him – though I hope for their sakes they managed to run and hide before he caught up to them.

No such luck for any of us, because I soon see all three of their heads bobbing over the top edges of the walls that make up the cubicles stretching from one end of the floor to the other. I barely have time to brace myself before he rounds a corner and comes marching straight toward me. "Does anyone want to explain why we have nothing? Am I the only one around here with a sense of urgency?"

Emma shoots me a pained look from behind him, while Daniel scrubs a hand through his hair, staring at the floor. He looks like he's already been dressed down this morning, shoulders sagging, a frown etched across his face.

"As a matter of fact," I tell them, "I was about to head down to the tech team and see if they found anything on Tamara's phone."

"It was left behind, right?" Agent Siwak asks.

"That's right. Her phone and car keys were still in the house when Mr. Higgins got home the night of the disappearance."

Daniel snickers, folding his arms. "You mean when he finally decided it was worth going home. I'm sorry, but I can't stomach the idea of staying at the office after someone called to tell me my wife was missing."

"We can't rule him out, but we can't focus all of our attention on him," Agent Siwak murmurs, shaking his head the way Daniel did. "I can't fathom it, either, but there's a world of difference between being a bad husband and being a threat to one's wife."

"You said you got a bad feeling from him, didn't you?" Emma asks me.

"He contradicted himself, he knew nothing about his wife's life, and he had yet to see his children the morning following their mother's unexplained disappearance. I don't like him at all – but that doesn't mean we can afford to lose all proportion and look only at him," I conclude. It's more for Agent Siwak's benefit than anyone else's. I know that's what he wants to hear.

Really, I would love nothing more than to follow David Higgins' every move. I want to know everything about him. Is there a girlfriend somewhere? Does he have financial problems, something he was hiding from

Tamara? I find it difficult to believe that a man who treats his wife like she's practically a stranger would be beyond keeping secrets.

"Let me know immediately once you've gotten information from the tech crew," Siwak concludes with a sigh. He's in his early sixties but normally could pass for ten years younger. Today, he's looking his age. Stress will do that. "There's no way two women from the same neighborhood vanished without a trace on the same day without anyone seeing anything. Somebody's got to know something."

His parting words ring out in my head as I jog down two flights of stairs to where people much smarter than me and with much more patience than I've ever possessed dig through phones and computers for evidence. They've had Tamara's phone since yesterday, once local officials secured a warrant for it. Our technology is head and shoulders above anything local PD could manage, hence the reason the phone is in our possession. After the way Chief Perkins treated me post-press conference, the idea of it sticking in his craw brings a genuine smile to my lips for the first time all day.

I've worked with Corey Blake in the past which, for some reason, gives him the impression we're buddies or something. He spins in his chair when I knock on the open door to his corner office, grinning as he looks me up and down. "There she is. How's the current today, River?"

He loves making jokes about my name. "It's moving pretty fast," I tell him through a forced smile. "Mostly because my boss is on my back about this case."

It almost feels like I've said the wrong thing. This is why it's preferable to be alone. His face falls slightly before he clears his throat. Which social cue did I miss this time? "Well, I wish I had some big breakthrough to share with you. I also wish for a few hundred million in my bank account."

My stomach sinks before he adds, "But there is something interesting."

Now he's speaking my language, his choice of words making the hair rise on the back of my neck. "What is it?" I ask, mentally crossing my fingers.

He pats a wheeled chair positioned at a darkened laptop. He and his teammate Josh normally sit back-to-back. He must read the confusion in my hesitation, because he explains, "Josh is out today. I wish he was here so I could show him this, but that means you get to see it first."

I guess now is not the time to bring up my aversion to being this close to people unless I can absolutely help it. This is not a bad guy. It's obvious he wants to be friends. Just why he would want to be friends with me, I have no idea, but now isn't the time to question him on his taste. Instead, I grab the chair and pull it close to his before plopping down.

He turns his attention to his screen. "See, I have the report here. I went through her Google location history. She never disabled her phone's tracking ability."

"Meaning... what, exactly?"

"Meaning I can trace her activity." When I'm still a little lost – which strikes me as strange, considering what

I do for a living – he clicks on one of the dots on the list, which takes us to a pinpoint on a map.

"Here's Shenandoah Elementary," he explains. "According to the app, she was there at 7:45 the morning she was abducted. After that ... " He clicks the next dot and I watch the map shift. "She went to the dry cleaner, the post office, then Starbucks," he announces, moving from one location to another to trace her morning.

"I get it. It's one of those things where an app asks whether it's okay to track your location. I always say no when it asks," I confess.

"Me, too," he agrees. "I don't want anybody following me around the comfort of their computer terminal. I miss the old days, where a stalker at least had to leave the house."

It's just a joke. He's only kidding. There was a time when a comment like that would have shut me down. Now, it's nothing more than a slight twinge, a moment of pressure in my chest that quickly eases. It's taken a lot of work to get me to this place.

"What did she do after that?" I ask, eyeing another dot in the list of locations.

"Her last stop was home." Sure enough, Tamara headed home after picking up her coffee. Now, a map of the neighborhood is on display, a blue pin positioned over a satellite image of the sprawling house.

I look at Corey, expecting more. "And then?"

"And then ... nobody knows yet, do they? After this, it's up to you to figure it out."

Like I didn't know that. Turning back to the screen, I have to sigh. This hasn't given me anything I didn't already know. "So this was her last known location. No other stops."

He leans back in his chair, folding his hands behind his head. "Maybe. Maybe not."

"What do you mean?"

"Well, she could have gone elsewhere with her phone turned off."

"Right. It wouldn't track her if her phone wasn't on," I muse, staring at the map and the pin designating the Higgins home. "But would she do that? She's such an involved parent. Would she take the risk of missing an important phone call? What if there were something wrong with the kids?"

"Good question." His thin, freckled face scrunches in a frown. "I wish I had an answer."

That makes two of us.

9

River

"So, what are you wearing for your date tonight?"

There are times when I feel like Emma and I speak two different languages. Our brains work differently, that much is for sure. She is practically bouncing out of her seat at Courthouse Cafe, where we stopped in for lunch to get out of the office for a while and shake up our brains a little. What a shame there's no shaking off the sense of growing desperation the longer it takes to uncover a serious lead.

"I thought we were talking about Beth Clyburn and going out to interview the husband." I narrow my eyes at her over the top of my chicken salad croissant. "What does my unfortunate date have to do with that?"

"There you go." She rolls her dark eyes at me, a gesture I'm used to seeing. "Why do you have to assume the worst? You're setting yourself up for failure before you ever leave the house. This could turn out to be great."

"Let's be honest. This sort of setup doesn't work outside of movies. And exactly what my brother-in-law thinks he knows about me, I would love to hear. How would he know the first thing about what I'm looking for in a relationship?"

"Do you even know what you are looking for?" she counters, arching an eyebrow.

"No, and that's just the point. I'm not looking for anything. Why is that so hard for everyone to accept?" I need to lower my voice. A pair of kids wearing backpacks give me a curious stare as they pass our table, telling me I'm attracting attention.

"River. You can't spend your entire life alone."

"Says who?" I whisper. "What if that's what I want?"

"Nobody wants to be alone."

That's where she's wrong, but I know she would never believe it. I could talk until I'm blue in the face, and there would be no way for her to understand how serious I am. That I don't say these things to be dramatic or to earn sympathy. She can't understand, because she isn't me. Just like I'm not her, and can't fathom caring for another living creature whose entire existence depends on me. The thought makes me shiver—and feel sympathy for my completely hypothetical child.

"My point stands." I set my sandwich down and wipe my hands on a napkin a little harder than necessary. "Chris doesn't know my type; and, I mean, Chris is a great guy and all that, but I would be bored out of my mind sitting around, listening to my boyfriend talk about the same sort of things he does. I can barely stand it during a normal family event."

When all she does is stare at me, I add, "If they're friendly, it stands to reason this guy is the same sort of person. That's all I'm trying to say."

"Is that the only argument you have against going out on a perfectly normal, no-strings-attached dinner? Because I hate to tell you, kid, but it doesn't hold water."

She likes to call me *kid* though I'm barely seven years younger than her. When I'm not bristling at the word, it actually feels a little nice. I never had an older sister.

"I'm not good at this." Saying it out loud brings a strangely freeing sensation along with it. I spoke my truth and the world did not come tumbling down.

"No one is born good at anything," Emma reminds me in that same big sister tone. Do I sound that way when I talk to Leslie? How could I, really? She's usually the one telling me what to do, bossing me around. "How do we get good at things?"

"Okay, I get it."

She is not letting me off the hook. "I need to hear it."

"Oh, this is just silly."

"Say the words." Before I can take hold of it, she snatches the other half of my sandwich off my plate and holds it out of my reach. "How do we get good at things?"

This is beginning to verge on humiliation. "Through practice," I mutter, grabbing the sandwich away from her when she offers it up. "Who says I want to get good at dating?"

"Quit it with the arguments." There are times like this when I feel sorry for her daughter. The woman can be downright scary when she puts her mind to it, eyes narrowed and nostrils flaring as she stares at me from across the small table. There are a couple dozen cops and agents sitting around, eating their lunch, gulping down coffee to keep themselves sharp before heading out to chase down a lead.

At this moment, though, it may as well be the two of us alone. She's that intense, unblinking. "Enough with the arguments, enough with the excuses. I know you haven't had it easy." Her voice drops to a whisper and her expression softens a little. "But you can't hold onto the past throughout your entire adult life. It's not healthy to devote all of your time and energy to work. You become obsessed, and you know it. Your sister is only trying to divert you in hopes that you'll have a more balanced life."

"Please, tell me the two of you haven't been talking about me. I don't think I could handle it."

She blurts out a laugh, shaking her head until her curls bounce. "Of course we haven't, silly. I don't need to talk to her to understand this. She loves you and wants you to be happy. There's nothing wrong with that."

The worst part is, I know she's right. But I also know I am not like other people. Why can't the world leave me alone?

Rather than sit around and lick my wounds, I check the time and push back from the table. "Chief Perkins takes his lunch from noon to one o'clock every single day. Which means he'll be back by now."

Emma laughs as she watches me grab my bag from where it hangs over the back of my chair. "How do you know that?"

"Not everybody over at Charlottesville PD is hostile. Sometimes, all it takes is offering a little something extra." I glance down at my wallet once it's in my hand.

"Like a few bucks?" I only shrug, which makes her laugh again before she waves her hands. "I don't need to hear anything else. I'll trust your methods."

After settling the bill, I step out into a sunshine drenched afternoon. It's at times like this that I wonder what the rest of the world must have looked like to my parents in the first weeks after I went missing. Was the weather beautiful? It had to be at some point. It couldn't have rained every day. Did they ever ask themselves how everything else seemed so bright and normal?

Is that what the families of our missing women ask themselves now? The idea gets me moving faster, with greater purpose as I walk the handful of blocks to the police station. Those women are counting on us.

There is nothing like walking into the station and knowing virtually everyone inside would rather swallow their tongue than say anything pleasant to me. Not that I care. If anything, it's better than pretending to be friendly for the sake of so-called professional courtesy. Rather than waste time with pleasantries, I show my badge to the officer at the desk before heading straight back to Chief Perkins' office.

Somebody mutters in a deep voice not far from where I walk, "Like they own the place." I should pretend I didn't hear it. The best I can settle for is shooting a look toward the cluster of cops following my progress. A few of them have the decency to look away, at least, though a couple stare me down. I probably wouldn't react much better in their shoes.

One thing is the same, ever-ringing phones, overlapping voices, the aroma of burnt coffee. Some things never change. I remind myself to think about that rather than the cold, almost aggressively disapproving looks all around as I make my way to the corner office. I see the chief sitting in there, he doesn't notice me until I'm too close to the room for him to pretend he's doing anything that might rule out an impromptu meeting. Sometimes, it's better to take people by surprise. I doubt it will earn me any points, but that's a sacrifice I'm willing to make.

"What can I do for you, Agent ... " He snaps his fingers a few times as I enter the room, scrunching his bushy eyebrows together. I don't know whether he genuinely forgot my name or if this is some weird power play. Like my name isn't important enough for him to remember. Either way, he hardly comes off as sincere, which doesn't do much for my level of respect for him. It's one thing for the officers outside this room to act like jealous school kids. I would've hoped for better from a man in his position.

"River Collins," I remind him, taking a seat in one of the two chairs positioned in front of his desk. They look almost brand new, come to think of it, in keeping with what I've seen of the decor around here. This is not an area where violent crime is the norm, and I have to wonder whether the chief and his officers can remember the last time they worked this hard on a case.

But are they working hard? That's what concerns me

most, and now I wish I had come up with a diplomatic way to ask what needs asking. "Do you have anything new for me?" I blurt out after a few awkward, silent moments.

His eyebrows shoot up before he sputters. "Right to business," he manages to choke out once he's composed himself a little. "I can appreciate that."

"But you still haven't answered my question. Our lab is currently digging deeper into Tamara Higgins' phone," I explain while eyeing the photos strewn around his desk. I recognize a few of them as coming from the Higgins home, including one of a minivan I noticed in the driveway during my first visit. Tamara's car.

His shoulders creep up closer to his ears. I'm skating on thin ice. "I'm aware of that, Agent Collins."

"Is there anything else that's come to light? Something we can pursue? Someone you aren't satisfied with and would like to revisit?"

"You know, we're capable of pursuing things down here, Agent Collins. My badge might not be as shiny and new as yours, but that's only because I've been carrying it as long as I have."

In other words, *don't question our abilities*. "I'm sorry you feel compelled to take my questions personally."

Color floods his cheeks and his mouth falls open like he's about to tell me off. Welp, I'm going to hear it from Siwak over this.

As it turns out, he's cut off before he can order me out and demand I never come back. A uniformed officer pokes his head into the room, barely glancing my way before his gaze fixes on the chief. "I just came back from the Clyburns'."

"Did you find something?" I ask while mentally crossing my fingers.

His head bobs. "I sure did. And it looked a lot like a bloodstain."

10

Beth

The Day Of

"Unfortunately for the twenty-two-year-old nursing student, what started as a routine overnight shift turned into a nightmare that would send a small town reeling."

As cheesy as the intros can sometimes be, I can never resist a new true crime podcast. I don't get as deep into them as some people do – going online, asking questions, pretending to be a sleuth. I'm not deluded, and I can't help but think of the family members of the people featured in the stories. They're real people. To them, this is not entertainment.

It's a cool morning, and I'm glad I wore an extra layer for my run. I'm glad I put sweaters on the kids, too. This time of year is so tricky. I am sure it will be warm as anything by the time I go for pick-up later on. Soon it will be warm all the time, which reminds me that I want to sign Clara up for swim lessons this summer. Yet another activity, another thing to check off my to-do list. Not that I have anything to complain about.

Though I do wish it didn't feel so much like I'm on my own.

I hate thoughts like that, and I push this one away like I always do, running a little harder like I can outrun the twinge of ... what is it? Not anger. I'm not angry, married to a doctor who provides me and the kids with a beautiful life. I'm not sad, either, and I wouldn't call myself discontented. So what is it? Why do I get this sick feeling in my stomach sometimes? A sense of ... loneliness, I think. Kissing him goodbye every morning, sometimes so early the kids aren't up yet. Knowing our days will go on the way his will, and that they will be almost completely separate. I doubt he's ever considered swim lessons or any of the other activities the kids participate in.

By the time I reach the familiar landmarks of my block, sweat rolls down the back of my neck and I'm nearing the end of the first episode setting up the circumstances of the case. Sometimes I wonder how women can be so naïve and oblivious toward their own safety in this day and age. But then I guess nobody thinks it will happen to them.

After a quick shower once I've made it home, I fix a smoothie and check my phone while the machine whirs in the otherwise silent kitchen. Normally, the sight of my best friend's name along with a new text would make me smile, but today is different. I know what it's about before

I read it, a continuation of the uncomfortable conversation we had last night. She's not going to let it go.

Sure enough, she wants to pick up where we left off, when she told me about a mutual friend's recent engagement. Not somebody I'm close enough with that I would expect an invitation. More like an old friend who time has turned into a warm acquaintance. One who is aware of the side hustle I've worked on the past year or so, picking it up when I have a little extra time.

Laura: Have you given any thought to shooting Sarah's wedding?

I love her, I do, but she's like a dog with a bone sometimes. She knows me well enough to know better than to push so hard when I tell her I don't want to talk about something. She also knows me well enough to know she can talk me into just about anything. Maybe one day, she should talk me into growing a backbone and not letting her order me around.

She has the best intentions. She might not be wrong, either. I'm not very good at pushing myself outside my comfort zone, which she knows very well and refuses to let me get away with.

Me: You know, it's never a good idea doing work like that for friends. It always gets sticky.

That's not even an excuse. Already, three different moms in Clara's class have mentioned a photo shoot for their family after stalking my Facebook page and finding the handful of photos I've posted there in the past. Your work is adorable. If you were looking for experience, you could take our photos. We would love to be your models. In other words, they expect it to be free because we know each other and because I'm not treating this like an actual business. At least, not yet.

Who am I kidding? I'm never going to have time for that. I barely have time to edit what I shoot now, and I'm not shooting all that much. Besides, it isn't fair to Greg or the kids to take so much time away from my work around the house. Especially if I'm not really making any money at it. It would be one thing if I was contributing to our finances.

She wastes no time getting back to me, and the response comes as no surprise.

Laura: You are so full of it. I know why you're skittish, and I'm telling you to knock it off. You need to have a little more faith in yourself.

That's always easy for somebody else to say, isn't it?

Me: But this is a wedding we're talking about. Not just a family photo shoot, something low stakes. This is the most important day of their lives. That's a lot of pressure.

Laura: I know you can do it.

She's probably right. I can probably do it. I was able to upgrade my equipment after the first few sessions, once I finally got up the courage to do something with the hobby I gave up years ago. It was only ever something I fooled around with, but it always interested me. Identifying moments that would make for a great shot, playing with light and shadow. Something for me, something satisfying. There's nothing like the feeling of a shot matching up to what I see in my head. Being able to capture it fully. It's a rush.

But turning it into a business? That sort of takes the

fun out of it, for one thing. And it's something Greg has mentioned more times than I can count. Just last night, for example, when I confided to him about the talk with Laura while we were getting ready for bed. "Remember, this is supposed to be fun. Don't stress yourself out so much." Again, easy for him to say.

I'm mulling it over as I empty the dishwasher, then head to the laundry room to pull a load from the dryer. I should take the offer and shoot the wedding. Heck, there's plenty of time between now and then. Who knows how much better I'll be if I practice consistently?

There are other concerns, though, and I type out the one closest to the forefront of my worries after sitting on the living room sofa with a basket full of pajamas, socks, and underwear waiting to be sorted.

Me: I wouldn't know what to charge.

Laura: You can figure that out. Just don't shut the idea down before you give yourself a chance. That's all. And please, don't let imposter syndrome win.

It's not the first time I've heard somebody mention imposter syndrome. It is, however, the first time I've heard it spoken of when I was the subject. Is that what's holding me back?

Laura: Think about it. You are always the first person to shoot yourself down. Sarah expressed interest in the work you've been posting online, and the first thing out of your mouth was a bunch of excuses. You're not being fair to yourself.

Maybe she's right. Maybe I need to stop coming up

with reasons why not and start coming up with reasons why I should. There's plenty of time to practice between now and then, and maybe I can get those interested moms to sign up for a session. If it means something like preparing for a wedding, a really serious job which could get me started on building an actual business, I'm willing to offer a reduced rate for the sake of experience.

Am I seriously considering this? A giggle bubbles up in my throat before I can help it. Me, a real photographer. Doing real work instead of goofing off for my own enjoyment. My heart is in my throat, but I'm not going to let it stop me. Before I can talk myself out of it, I send Laura another text.

Me: Tell Sarah I would love to talk with her about it.

Laura's response comes in the form of a GIF of a little girl dancing and clapping. It makes me laugh before I set the phone aside and turn my attention back to the pile of laundry waiting to be put away. Funny how the job seems a little easier now.

11

River

Chris and I are going to have a long talk. The chief topic of conversation, what in the world he was thinking when he suggested I go out with this guy. I don't know if he's a really bad judge of character, or if this is some sort of message. There I was, thinking we liked each other.

Gazing across the table at my date leaves me thinking otherwise.

It isn't that there's anything wrong with him on the surface. He's pleasant, he's personable. He's good looking, too, with a sporty build and a solid tan. He hasn't spent the entire time talking about himself, which is usually a plus.

Instead, all he wants to talk about is me. Somebody should have told him a little of me goes a long way.

"I have so much respect for you." His dark eyes are practically shining as he folds his arms on the table and offers a grin. He's definitely a type, right down to his square chin and the dimple in it. Golden hair gleams in the light from the candle in the center of the table. Should I swoon?

Give the guy a chance. I want to, if only so I can tell Leslie and Emma I tried my best. I don't want them to come up with some reason for it to be my fault that we didn't make a connection.

"There really isn't that much to admire," I insist with a weak smile. A nice, crisp Chardonnay makes this a little easier to deal with, and I take a delicate sip while trying to come up with something else to say. This is exhausting. And people do this all the time?

"Not from where I'm sitting – and I don't only mean because you're so gorgeous." Before I can even blush, he adds, "I mean, Chris has pictures of your sister on his desk, so I figured the two of you had to resemble each other. I'm glad I was right."

Again, everything coming out of his mouth is pleasant enough, but it's like a song being played slightly off-key. Just a little flat, not enough to be a disaster but enough to make a skilled listener cringe.

I know exactly what Leslie would say if she heard what I'm thinking right now. You need to stop obsessing over work for once, or you'll always find a reason to not trust somebody. She wouldn't be wrong, either. My line of work precludes me from accepting most people's words at face value. I've interviewed too many victims and heard too many charming lines that they fell for and wound up regretting. I mean, it's not like I'm imagining dead bodies in this guy's basement or anything. I don't deliberately sabotage dates that way.

"It's okay to say thank you," he murmurs in an indulgent tone when I don't offer a response.

"Pardon?" Time for another sip of wine. Maybe another glass. How much is left in the bottle?

"When you're complimented, it's okay to thank the person who offered it."

That's all it takes for my skin to start crawling. It didn't take very long at all for him to reveal what's under that overly complimentary attitude. I should probably go. We haven't been served our entrées yet. Nobody could accuse me of using him for a free meal.

But now I'm intrigued. I mimic his posture, folding my arms on the table, offering a smile that makes his smile widen. "Is that what you think the problem is? I don't know how to take a compliment?"

He scoffs gently, his mouth tipping upward at the corner in a smirk. "Come on. Let's not kid each other. The world you live in, the way I'm sure you have to be for work, you must always feel like you have to be on your guard."

"Against what?"

Lifting a shoulder, he says, "Against, you know. Being too feminine. You have to act like one of the guys."

I've changed my mind. I'm going to have to thank Chris. It's very rare to have an opportunity like this. "That can be a problem," I murmur, nodding slowly. "The first sign of emotion, and some of the guys I work with call me hormonal."

He wrinkles his nose, though I don't know whether it's in response to that attitude or to my mention of hormones. With some guys, you can't tell. "That's what I mean. It must be an awful challenge for you, dealing with those jerks."

"It can be a real nightmare."

"That's why I've never been able to understand why a woman would put herself through it. Why go to the trouble?"

Wow. It's like he's determined to miss the point. "You think the problem is with women taking on a career like mine, and not with the men who refuse to take us seriously."

"Let me put it this way." His eyelids lower slightly and his smile turns to something much more serious. "If we were together, you would never feel like you have to go out there and prove yourself to anyone. I would make sure of that."

"How?" Because now I need to know whether he honestly believes the things he's saying. Like I'm out here looking for a savior. I learned a long time ago there's no such thing. If I'm going to get anywhere, I need to get there myself.

"I would step into my role as your protector. I knew the second I set eyes on you that's what you need. You need to rest. You need to know it's okay to stop battling. You don't have to carry the whole world on your shoulders, you know?"

"Wow. You really know how to read me, don't you?" Instead of throwing up, I finish my wine.

"Let's say I've met plenty of women like you," he assures me with a wry chuckle. "But you are something special."

"You flatter me."

"It's the truth." I'm sure that warm, intimate tone in his voice is supposed to get me all flushed and giggly, but it has the opposite effect, setting my teeth on edge while he rambles on. "I mean, look at you. You're this skilled FBI agent, but you manage to come off so pretty and feminine. I can imagine what it would be like, coming home to somebody like you at the end of the day. I wouldn't be able to stay late at the office anymore, I'll tell you that."

"That's very kind."

"I'm not trying to be kind. I'm trying to let you know that you deserve so much more than a life spent shuffling papers, and that's when you aren't potentially putting your life on the line. You're not meant for that. You're meant for better things. I feel it, and my instincts are never wrong." He offers a wink before leaning back a little in his chair, so our server can place our entrees on the table. I'm surprised Lucas didn't order for me, convinced he would know exactly what I would enjoy.

"Don't get me wrong," he continues before cutting into his porterhouse. "I have nothing but respect for the work you do. I know I certainly would never be able to make it through training alone, but I hear you made it look easy."

And now I will have to thank Chris for sharing personal details of my life. "I was determined to prove myself."

"You have no idea how much I admire that. I'm a little overwhelmed by you," he admits with a self-deprecating laugh. "I can't believe I just admitted that. I don't know what it is about you, but I feel like I can say things without worrying what you might think."

He would not like to hear what I'm thinking. The idea of giving him a look at what's happening inside my mind makes my lips twitch with a barely suppressed smile as I cut into my filet. "I'm flattered." It's getting harder to come up with responses.

"With beautiful legs like yours, I bet you like to dance."

He needs to be careful, or I'll end up choking. As it is, I can barely swallow the mouthful of meat before asking, "Excuse me?"

Holding up a hand, he murmurs, "Sorry. That was rude of me. But I'm not going to pretend I didn't notice your beautiful legs in that dress. I was thinking we could maybe go out this weekend to a club in town that's a favorite of mine. It's not too loud, and the vibe is casual but fun. I know after a busy day, you wouldn't want to be surrounded by hundreds of people pressing in on you."

That might be the first accurate assumption he's made tonight. "I'll be honest with you. I have two left feet and no sense of rhythm. But I do appreciate the suggestion."

"Everybody can dance if they have the right partner," he informs me with a wink.

"I guess that must be my problem," I muse, once again fighting off laughter. It's going to be so much fun telling Emma about this. "I've never had the right partner."

"Don't worry. I'll take care of that for you."

Oh? Are you going to find somebody for me to dance with? The fact that the words come dangerously close to dropping off my tongue tells me I should let the guy down easy sooner rather than later, before I say something unforgivably rude. "That's really nice. Unfortunately, I've just started a big case. I don't know when I'll have any free time – as it is, I had to make up a story for why I couldn't be in the office tonight with everyone else." That part is true, though Emma knew exactly where I was going. She's so determined for me to find somebody, it didn't even bother her to watch me slip out early so I could head home and get ready.

At first, I think I might have broken his brain. He goes still, freezing solid before barking out a dry laugh. "Really? That's all you have to say? I take you out for one of the most expensive meals in town, and all you have to say for yourself is you're busy at work? Newsflash. Plenty of people are busy at work, but they make time for other people. I guess you're too special for that."

Wow. I figured there was something darker lurking under the surface, but I had no idea it was that dark. If anything, I'm a little disappointed. He could've tried a little harder, hung on a little longer.

"I'm sorry I have upset you, but this is a really busy time, like I said." Looking down at the table, I add, "I would be more than happy to pay for my share of the meal."

"I'm sure you would love that. Then you can tell all your friends about the cheap guy you went to dinner with. I've got it." He continues muttering to himself about a ruined appetite while pulling out his wallet, shooting me a couple of dirty looks in the process.

And people wonder why I don't like wasting my time this way.

12

River

Mom and Dad are going to kill me.

My stomach's been hurting all day, but it's worse now that I'm off the bus and on my way home. I should've studied. Why did I think I would do okay on the test without studying harder than I did? I can just hear Dad now. You're better than this. Can't we trust you to handle your schoolwork responsibly? You are not a D student.

Instead of walking straight for a block and turning right on my street, I take a different route from the bus stop. A longer one. Sure, I have to go home, and I will. It's just that my insides are shaking. I feel a little sick. Why didn't I study harder? I even had the TV on the whole time I was supposed to be reviewing parts of the cell.

It's been gray and drizzling all day, which definitely works with my mood. I pull up the hood on my jacket to keep my hair dry and bury my hands in my pockets. I'm probably going to end up grounded. I know I won't be allowed to watch TV – they took it away for a week when I got a C on a math test almost nobody passed since it was so hard. It didn't matter. I still lost TV privileges for a week, and now I have to tell them I got a D. Two weeks? I don't even want to think about it.

My feet get a little heavier with every step, but soon I've reached the overgrown wooded area that separates one half of my neighborhood from the other. I can see my house through the trees from where I'm walking, though pretty soon that won't be possible anymore. Once the leaves come out, everything will be too overgrown to see very far into the woods. It's not easy to take a deep breath without whimpering a little, but I know what I have to do. And I'll need to remember this the next time I want to flake off instead of studying.

"Excuse me! Can you help me?"

I have to pull my hood aside to see the woman in an old, black car slowly rolling my way. The woman driving looks friendly, but embarrassed. She's probably around Mom's age which somehow makes me feel safer than if I were facing somebody younger. "What do you need?" I call out, folding my arms and shivering when a gust of wind blows past.

"I am so lost. Do you live around here?" She chews her lip, looking over her shoulder, shrugging. "I know I missed a turn. I'm trying to find the mall. Somebody's meeting me there, but I know I must be driving past it."

"Oh, sure. It's not far from here, maybe ten minutes." Turning, I point down the street in the direction I came from. "Go down... four blocks, then make a left. Follow that out to the first light and make a right. Take that down to the McDonald's, make a left –"

"Hang on, hang on." She waves her hands and shakes her head, laughing. "No way can I remember all that. You said go down four blocks and make…"

"A left." I step up to the curb so I won't have to yell anymore. "It's actually really easy."

"Yeah, that's what my friend told me when she gave me the directions, and here I am." She taps her fingers on the steering wheel, looking around again, grimacing. "I am so late. Hey, here's an idea. Could you show me how to get there? I promise, I'll drive you wherever it was you were going. I am just the worst when it comes to following directions, but if you show me, I'll remember."

"No!"

My eyes snap open in time for me to hear the echo of my own broken cry still filling the air in my darkened bedroom. It's always like this in the moments after I wake up from one of those dreams. I'm frozen, barely able to breathe much less make a move. Cold sweat is soaking into my pillow, but there's no hope of making myself comfortable. Not yet. All I can do is stare up at the ceiling and count the stripes of light created by the blinds over my windows.

It was so vivid, like it always is. I can still smell the rain in the air, can still feel drizzle hitting my face when the wind blows just right.

I can hear her voice.

I might have woken up before the memories played themselves out, but I've suffered through it enough times to remember every moment. I had two whole years to go over it, to blame myself, to curse myself for being so stupid. For getting in that car, for believing a stranger who promised she would take me home if I showed her how to get to the mall. I was supposed to be a smart kid, the sort of kid parents trusted thanks to good sense and intelligence.

Yet there I went, making the most unintelligent move of my entire life and setting myself up for a lifetime of repercussions.

Slowly, my body loosens and my pulse slows to a more normal rhythm. Now I can hear faint nighttime noises outside my bedroom window – the occasional car passing by, rattling in the trash cans in the alley as raccoons put together their nightly feast. I'm safe, right down to the pistol under my pillow. Nobody's going to hurt me.

But in my head, the memories play like a movie I can't stop. Her cheerful, friendly attitude while I directed her, sitting in the passenger seat of a car that reeked like cigarette smoke. We rolled further and further away from my house, but I wasn't in any hurry to get home, anyway. It never occurred to me I might be in trouble.

Not until we passed the mall.

"Now, all we have to do is turn around here." For the first time since I got in the car, I went ignored. "Up here," I repeated, pointing to the light up ahead. "You'll just want to get in the right lane –"

When she blew through the light, continuing straight, dread started leaking into my veins. "I need to go home," I whispered, looking at her from the corner of my eye, barely able to breathe while my heart pounded out of my chest. "Take me home. You said you would take me home."

The worst part of all was her silence. She was cold now, totally unmoved. Her only reaction to anything I did or said was to lock the door when I reached for the handle, then floor the gas pedal. It wasn't long before she pulled off the main road, meaning there was little traffic around us. Less chance of anybody spotting me if I freaked out.

My fault. This is all my fault. Those words ran on repeat in my panicked, overwhelmed mind as we drove to the middle of nowhere and the entire course of my life changed.

And there's nothing for me to do now but spend the next few hours waiting for the sun to rise and the last fading memories to give way to morning.

Only to return tonight, the way they always do.

13

River

There is nothing like an elementary school at drop-off time. I've been through FBI training less intense than what I witness in front of Shenandoah Elementary the morning after my disastrous date and the almost crippling nightmare that followed. Maybe I'll tell my sister about the nightmare and pretend it had something to do with him. Maybe then she'll leave me alone and let me live my life, which is just fine as it is.

All right. It's not just fine in many ways, but it's good enough for me.

Taking a pull from a cardboard cup of coffee, I observe the activity unfolding on a busy morning. Cars line up, moving slowly and systematically toward the school entrance. Kids pour out of these vehicles, sometimes racing so fast it's like they're afraid of what will happen if they don't. A little boy with a backpack roughly the size of his body trips and almost falls in his haste to get out of his mom's SUV before she pulls away.

Here and there, parents call out to each other. It's not only women, I know, but the majority of the parents are mothers. Many of them remind me of Beth and Tamara; young, healthy, involved. Somebody asks a loud question about a bake sale, calling out to a woman several cars further down in the line, and part of me is glad I've never seriously considered having kids. Not that there's anything wrong with children – I love Leslie's kids. We get along great, maybe because they don't ask more of me than I'm able to give. They're happy to take me how I am.

That doesn't mean I can imagine juggling homework and projects, volunteering and chaperoning trips. And I certainly couldn't feign interest for the sake of fitting in.

I get the feeling fitting in is very important around here. Like the apparent mom uniform, which mostly involves perfectly coordinated workout clothes and matching Stanley cups. I would never make it here. Nobody would ever call me a slave to fashion, for one thing. I've never imagined myself having a personal style beyond whatever is clean and reasonably unwrinkled. Otherwise, I can't bring myself to drum up enough interest to follow trends. Trends pass.

And two years spent wearing filthy rags have a way of adjusting a person's priorities. There were nights I would dream of pulling a t-shirt from the dryer and putting it on, pleasantly warm and fragrant against clean skin.

I need to get a grip on those memories. More and more often lately, I find myself sinking into them, referring back to them at random times and for seemingly no good reason. Is it any wonder I have awful nightmares when my waking thoughts are full of ugly, brutal memories of a time I would give anything to forget?

At the moment, forgetting means being able to return my focus to the reason I'm here in the first place. After conducting my preliminary observations, I climb out of my car, parked in one of a handful of visitor spots in the lot running beside the school. On the opposite side is a huge playground which I drove past when I arrived. As I round the school, silently observing, keeping to myself, I come upon a pair of young women wearing long cardigans over blouses and slacks. The lanyards around their necks tell me they work here at the school, and this morning they're overseeing the playground until the bell rings in around fifteen minutes.

I can't really make out what they're saying as I approach, but they sound pleasant enough to give me confidence as I clear my throat behind them. The sound makes them turn to face me. According to her name badge, the younger blonde is named Jeannie. She's fresh faced enough to be straight out of school herself. The slightly older brunette is named Marissa. Marissa is sporting a baby bump which she covers with one hand at the sudden presence of a stranger. When she glances at my badge, hanging from a lanyard not unlike hers, she loosens a little bit but is still on guard.

Jeannie, though, immediately figures out why I'm here. Her eyes go soft, her mouth twists in a frown. "Please, tell us you found something."

"I wish I could," I admit. After introducing myself, I

ask, "Do you have a couple of minutes between the two of you to answer a few questions?"

"What kind of questions?" Marissa asks, one eye on the kids at all times. "If we lose sight of them, there's literally no telling what they could do."

"You're monitoring the school yard today?" I ask, raising my voice when a group of little ones nearby start shrieking for seemingly no reason, running around, chasing each other. I hope for their teachers' sakes they get all that energy out now.

Jeannie's golden head bobs. "But really, whatever you need. I don't know how we can help … " The two of them exchange a look, shrugging.

I step in place beside them, the three of us facing a sea of children. "What grades do you ladies teach?" I ask, pulling out my notepad to jot down anything worth remembering.

"Jeannie teaches Molly Higgins in the fourth grade," Marissa tells me. "I have Josh Higgins in the second grade."

"Brandon Clyburn is in the other fourth grade class. I don't know him well," Jeannie tells me before delivering the surprise of my life by putting two fingers in her mouth and blowing out a sharp whistle that cuts through the wall of noise. "You know we don't tolerate that," she calls out, wagging a finger and shaking her head at a pair of girls. "That's not very respectful. Don't let me see you do that again."

"What do you think about the kids?" Because in the end, the odds are still in favor of this being a crime committed close to home. I'm planning on visiting Beth

Clyburn's husband shortly, but could use a heads up on any red flags a teacher might have noticed.

Marissa's expression melts into one of fondness. "Josh is a sweetheart. A very serious little student. He wants to be a doctor like his daddy – he announced that on the first day of school, when I was going around the room to learn about the kids."

"Is he here now?" I ask while scanning the crowd.

"No, I don't think so. Though he may have gone straight into school to spend quiet time in the library, instead." Marissa drops her voice to a confidential tone. "Administration is sort of looking the other way right now when it comes to tardiness and absence. Nobody expects a distraught husband to drop the kids off on time in a situation like this, you know?"

"I understand Tamara's kids are staying with her mother right now," I offer, waiting for a reaction. I'm not sure what I'm looking for. A quick glance at each other, rolled eyes, anything that might point to David Higgins as being a less-than-stellar husband. Word gets around in a small town. Maybe somebody knows something about him I could turn into a lead.

No such luck. "It's all just so sad," Marissa murmurs, shaking her head. "A mother taken from her babies. I only hope they both come back soon. What are the odds of something like this happening to two women at once?" The way she's rubbing her belly, almost like she doesn't know she's doing it, makes me think she's asking herself what would happen if someone took her from her child.

"I can assure you, we're doing everything we can to

answer that question." My head snaps up when a high-pitched, whining noise fills the air. The kids start to head toward the doors leading inside.

Marissa turns my way while Jeannie claps her hands briskly to encourage a few slowpokes. "Time to go in. Is there anything else we can do for you?"

"I have one more question. Did you ever see Beth and Tamara interacting together around the school? Were their kids friendly?"

"Molly and Brandon aren't in the same circles, if you know what I mean. Nothing bad. They're just not the same type of person." Jeannie starts off after the last couple of stragglers cross the threshold.

"And I've never seen Beth and Tamara together at school," Marissa adds, while Jeannie shrugs like she agrees. "As far as I know, they weren't friends."

"Thank you." I hold up a hand, offering a brief smile as they turn away and quickly cross the playground. The way their heads are slightly inclined toward the other tells me they are whispering something. I'm sure half the town will know by lunchtime that an FBI agent was at the school, asking questions.

I have to wonder if the gossip will send a chill down the spine of one of the people who hear it. If maybe the person or people responsible for this are hiding in plain sight.

14

River

Dr. Greg Clyburn is a handsome man. Tall, trim, with dark hair and bright blue eyes that look even brighter thanks to the bloodshot quality of the whites. I'm struck by his good looks and his distraught expression when he answers the door, wearing an old polo shirt that looks like it's seen better days and a pair of sweatpants with a small hole in one knee.

"Agent Collins?" he asks in a voice thick with tears.

"That's right. I'm sorry if this is a bad time," I offer. It's social conditioning nonsense and I know it, but there's something distinctly uncomfortable about the sight of a man – a doctor, at that – breaking down openly. The tears in his eyes are fresh, just like the stains on his cheeks.

"Between you and me, there's no such thing as a good time right now." He runs a hand under both eyes before stepping back, motioning for me to enter. "Mrs. Fleming, my neighbor, took the boys for the morning. I don't have to put on a brave face when they're not here."

"I understand. You want to get it all out while they aren't here." His head bobs as he closes the door, and I take a quick glance around the foyer. It's pleasantly cluttered – a few pairs of kid's shoes lie where they were kicked off from the looks of it, there's a handful of what looks like junk mail strewn across a table inside the front door. A knit scarf looks like it was intended to hang over a peg embedded in the wall, but it sits on the floor instead.

He notices my curiosity and grunts softly. "I just don't have it in me to keep things the way Beth always does. She would never leave a scarf on the floor like this." He picks it up and drapes it over the peg with a sigh.

"I don't think anyone's going to judge your housekeeping skills at a time like this."

He offers a brief, half-hearted grin before asking, "Why don't we sit in the living room? Can I get you something to drink?"

"No, I'm fine. Thank you." From what I understand, the bloodstain found in the home was located on a curtain covering a window near the front door. It doesn't take much investigation to tell which one it was – an entire panel has been removed, leaving the window looking lopsided.

"We sprayed luminol over the entire area," the cop back in the chief's office had explained, "but we only found blood on the curtain. Not a trace anywhere else. Like somebody was passing by and brushed against it."

In other words, not enough to point to signs of a

struggle here in the foyer. Considering there was no blood anywhere else in the house – at least, according to local PD – that single stain carries a lot of weight. It might change the direction of the entire case.

I follow him into the living room to the right of the foyer. Like the Higgins house, the Clyburn home is stately, comfortable, tastefully decorated. My sister would go wild over the perfectly coordinated furniture, area rug, curtains. "What do they call this?" I ask, indicating the wall full of photos above the sectional sofa. "A gallery wall?"

"Beth put so much time into that arrangement," he explains. "She had this big roll of paper spread out on the floor and arranged everything on it, then traced the outlines and positioned it on the wall so she could see where the nails should go."

"Pretty clever. I would just put them up there without giving it much thought." Who am I kidding? I wouldn't hang anything. The walls of my apartment are bare.

Enough small talk. "Dr. Clyburn, when was the last time you saw your wife?"

He sniffles as he sinks onto the sofa. "The morning she disappeared. I had to head in early to the hospital, before dawn, and she was still in bed. I let her know I was leaving and gave her a kiss. I assume she went back to sleep for another hour or two."

"Was that frequently the case?"

"Are you asking if my wife was alone a lot?" Instead of taking Greg Higgins' attitude, there doesn't seem to be anything but sadness in his voice. "I'll be the first to say yes. Not through any choice of my own," he adds.

"Doctors typically have busy, sometimes unpredictable schedules," I muse, and he nods. "Was that ever a problem for you two?"

"I won't pretend Beth was thrilled that I would end up getting called in at random times, but it wasn't an ongoing issue. We are happy. We have a good marriage. The sort of marriage other people envy."

He's intense enough that I wonder if he's trying to convince me ... or himself. "Where could she be?" he asks, covering his face with his hands. His shoulders shake, and the sound of muffled weeping soon fills the air.

There's a box of tissues on the coffee table, which I lean over to slide his way. "I'm sorry," he mumbles, grabbing a tissue and blowing his nose. "Sometimes I can't stop it before I start blubbering all over the place."

"This is an extremely difficult time. It would be surprising if you weren't emotional."

"It's like all I can do is think about what she must be feeling. I keep telling myself not to think too much about it, because all it does is make things worse. It's morbid." He balls up the tissue and shoves it into his pocket before blowing out a deep breath. "I'm sorry. I know you have a job to do."

"It's all right, believe me." After giving him a second to compose himself, I continue. "How did your wife strike you recently? Was there any change in her demeanor, her habits? Was anything slightly off? No matter how small it seemed at the time. Anything could be important."

He stares at the dark TV across from us, furrowing his brow, narrowing his eyes. "I'm trying to think back, but nothing comes up. Everything was the same around here. There was no slacking off on the housework, the kids were their normal selves. Dinner was always on the table on time."

Then he chuckles, closing his eyes and shaking his head. "I just listened to what I said, and heard myself the way a stranger would hear me, and I realize how idiotic that sounds."

Interesting. "What makes you say that?"

"It's all I have to tell you. Everything was the same. She did the housework, she kept the kids clean, she cooked the food. I can only imagine what he must be thinking."

Now that he puts it that way, I see where he's coming from. In this respect, though, I'm not surprised. Few people understand the real cost of the labor housewives and stay-at-home moms provide. Could Dr. Clyburn maintain his career at the hospital if it weren't for his wife managing the rest of his life? She's live-in childcare, a housekeeper, a private chef. She's a personal assistant, keeping the kids' schedules in check, a chauffeur, and so many other things.

In this case, it seems the good doctor appreciates his wife. Though whether that's a new development based around her disappearance, I can't say. Too many people don't know what they've got until it's gone, like the song says.

It's like the man reads my mind as he drops his hands into his lap with a defeated groan. "I'm lost without her. I swear. Not only around the house, but in general. She's always the person I go to first with a decision I need to make. When something good happens, she's the first person I want to tell. How is the world still turning?"

"It's all been so sudden," I point out as gently as I can. The man is distraught, to say the least. I can't rule him out just yet, but that doesn't mean I want to treat him like a suspect just yet, either.

"In a second." He snaps his fingers, the sound sharp in the otherwise quiet room. "I know this doesn't have any bearing on anything, but Beth was waffling over something the night before she vanished. Again, I'm sure it doesn't mean anything."

"You never know," I remind him.

"She has always been into photography," he explains, gesturing at the wall behind him. "She took a lot of these photos herself."

Now I examine the wall through different eyes. Most of the pictures revolve around the kids – standing near the water's edge down on the beach, playing in the snow in what looks like a ski resort, somewhere with mountains in the background. There's a photo of a one-year-old smashing their first birthday cake. It's crisp, gorgeous, even with the messy icing smeared all over the baby's chubby cheeks.

"She studied photography in college," he explains. "After we were married and we started our family, she put all of that aside. It was more of a hobby until a friend of hers asked if she would take family portraits for them. She did, and the friend posted them on Facebook afterward. All of a sudden, everybody wanted to know if Beth could take pictures for them."

"Did she?"

"Sure. She started posting them herself, sort of drumming up a little business. Recently, though, a friend of hers asked if she would be interested in shooting a wedding. An actual, professional gig."

I can't tell how he feels about that. "And she was conflicted?"

He lifts a shoulder. "I guess it's one thing to treat something as a side business, something you do in your spare time, but it's another to photograph someone's entire wedding. She didn't think she could handle it."

"What do you think?"

"Honestly? She has so much on her plate. She volunteers at school, she's always helping out people in the neighborhood whenever she can. She gets involved in causes – fundraisers, donation drives, that sort of thing. Why add that kind of pressure? If it wasn't making her happy, I mean. I told her she's allowed to say no and keep things simple if that's what she wants."

Not unsupportive, but not exactly enthusiastic, either. He makes a point, though. It sounds like a reasonable reaction. "Do you know the name of the person who asked her to do the wedding?"

"Her friend, Laura Barnes. It's not her wedding," he explains. "The bride is a mutual friend. Do you think this might have something to do with her disappearance?" Confusion hangs heavy in his voice, understandably.

"Oh, no. Not exactly. But since I haven't had a chance to speak to Beth's friends yet, I thought this would be a good place to start."

"I see. I would hate to think … " He shakes his head.

"Well, there isn't a single thing about this that I like to think about. It's a nightmare."

"I can only imagine. We're doing everything we can, I assure you." That much is true.

On the other hand, this is another man who has no idea exactly what his wife does with her life. For all I know, Beth could have an entirely separate life lived while her husband spends countless, unpredictable hours at the hospital. The same is true of Tamara.

Speaking to Laura Barnes will be a first step toward learning more. With that in mind, I stand, handing the doctor my card. "If you think of anything that might be helpful, something you didn't remember just now, don't hesitate to call. Anytime, day or night."

"Thank you. I'll do that." He clutches the card in his hand, showing me to the door. Before I can leave he turns to me, and again his eyes are full of tears. "Please. Find her. Find out what happened. I'll do anything to get her back, whatever it takes. If they want money, I'll give it to them. Anything."

"You'll be the first to know the second there are any developments." That's the best I can come up with, since I'm not sure how to respond. I can understand him being intense at a time like this, but it's almost a little too much. Enough to make me glad to be on my way.

Enough to leave me wondering if he's for real.

15

River

"I know you aren't serious. Leslie, how could you do this?"

"How could I do what?" Even while over the phone, I can practically see my sister's overly innocent expression. The way she always looks when she knows she's messed up and is caught dead to rights, but refuses to drop the act.

"I called you before I made it home last night to tell you how awful it was at dinner." The thought alone makes me shiver as I sit in the parking garage, where I took Leslie's call before going in to report this morning's findings. "How could you set me up on another date? How many single coworkers does Chris have?"

"Several." Her tone is chilly, touched with a little bit of hostile superiority. Right on schedule. This is step two, where Leslie turns herself into a victim. "I'm so sorry your happiness is so important to me. What am I thinking?"

I stare out through the windshield, watching a pair of agents emerge from the elevator. They're laughing, joking about something. How is it so easy for some people to connect with others? It can't all be a matter of my trauma. Can it? I was never exactly a loner in the Before Days – the way I think about it sometimes. Back before everything changed

But now that I look back, it was never easy for me to feel like I was a part of a group. There was always a reason to feel like I was standing on the outside, looking in. The way I am now.

"Could you not turn on the guilt?" I ask, irritated. "Sorry if I'm a little hesitant, considering the winner you set me up with already. Mr. Misogyny himself."

"I wouldn't call him a misogynist based on how you described him." Leslie snorted. "Chauvinist, maybe."

How nice for one of us to find this amusing. "And yet you wonder why I don't want any part of this?"

"All right, last time was a misfire. It'll be better this time." I have to groan at her assurances, while she powers through. "I've met this guy myself at a couple of holiday parties. He has a great sense of humor, a really nice personality, and he's cute."

Wow. He's really checking all of my boxes. "What's his name?" I ask with a sigh, closing my eyes. I know darn well I'm not getting out of this without accepting, and I don't have the time to sit here and argue in circles any longer.

"Tom Aten." She gives me his number so I can text him, and I enter it into my phone even while silently wondering what I did to deserve this. "You're going to have a great time – if you allow yourself to have a great time."

"Hey, listen. I walked into that dinner with a good attitude. I was determined to keep an open mind, but that was before I found out he would rather I didn't use my mind at all."

"I get it, I get it," she grumbles. This is the final stage, where she admits she messed up, but wants to gloss over it and forget the whole thing. "All I ask is you don't let it ruin the present. Okay? Move on and give someone else a chance."

Move on. If only she knew how hard I try to move on. I try every day.

"I'd better go. I just came back from an interview and need to touch base with my boss." It's a relief to get off the phone. I don't have to listen to Leslie's voice while imagining how good it would feel to strangle her.

There's no time to think about that right now. Agent Siwak wants progress, and I don't have nearly enough to report after spending the morning out and about. It wasn't challenging to find Laura Barnes, considering she and Beth are Facebook friends. Laura made it a point to be the supportive pal, always commenting on the portraits which Beth shared. She's as aggressively supportive as Leslie is toward me. I wonder if she's as pushy, too.

Special Agent Siwak barely glances up from his keyboard when I knock on his open door. "Tell me you have something good for me."

Hello to you, too. "I would love to."

His rapid typing stops, his head slowly lifting until his

narrowed eyes find me. Strangely, they weigh around a hundred pounds each, crushing my skull while he stares holes through it. "And yet?"

"And yet, all I know is Dr. Greg Clyburn is a weepy mess without his wife. Whether it's an act or not, I couldn't tell you. Beth was thinking about expanding her little photography business, and a friend of hers was encouraging her to do it. I plan on going to this woman's house after checking in here with you. I want to know more about what Beth's mindset was before she disappeared. And how much Laura knows about the Clyburn marriage."

"You're suspicious of the husband?' He asks it while wearing a wry smirk, more than a little jaded. "He would hardly be the first."

"I want to know more about him," I explain. "Some people underreact when they are in a situation like this and they wind up painting a target on their backs. Then there are men like him who almost go overboard."

"Then by all means, check in with the friend." He pushes his chair away from the desk and crosses his ankles on its surface. As always, his shoes are well polished, his slacks crisp and unwrinkled. I admire his discipline, born from decades of keeping himself in top shape for the job. Reaching his early sixties hasn't changed things.

"Aside from that, I spoke to a couple of teachers over at Shenandoah Elementary today. It didn't lead anywhere, really. There doesn't seem to be a connection between these women aside from geography and the fact that their kids go to the same school."

"Who knows?" he suggests, scrubbing his hands over his smooth shaven cheeks. "It could be they decided to run away together. To get away from their responsibilities. The pressures of being the perfect wife and mother."

I know he's only half serious, brainstorming in a desperate attempt to bring us closer to resolution. But something about his choice of words rings true. "I have no doubt there's a lot of pressure in these women's lives. Drop-off line alone is like something out of a war movie."

He snorts softly. "You're not kidding about that. I've driven past there that time of morning and I would swear my blood pressure rises every time. When it comes to an area like this one, there are too many people with too much to do. They don't have enough free time for hobbies to fulfill them, so they turn scrutiny into a sport."

"I guess it's possible one or both of them decided to walk … but it would mean leaving the kids too. And in the worst possible way, with no explanation. Even though their husbands could be a little more present in their lives, I can't believe either of them would run away."

"Fair enough." Heaving a sigh, he asks, "What does that leave us with? The husbands? Anyone else?"

"So far, that's the most we've got. Unless local PD is withholding information from me. I would think they would know better, but I wouldn't put much past the chief right now. I've seen people look happier on their way to a root canal than he looks when he sees me coming."

His lips twitch knowingly. "Who can blame him, as charming as you are?"

"I have been nothing but professional. He's the one who came at me with his crummy attitude."

"Which is nothing new, and we both know it. I would hope they would know better than to withhold information."

"Right now, all I can do is talk to this Laura woman and hope she sheds a little light. She might be able to steer me toward additional people who know more about Beth's life than her husband does."

"Let's remember being a distant, distracted spouse does not make a person a murderer. Men like him tell themselves they're doing right by their spouses every day they get up and leave the house for work. They're providing. Their job is done. A lot of them simply don't stop to think about how much work it takes to keep things running."

"Or about how lonely and isolating that kind of thing can be. Thankless, too," I add.

"Yes, I'm sure it can be."

We both look at the phone on his desk when it rings. He holds up a hand while answering to stop me when I begin backing out of the room. Darn it. I was hoping I could get away before he takes his frustration out on me.

His gray eyebrows lift. "Oh? Yes, send me that information immediately. We'll have the CSI team run it through the database." By the time he hangs up, I already have a feeling what he's going to announce. "The bloodwork came back from that stain in Beth Clyburn's house."

16

River

"All we know so far is, there haven't been any hits on the DNA?" Daniel tips his head back until he's staring at the ceiling of Siwak's office. The boss called him in along with Emma after receiving the call from Chief Perkins. *I can't pretend I'm surprised the man didn't reach out to me and won't bother pretending to be insulted.*

"That was always going to be a possibility," Emma reasons. She doesn't look happy about it, but then why would she? *Since yesterday in the chief's office, I've held onto the hope that the bloodstain would lead us somewhere. That at least one of these women could be located based on what the stain tells us.*

Here we are, back at square one. No, that isn't exactly right, since we've been at square one all along. How is it possible? People don't vanish into thin air.

"But we can at least confirm the blood came from a male." Agent Siwak sits back, clasping his hands on top of his head of salt and pepper hair. "So we've narrowed the suspect list down to roughly a hundred-and-sixty million. And that's just in the United States."

At least he's trying to keep it light. That isn't always the case.

"There has to be something we haven't considered yet." Pacing the length of the office doesn't help anything, but neither does standing still. Chewing my thumbnail, staring at the floor, I do my best to view the situation through fresh eyes. "We have a pair of wives with successful husbands. Stay-at-home moms, young children. Everything perfect on the surface."

"Nothing is that perfect," Daniel murmurs. A quick look his way reveals his scowl.

"You sound like you're speaking from experience," I point out.

He only smirks. "Come on. I stopped believing in the concept of perfection around the time I found out Santa Claus isn't real."

"He isn't?" Emma winces. "Now you tell me."

"I didn't know I would be treated to a comedy routine this morning." Agent Siwak folds his arms, arching an eyebrow. "By all means. Keep going. I love a good laugh." The man is a master of making a person feel about two inches tall when he puts his mind to it. He makes it look effortless, in fact. Both Daniel and Emma are slightly shamefaced, Daniel scuffing the floor with the toe of his shoe, Emma clearing her throat and jamming her hands into her pockets.

"But Daniel makes a good point," I continue, exchanging a glance with Emma. She looks like a kid blushing after getting hollered at by the teacher.

"Nothing is that perfect. And anybody who thinks a stay-at-home mom has it easy has never tried to do it. Sometimes, I don't know how my sister gets through it without going crazy. There are all these standards she holds herself to."

"You get the feeling Tamara and Beth held themselves to the same standards?" Daniel asks.

I wonder if he realizes he used past tense when talking about them. "Most definitely. From the looks of it, Leslie would get along great with Beth. They could obsess together over coordinating the drapes and the throw pillows, or whatever people like that care about." I have a hard time thinking about my sister without irritation flaring up in my chest. It must leak into my voice, since I catch Emma giving me a curious look. I'll ignore it for now, though something tells me she won't allow me to ignore it forever. She wants to know what that meant. I gave her a quick rundown of last night's debacle when we first caught up here at the office, before I drove down to the school. At least she'll show me a little empathy, which Leslie seems unable to do.

"What else do these women have in common?" Siwak asks.

"Neither of them seem to have a lot of friends," Emma points out, looking around the room like she's looking for backup. "Has anyone noticed that?"

Now that she mentions it, that does stand out as being an odd coincidence. "That's true. They have plenty of acquaintances. The other moms, for sure. They're both involved with the PTA, volunteer work, that sort of thing. They know a lot of people, a lot of people know them. That isn't the same as having friends."

And I of all people understand that. I know what it means to have plenty of associates but no friends. Emma is somebody I depend on at work, and we know a lot of each other's lives, but I wouldn't necessarily call her a friend. Neither of us has ever asked the other one to do something social outside of work. I wouldn't consider grabbing lunch or a cup of coffee a social outing. Even so, it's always while we're working. Not that I have a social life, and she certainly doesn't have the time right now with the baby.

"That's an interesting distinction." Agent Siwak nods sagely. "In their own way, they are both isolated. Though to be fair, would their husbands know if they had close friends? From what you're telling me, they're both fairly uninvolved in their wives' daily lives."

Emma has a quick answer for that question. "I observed the school at pick up yesterday," she reminds him. "I stood there out in the open, my badge plainly visible. I can't tell you how many people drifted my way, asking if there was any news about the disappearances. I heard a lot about the two of them being missed around the school, about how they were in everybody's prayers. You know what I didn't hear?"

"You didn't hear anything personal," Daniel concludes.

"Bingo." Emma touches a finger to the tip of her nose. "You know how people get at times like this. They tend to place themselves in the center of the events. All of a sudden, a warm acquaintance becomes a best friend. Showing up at Starbucks at the same time once or twice a week turns into regular coffee dates. That isn't the case here. There's a lot of concern, but not a lot of personal connection with either of them."

"Maybe they both felt like outsiders," I murmur, going back to my pacing. "Or maybe they really do have secrets they were keeping. Maybe they don't trust a lot of people."

"Sometimes it's smarter to keep things to yourself," Emma muses. "It's not easy, learning to trust people. Especially if you've been burned in the past."

"You're going to talk to that friend of Beth's, aren't you?" Siwak asks. When I nod, he says, "That's our first step in finding out the kind of social life Beth really had, not the version her husband is aware of."

"The version he isn't aware of," I remind him. "Don't get me wrong. He seems like he could be a decent husband. He didn't get defensive the way Tamara's husband did. He seems in love with his wife. But…"

"But?" Daniel asks.

"But … I don't know. I can't put my finger on it. I was glad to leave the house," I admit, looking around to gauge everyone's reactions. "He was a little too much. Telling me he'll even pay ransom if it's demanded."

"What a strange possibility to land on," Emma says, frowning, wrinkling her nose. "It's not tacky, exactly. That's not the right word. But it gives me that vibe."

"Right." It's my turn to touch the tip of my nose the way she did. "It was tasteless, almost. I should've asked him what made him say that, but who knows? Maybe he's seen too many episodes of *Law and Order*."

"If that were true," Daniel points out with a snort, "he would be telling you how to do your job. There's nothing I love more than someone telling me how to do my job. Do I walk into a surgical theater and tell the guy holding the scalpel how to cut?"

"Why does it have to be a guy?" Emma mutters.

"Focus." Agent Siwak's sharp rebuke snaps us to attention again. He didn't direct that comment at me, yet somehow I'm suffering secondhand embarrassment. "You'll find out more about him from Laura Barnes. Why don't you take care of that, then report back?"

I'm being dismissed, and I couldn't be happier about it. It's a wonder my hair doesn't blow back, I duck out of the office so fast. Emma and Daniel follow me, with Emma joining me at my desk while I grab my shoulder bag tucked into the bottom drawer.

"Is everything okay with you?" She perches on the corner of the desk, uncomfortably close. She knows I don't like it when people get too close. I guess it's easy to forget, sometimes, especially when you spend enough time with somebody. She feels comfortable around me, and I'm glad she does. I wish I could say the same, not that it's anything personal. I rarely feel comfortable around anybody.

"Oh, just fine." I shove my phone into my bag before slinging it over my shoulder. "And already looking forward to another date tonight."

"What?" She comes as close to a full-body cringe as I've ever seen. "Wasn't last night enough?"

"So at least you're on my side now? Because yesterday, you were all about me going out and meeting somebody new."

Rolling her eyes, she retorts, "And I would encourage this if anybody but your sister was doing the matchmaking. What's so different about this guy? She thought last night's caveman was a good idea."

"Thank you. I feel a little less like I'm being unfair. She must have set this up in advance," I decide, shaking my head at both Leslie and myself. "How else would she magically have another date lined up for me tonight? I should have turned her down flat. It's not my fault she makes promises for me without checking in first."

Shrugging, she says, "Hey. It's a free meal."

That's a less positive spin than she put on last night's date. "What about you?" I have to ask before heading out. "You seem a little off."

"Another night of broken sleep. I have to believe it's going to get better soon." Then she yawns, which of course makes me yawn.

"I'd better get out of here before I fall asleep." At least I can leave her laughing. She's one of the few people I go out of my way to cheer up. It's the least I can do after everything she's put up with from me. I know I'm not easy.

The visit with Laura Barnes is enough to help push all thoughts of tonight's dinner to the back of my mind. If there's one thing I'm good at, it's compartmentalizing.

Otherwise, there's no way I could function.

17

River

Laura Barnes lives equidistant from Tamara and Beth in an equally impressive house that bears a resemblance to both. There isn't much room for originality out here, I guess. Like the building company responsible for these homes worked from a handful of templates when it came to size and features.

The one thing that sets Laura's house apart from the others is the bright yellow door which looks sharp against black trim. I wonder if the homeowners association had something to say about that. Whenever I hear about them, I'm grateful to live in an apartment. It might not be much, but I don't get harassed over grass that's a quarter of an inch too tall.

The presence of a few toys scattered across the lawn gives me insight into the cherubic twin girls she's featured on her Facebook page. Blue eyed, dimpled, with blond, Shirley Temple curls and ridiculously sweet smiles. From the looks of it, they like to play hard. There's a soccer ball, a baseball bat, a skateboard. Appearances can be deceiving.

Beth casts a look over my shoulder once she opens the front door. "Sorry everything is such a mess out here," she frets, joining me on the front porch. "I told them to pick up their things. I must have overlooked them this morning after I took them to school. I'm a little distracted." Her chin quivers and she folds her arms over her trim body. Like so many of the moms I observed this morning, she's wearing yoga pants, a tank, a zippered sweatshirt over top.

"Thank you for taking time out to speak to me." I'm reminded of the interview with Beth's husband, watching him cry. She fights off her emotions better than he did, blinking hard until her eyes aren't so watery anymore.

"It's the least I can do. Have you heard anything?" There's breathless hope in her voice. I hate to disappoint her. "Even if it's bad news. I can take it."

"I don't have anything to report." I gesture toward a pair of rocking chairs close by. "Maybe we should sit down. Take a breath. I've been up and around all day, and I imagine you have, too." She is wound about as tight as her slicked back, strawberry blond ponytail.

"I was surprised when you reached out." Laura arranges herself in one of the chairs, crossing her legs, her foot swinging in a quick rhythm. "I didn't think Greg would remember my last name so you could track me down."

That saves me having to ask about him. She brought him up with no prompting. More than that, she sounds downright sarcastic. "Have you and Beth been friends for long?"

"Years. I've been to the house a hundred times. We've had dinner together, attended birthday parties for each other's kids. But I swear, every time we get together, it's like there's this moment of confusion where he has to remember my name."

"Do you think it's cognitive?" I ask, intrigued.

Her laughter is soft, disarming. "No, that's not what I mean. He can't be bothered to remember. He's so important." She adds a dramatic roll of her dark blue eyes. "How could he possibly be bothered to remember a name when he has so many important things on his mind already?"

"Did you ever get the feeling it was personal? Or was this more of a normal thing for him?" I don't want the entire focus of this interview to revolve around Greg, but the insight into their relationship is valuable, as well.

"Oh, it wasn't personal. Beth jokes sometimes about having to remind him to brush his teeth and put on his shoes before he leaves the house. He's always reminding her how busy he is, how much he has to do. Coincidentally, that usually occurs when she asks for help around the house."

I can't say I'm surprised. There's a reason the helpless, clueless husband cliché is so common. "Do you think this is a problem for them? I mean, as far as Beth is concerned? Is she joking, or is she complaining?"

"A little from column A, a little from column B." She gives me a meaningful look before lowering her brow. "If you ask me, there's something off with him."

We are definitely going to come back to this. I can't afford to lose focus on what this was supposed to be about. "Let's talk about Beth's mental state as of late," I suggest, steering the conversation. "I understand you were talking to her about a possible business opportunity?"

"Oh, yeah. The wedding. She wasn't sure she wanted to do it at first, but she told me … "

She looks away, staring out at the kids' toys while her throat works and her chin trembles. I wait patiently for her to continue. "She told me she wanted to do it. That was the last time I talked to her. The day she … disappeared." Her gaze drops to her lap, her cheeks going red like she's about to cry.

"Did she decide to take it?" I ask gently, and Laura nods. "Did she say why she made that decision?"

"She didn't think she was good enough. She never thinks she's good enough." Running a hand under her eyes, she sighs the way Leslie sometimes does when I frustrate her. "I tried to talk her out of that, and I guess it worked, because she decided to do it. She just needs a little more confidence."

I appreciate the way she uses present tense to talk about her friend. She is still hanging onto hope. "Is that normal for her? That lack of confidence? Or does it only extend itself to her photography?"

"Beth … She's so smart. She's so determined. And she frets all the time about not doing a good enough job with everything in her life. As a wife, as a mom, she feels like she's pretending to be a grown-up, and everybody's going to see through her someday."

"I think most adults feel that way," I murmur, and she nods with a short grin. "This might sound like a leading question, but based on what you've already told me, I have to ask, do you think her relationship with Dr. Clyburn plays into this at all?"

Rather than give me a quick, thoughtless sort of answer, she sits with the question and mulls it over. I wait while birds sing in the trees nearby, adding to the picturesque quality of my surroundings.

Finally, she shakes her head. "I never got any sort of sinister feeling. There's being self -important and self-absorbed, which he can be, and then there's being neglectful or abusive. I don't think he's either of those things. I can't remember any red flags, anyway."

"What about other friends? Is there anyone she was close with, that she might have shared personal information with?"

"Like I said, she's too hard on herself. It's not easy for her to get close to people, you know? I'm that way, too," she admits with a tiny shrug.

"I can relate," I admit. Can I ever.

"I always figured having one or two really good friends is better than having ten friends I don't quite trust anyone not to talk about me behind my back." While I nod in agreement, she adds, "And if there's one thing people like to do around here, it's talk behind other people's backs. Don't even think about not participating in a fundraiser, and you had better not dream of bringing something to the bake sale that you bought in a store."

"Honestly, I would rather have something store-bought. You just don't know what people are doing in their kitchens."

She blurts out a laugh, nodding. "Right? Anyway, sometimes it's better to be picky when it comes to who you trust."

Sometimes? I find that to be true all the time. "So you were well aware of Beth's day-to-day life?"

"You mean, do I think she was keeping secrets?" Her ponytail swings back-and-forth when she shakes her head. "Not at all. What you see is what you get." Unlike someone telling a lie, Laura doesn't go into detail. She's not overly elaborate. The fact that she's so straightforward gives me confidence she's telling the truth.

Her Apple watch chimes and she checks it, then frowns. "I'm sorry. I have to run a couple of errands before pick-up. Is there anything else? I want to help, I really do. I miss her," she adds.

"If I think of anything, I'll ask. And in the meantime, don't hesitate to call me." For the second time today, I hand out a card before retreating to the car. She seems like a decent, straightforward sort of person. Unpretentious. Real, for lack of a better word. That gives me an idea of the sort of person Beth is — if they're close, it stands to reason they have a lot in common.

Though nothing she told me points me in any new direction. It's almost enough to make me wonder if Agent Siwak's half-joking theory holds a note of truth. How does a person disappear without a trace unless they planned everything in advance?

18

River

Tom Aten is a decent-looking guy in his mid-to-late thirties. Probably around six-two with a fairly athletic body – maybe a cyclist or a runner. His smile is warm and friendly when we meet in front of a seafood restaurant whose outdoor patio is bustling with activity beneath strings of white lights spanning the space. It's charming, which is a word I rarely use.

"I hope you don't mind, but I asked for a table outside," he tells me in his deep, rich voice as we step up to the host stand. I'm glad I wore a sundress, since it's unseasonably warm tonight.

"I'm sorry you got set up on this date," I offer once we're seated at a table overlooking a man-made lake where fountains shoot water into the air and a handful of kids feed ducks over the side of a footbridge. Again, charming. Things are looking up.

He laughs softly, almost in disbelief. "Why would you

apologize? There's nothing to apologize for. I'm lucky to be here with you tonight."

Down, boy. The way he says it, it doesn't come off as a throwaway line. Something cheap and cheesy a man might say to break the ice and make a girl feel good. It shouldn't creep me out, should it?

Maybe Leslie has a point. I need to stop profiling every man I meet. An occupational hazard for sure. "That's nice of you to say. Anyway, how long have you known Chris?"

"We've been working together a few years now. What about your work?" he counters as a server fills our water glasses before dropping off a drink menu. "I would love to hear about it."

"Oh, there isn't much to tell." He waves a hand, laughing in a way I'm sure is supposed to sound carefree, but comes off as sort of creepy.

"I find that hard to believe." The strings of lights crisscrossing overhead make his dark hair gleam as he leans in, lowering his voice, winking. "It's okay. You can tell me."

"Tell you what?" I ask with a nervous laugh.

"About your work." His eyes dance like we share a fun little secret. " I won't tell anybody. Scout's honor."

At first, during last night's debacle, I was a little offended. Wondering if Chris has a poor opinion of me, considering who he thought I would want to go on a date with. Now, I'm starting to wonder if it's Chris himself who's the problem. How does he attract these weirdos?

"So you know what I do for a living?" I'm going to need wine, and I'm going to need it fast. After ordering a glass of Chablis, I start plotting. How do I get out of this? I'm willing to give the guy a shot, to at least stay through our entrées, but I would like to have a backup plan just in case.

"Are you kidding? Your Leslie's sister, the FBI agent. Is it like what you see on TV? Probably not," he concludes before I have the chance to say a word.

"Truthfully, I don't think it matters what the profession is. There's never going to be a ton of realism on TV."

He nods slowly, like I just dropped some pearl of wisdom instead of regular common sense. "What do you do with your free time? If you have much of it," he adds, sounding sympathetic.

"I don't get a lot of free time," I admit, gratefully taking my glass of wine when it arrives. The skin on the back of my neck is prickly, and all of a sudden my dress doesn't fit right and my chair is uncomfortable and I would very much like to get out of here. I've never understood what a suspect feels like under questioning until this moment. He may as well shine a spotlight in my face.

"I guess not. Always at the office, doing research, analyzing evidence." He holds my gaze as he speaks, eyes shining like he's looking at his hero.

"Have you ever considered getting into law enforcement?" I ask, gritting my teeth in the closest I can come to a smile. "You seem so interested in it. Maybe that's what you're meant to be doing?"

His laughter is self-deprecating as he shakes his head. "Between you and me, I came really close to taking the test for the police academy straight out of high school. My parents talked me into going to college." He actually rolls his eyes, like he doesn't have a cushy job as a web programmer or whatever it is Chris does. I've never been quite sure. Maybe I should pay more attention.

"You don't seem to be doing too badly for yourself," I offer. "Tell me more about your work. What is it you like to do with your free time? Please," I add when he looks like he's going to brush off my questions, "I need a little bit of normalcy for once. It doesn't matter how boring you might think your work is. I want to hear about it."

Before he can launch into a story, our server arrives, wearing an expectant expression. "Did you have any questions about the menu? Can I send an order back to the kitchen for you?"

Darn it. Well, I told myself I would give him a chance. No ducking out before I'm locked in by ordering food. I settle on grilled salmon before Tom asks about the sourcing of their tuna. It's the perfect opportunity to reach into my purse, sitting on my lap, and set a twenty minute alarm on my phone. I deliberately use an alarm sound that mimics a generic ringtone, so it should come off as legit when I pretend there's an emergency phone call. If things get better between now and then, I can always dismiss the call and get back to our meal.

"So, I hate to disappoint you." Tom takes a sip of his beer, shrugging. "I have nothing interesting to share. I sit behind a computer all day, running tests of our code, praying I don't see too many red lines."

When I tip my head to the side, since I have no idea

what he's talking about, he explains, "A red result means the test failed."

"Oh. I see. I'd pray for the same thing."

"It must seem painfully boring compared to what you do. I'm almost embarrassed to explain it." He laughs before drinking from the bottle again.

"I don't see it that way at all," I insist. "That's the truth. You don't know how many times I've wished I had a regular, nine-to-five job. Something predictable I can build a life around."

"I guess there are drawbacks to everything." The arrival of our food gives him a reason to stop staring at me with that unnerving intensity. It's a relief to break eye contact. I can breathe again, something one wouldn't imagine to be a problem while sitting outside.

Twenty minutes can't pass quickly enough. How long has it been since I set the alarm? Hours? Half a lifetime? How much longer can I sit here with this pleasant expression plastered on my face?

"So really." He cuts into his tuna, staring at me instead of at the fish. "Tell me. Is it hard, doing what you do? The sort of thing that sticks with you after the day is done?"

Am I imagining the almost breathy tone in his voice? Again with the hero worship stuff. Part of me–an extremely large part–wants to tell him it's horrible. Nightmarish. That I've seen things nobody ought to see. I want to mess with him, in other words, have a little fun with his silly notions.

"It's challenging to separate work from my personal life," I admit. "Which is why I don't like going over it when I'm not there." Will he take the hint and drop the subject? Something tells me no, but I had to try. When I tear Leslie a new one over this, and I most definitely will, I want to honestly tell her I did everything I could to turn the conversation in another direction.

I'm almost glad when he frowns, while I take a few bites of salmon. Might as well get everything I can out of the meal. Why won't the alarm ring? "You won't make an exception? Even for me?"

I don't know you. "I'm not sure what you want to hear." The rest of the wine is nice and cold when it goes down my throat all at once.

He lifts a shoulder before a smile touches the corners of his mouth. "Oh, you know."

"I don't." And I won't look away. Let him feel uncomfortable. Put on the spot. "What is it you would like to hear about?"

The problem is, he doesn't seem to mind or even notice. Setting down the knife and fork, he looks me straight in the eye and asks, "Have you ever killed anyone?"

I could cry with relief when the alarm rings, making me jump before I just about claw the phone out of my purse. "Sorry," I murmur with a brief smile. "I have to take this. It might be important."

Pretending to listen to somebody telling me about an emergency, I gasp, touching a hand to my mouth. "No. Seriously? How many people were in the building at the time? Did any of them make it out?"

He doesn't have the first clue that I'm making this up

to mess with him, hanging on my every word. "Okay. I'll be there as soon as I can."

"What's happening?" he asks, breathless, once I've ended a call that never started and pushed my chair away from the table.

"I … no. I can't talk about it," I tell him in a hushed voice. "You might hear about it on the news. You might not. Let me give you money for my half of the meal."

He doesn't keep me from taking cash from my wallet and dropping it on the table. "Be careful," he warns, wide-eyed and hushed before I head for the parking lot like my life depends on it. For all I know, that might be exactly the case.

19

River

After last night's disaster of a date, there are a few sweeter things I could hear on walking into the field office than what Daniel Brennon practically shouts as soon as he catches sight of me coming down the hall. "We got the financials!" He throws his hands into the air like a referee signaling a touchdown.

"Finally." Suddenly, there's a spring in my step, when only moments ago I fought through brain fog resulting from yet another night spent wrestling the past. If this keeps up, I'll have to fess up and let Leslie know her attempts at matchmaking are robbing me of sleep. For some reason, these awful dates have the ability to dredge up ugliness I've worked hard to suppress. Maybe because in both instances, there's been a sense of powerlessness.

All of that can be pushed aside for now, knowing we have a direction to move in. I was starting to think we would never get our hands on the Higgins and Clyburn financial records. Both husbands have sworn up and down there can't possibly be anything incriminating in the accounts – they both insist they keep a close eye on the family's finances. I have to wonder if either of them could estimate how much the family spends on groceries every week. Or what it costs to replace a pair of kids' sneakers. It isn't that I look down on them, exactly. I have to raise an eyebrow at their certainty, is all, especially when neither of them can come up with much insight into their wives' daily lives.

"Have you found anything yet?" I ask Daniel while dropping my things off at my desk. It's a good thing I went with an extra shot of espresso in my latte this morning. I'm going to need every ounce of concentration, since poring over countless transactions isn't exactly the most exciting work. We asked for a full year's worth of records from both families, meaning there's going to be a lot of squinting and cross referencing in my immediate future.

The man has a way of looking at me like he's wondering which planet I flew in from. "Are you kidding? I've only been here for ten minutes, myself." He checks his watch, snickering. "I'm good, but I'm not that good."

"Sue me for being hopeful," I mumble before taking a deep swig of my coffee. "Is Emma in yet?"

"Emma is right here." She holds up a paper bag while approaching my desk. "It was my day to pick up sandwiches, remember?"

"Good thing. We're going to need our energy." I look around the increasingly busy floor, a plan forming in my head. "Let's take everything to one of the small conference rooms to spread out. It will make more sense for us to go through this together rather than breaking it up and working separately." Now that we have a direction to go in and tools we can use, my determination is at an all-time high. I'm sure the coffee is helping matters.

"How did last night go?" Emma asks in a soft voice as we grab our laptops to take to the conference room.

"Daniel, can you get those documents printed out if you haven't started already?" I ask, pretending I didn't hear Emma's question. It's bad enough I don't like discussing my private life in the first place – with Emma it's more of a necessary evil, since she's the kind of person who genuinely cares. If she were being nosy or curious for the sake of being critical, it would be easy to brush off her questions and move on. I've sort of made an art form out of it.

She isn't like that, unfortunately. She wants to be supportive. I don't know why she cares. My life isn't that interesting.

It's obvious when she won't quit staring at me that she won't take a hint. "Honestly?" I ask, setting my machine down on the table and placing my coffee beside it. "The night was effectively over when he asked if I've ever killed anybody."

I'm surprised her jaw doesn't hit the table. "No way. You're making that up."

"I wish I were, to tell you the truth. I'm starting to think Chris's company only hires sickos, which makes me seriously wonder about the sort of man my sister is married to."

"Please." There's laughter in her eyes when she

narrows them. "Like you didn't run a full background check the second she had a ring on her finger."

That is surprisingly close to the truth, though I never shared it with anyone. Call it an occupational hazard. I know too well what human beings can do to each other. How they can hide things. I doubt any of my captor's coworkers knew they kept a girl in a basement cell for two years. They would have caught up over coffee in the break room or discussed last night's ball game while I rocked myself in a corner, desperate for a little comfort.

Emma shakes her head with a sigh while unpacking our breakfast sandwiches from the Courthouse Cafe. I'm glad to see my sandwich features one of their jalapeno cheddar bagels, which normally sell out within an hour of opening. "I didn't know people honestly thought that way," she says. "In what universe is it okay to ask somebody a question like that on a date?"

"What kind of question?" Daniel asks as he joins us, closing the door behind him before dropping a stack of paper on the table. "Who went on a date?"

The look I shoot Emma leaves nothing to the imagination. It's one thing to open up to her, but there's a line I'd rather not cross. All of a sudden, he'll think he's entitled to all sorts of personal information I would rather not share. Some people only need the door to be slightly ajar before they take the opportunity to kick it wide open.

Emma is either unaware of this or doesn't care, because she ignores my sharp look and explains, "River was set up by her sister and brother-in-law. He asked if she's ever killed anybody on the job."

Did I ask her to announce my private business? Yes,

we work closely with Daniel, he's part of our team, but that doesn't mean I want to air my personal messes in front of him. Besides, he's a man. I don't need him defending these weirdos.

As it turns out, that's one thing I don't have to worry about. "What a loser," he snickers. "One of those idiots who think there's anything glamorous about what we do. I hope you told him you make a notch on the grip of your service weapon every time you blow somebody away."

I have to laugh when I imagine Tom's expression. "I sort of wish I had. Anyway, let's get cracking on these bank accounts. I would love to put that behind me."

It's a relief to settle into work, and for a long time, the only sounds are that of our fingers striking keys, flipping pages, the rustling of wax paper as we unwrap and eat our sandwiches. Daniel handles the Clyburn files while Emma and I comb through the Higgins accounts.

"I don't understand why people have to make this so complicated," Emma muses, clicking her tongue and shaking her head. "Who needs this many accounts to keep things straight? Money is so simple."

For some people," Daniel points out. "Don't forget, money issues lead to more divorces than any other cause. At least, according to statistics. For some couples, it might be easier to separate things out like this."

"Are there multiple accounts for the Clyburns, too?" I ask. Leaning over, I take a look at one of the printouts Daniel is studying.

"There's the household account, the savings account, an account for both boys. There's also an account which

Beth earmarked for her photography. That hasn't been heavily used," he concludes, passing the monthly statements my way.

Even then, it doesn't look like Beth was charging much for her services. "I guess because she's so untested," I muse, answering my own question. "Laura Barnes did mention her lack of confidence. But it looks like all of these deposits were then transferred into the main checking account, aside from the money she spent early on, not long after the account was opened."

When I look up the phone number associated with the account the payment went to, I end up on a site geared toward photographers. She must've bought equipment once she got serious about continuing with her business.

"I'm actually a little disappointed for her," Emma muses. "You would think she would use a little of that money for herself."

"It could be Dr. Clyburn provides her with everything she needs," Daniel counters. "She might not need to keep money aside for herself."

"Every woman should keep money aside for herself," Emma insists with fresh, surprising intensity. "What happens if—"

It's time to slash a hand across my throat. "All right, all right." We don't have time for this to devolve into an argument about marital finances and what a stay-at-home partner should do to protect themselves in case the marriage falls apart. Everybody has their own opinions, and something tells me a man and a woman would naturally diverge.

"Here's something interesting." Emma rotates her machine slightly so I can get a look at what she's referring to. "This is the third entry in as many months. Money comes in from another account."

"Is there a corresponding transaction in any of the other accounts? Somewhere the cash transferred in from?"

"It doesn't look that way. Maybe I'm missing something." She sits back while I conduct my own search, cross referencing dates on which the money was transferred in. It doesn't come from any of the savings accounts, retirement accounts, household accounts.

"Maybe Mrs. Higgins has been hiding a secret," Daniel suggests. "I don't see anything like that on this end."

"It wouldn't be the first time a woman kept an account on the side," Emma points out. I'm going to ignore the darkness in her voice when she mutters that. I have a bad habit of reading too much into little comments which probably mean nothing. There's no time to waste sitting around and prying into someone else's privacy—we're already prying into these families' private matters as it is. Besides, she makes a good point.

"Frankly, I could never leave my entire financial future in the hands of my spouse. There would be way too much trust involved." I can only shake my head as I continue combing through and clicking back and forth between accounts on the bank's website.

"What if Tamara felt the same way? She might have been siphoning money here and there to pad a secret savings account," Daniel suggests. "It could be she figured her husband would never notice."

"I doubt he would have, but it still doesn't explain why she would sock the money away," Emma points out.

"She might've been using the money for something she didn't want him to know about," I muse, tapping out a rapid rhythm on the table with my nails. "I think we need to find this account. Contact the bank, let them know what's going on, and track down this account. Why wasn't this information included with everything else we received?" I feel it in my bones. This could be what does it. Something as simple as a hidden bank account can sometimes be the key to unlock an entire mystery.

I hope this is one of those times.

20

River

The bank was more forthcoming than I expected.

"I wonder if David Higgins knows about this," I murmur while scrolling through a lengthy list of transactions. It only took a couple of hours to unravel the mystery of Tamara's hidden account. Unlike the others, this one is in her name only. It's through the same bank, which makes sense. Transferring funds between accounts in the same institution is instantaneous, while going through an outside bank can take days. She would want to keep things as simple as possible. Painless.

Daniel leans back in his chair, his hands clasped behind his head. He could be posing for a spread in a sales flier, something advertising men's dress shirts and pants. "Based on everything you've told me about him after your interview, I'm going to say no, he didn't have the first clue."

His grin quickly fades, though. "If this case is teaching me anything, it's how clueless people can be when it comes to what they believe goes on in their relationship."

"This could still be perfectly innocent." Granted, I find it hard to believe, but one of us needs to keep a clear head rather than jumping to conclusions. I mean, have I already jumped to them? Headfirst. But we have to at least entertain other possibilities.

"It's not only that." He runs a hand over his jaw, snickering softly. "It makes me think about what I don't pick up on at home. I couldn't tell you what size soccer cleats my son wears. Granted, I could brush that off, make an excuse about how fast his feet grow. It's not easy keeping up with growth spurts."

"I don't know. We're pretty busy around here. I think you could be forgiven for not knowing the details." And that is as close as I can come to comforting someone when I'm champing at the bit to get to the bottom of this new mystery we've uncovered.

"Is that sympathy I hear?" He has the nerve to arch an eyebrow, his lips twitching in a smirk.

"It doesn't have to be," I remind him, and either my voice or the look on my face when our eyes meet convinces him to get serious.

On the surface, there's nothing out of the ordinary about this account. It could be Tamara wanted to put a little something aside for herself, an instinct I agree with. I am not a trusting person by nature, something which I doubt anyone could blame me for. I can't imagine leaving myself unprotected in case my spouse decided to walk out on me or fritter away the money I worked so hard to keep under control.

Then again, I doubt I could strike up a long-term relationship with anyone who would insist on me not having a job of my own. I know not everybody thinks the way I do. Lucky for them.

It does seem strange that she would keep an account solely in her name, not to mention one which David Higgins didn't have the first clue about. That was his attitude when I called to ask him about it, anyway. "What do you mean, she had a separate account? Why? Where?" His rapid-fire questions and the tension behind them sent up a multitude of red flags. Financial abuse might be the most insidious kind, since it's so easily hidden from the public.

Daniel cracks open a can of soda and takes a deep gulp. "What do you think about this?" he asks, highlighting a few lines of transactions. "There's a payment made to this external account once every two weeks."

I've noticed that, myself, going back for months. "It's not so much the transactions," I point out. "It's the lack of info." Normally, in the case of the other transactions in the long list, there are obvious clues pointing to the nature of the company or vendor taking the payment. That's not the case here. Instead, there's a series of letters following the word *payment*.

Daniel leans in, his shoulder brushing mine as he squints at the screen. I need to find a way to get past my immediate aversion to his nearness. It's not his fault I once got into a car with the wrong person.

"I'm going to look this up," he announces, and I read the letters off to him so he can do a little digging while I continue combing through transactions. None of them involve much money. Neither do the transfers out of the Higgins' shared accounts. That much, I can understand. Tamara would want to avoid getting her husband's attention by taking larger sums at a time. Up to this point, it doesn't look like anything sinister is happening here.

That is, until David gets off the phone, wearing a knowing grin. "I think we're in luck here," he announces, and I hear the excitement running under his words. It's enough to make me remind myself not to get my hopes up.

"Are you going to share with me, or do I have to guess?" I might as well be talking to myself as he types furiously on his keyboard. He's digging through old files on the Bureau network. There aren't many things I dislike more than sitting on my hands and waiting, meaning my teeth are grinding by the time he releases what I'm hoping is a triumphant grunt.

"I knew it sounded familiar." He swivels his chair, facing me, and I recognize the excitement in his eyes. The way they gleam. "They named the company in a very unique, memorable way. It reminded me of a case I worked, I don't know, five years ago. They take the first three letters of a last name, like Smith or Jones, then the first five letters of a city. In this case, it's J-O-N-R-I-C-H-M. Jones-Richmond."

His triumphant grin precedes his conclusion. "They're shell companies, and if I'm right, the same group of lowlifes is still operating."

"What were these guys into?" I ask, my curiosity growing.

"You name it. Whatever they could get into. Money

laundering, for the most part—that was what we put a handful of them away for, but we never did uncover the names of the guys at the top of the pyramid." The anger winding through his words isn't lost on me. I'd be angry, too, reflecting on a group of criminals who got away. "They were running crypto schemes last I heard, though I didn't know they grew the guts to show themselves in the States again."

What does my gut think about this? "They must be running something that looks legit." I look his way, gauging his reaction. "Tamara doesn't fit the profile of someone involved in shady schemes."

"Agreed." He checks the time, then clears his throat while wearing a guilty expression. "If you wouldn't mind, I think this is a good time to stop for lunch. That sandwich I had earlier only did so much for me."

How is it almost two o'clock already? "That would explain why my stomach's growling." Yet I don't make any effort to get up.

He lets out a soft groan and clicks his tongue. "Tell me you're not going to sit here and starve yourself. All of this can wait until you get some food in your system."

"You're starting to sound like Emma, and that is not a compliment." She had to take a couple of hours for a pediatrician appointment but will be back later.

"I'll bring you back a sandwich," he offers. I'm not going to bother talking him out of it, since I know it would be a waste of time. If anything, the harder I argue, the more food he'll bring. I'll end up buried under a pile of different salads, sandwiches, maybe pizza to top it off.

While waiting for him, I place a call to the bank,

asking for the same manager Daniel has been dealing with. "There is a company our missing woman has made several payments to on a regular basis over the past several months. I need more information on them."

Once we're on the same page, I hear tapping in the background. "They're classified as a service provider," the man tells me. "But I can't locate information as to the sort of service they provide. I do, however, have an address linked to the account."

Unfortunately, when I look up the address, I'm led to a satellite image of an abandoned building in a block of similar buildings. Something tells me no one is doing business out of any of them – not legal business, anyway. Nothing that would look remotely legitimate.

By the time Daniel returns with what smells like a meatball sub, I'm ready to burst out of my skin. "The address on record for the bank is no good, but I hunted down the address they forward the mail to."

He leans in to study the satellite image of a small building, one of many which take up a block of properties in a commercial district on the outskirts of town. "It might not mean anything," I conclude, "but I would like to know who these people are and why Tamara was paying them twice a month."

"If I know you, you already have an idea in mind." He sits down and starts unwrapping his lunch, one eye on me and a smirk tugging the corners of his mouth.

He's right. I do have an idea in mind.

And it's going to involve a trip to the store to buy some workout clothes.

21

River

"Stop fidgeting so much." Emma's soft laughter filters through what is meant to look like an innocent AirPod in my right ear.

"These pants are so tight," I mutter through clenched teeth, keeping my voice low and my eyes sweeping the area as I wait for cars to pass before crossing the street. Now that I am here in person, one thing is clear, the business looks legitimate, blending into a row of similar storefronts. The only thing setting it apart from the others is a green-and-white striped awning. There's no name on the plate glass window spanning the front of the building, which is slightly tinted like somebody doesn't want what goes on inside visible from the sidewalk.

"You're the one who wanted to look like the sort of woman who would hire a cleaning service," Emma reminds me. She's around here somewhere, watching me, keeping an eye out for anything that looks out of place.

Sure, it was one thing for me to get into character,

but it's another to feel like my whole backside is exposed in these tight workout pants. I'm carrying one of those big Stanley cups in one hand and sort of wishing there was something stronger than plain water inside. It isn't as if this is my first time going undercover – and really, it isn't like I'm planning on making this a long-term thing. I am only posing as a potential client for the sake of getting a closer look at the place and the people who run it.

I barely recognize myself once I reach the glass door leading into the small office. My dark hair is pulled back in a ponytail, and I'm even wearing mascara and lip gloss. As my hand closes around the handle of the door, I call to mind Laura Barnes and the other women I've interacted with since Tamara and Beth went missing. I need to be like them.

"Looking good," Daniel murmurs, reminding me he and Emma can see the reflection in the door just like I can thanks to the small camera embedded in a charm resting on my chest, hanging from a delicate chain.

The first word that comes to mind on stepping inside is *cheerful*. There's upbeat music playing softly through a speaker I can't locate. The space is brightly but warmly lit, and there are plants all over the place. One of them is currently having its leaves wiped down when the woman working on them turns at the sound of my entrance. She could be around forty, dressed in a skirt and blouse that don't quite fit right. I can't put my finger on it, but something is off with her.

"I'll be with you in just a minute," she offers from the other side of a waist-high wall separating the waiting room from her desk. Her bright, cheerful smile is almost aggressive. She's trying too hard.

She steps down from the stepladder she used to access a hanging plant in the far corner of the room. There are a couple chairs placed close to the wall behind me. Why would a small cleaning service run an office clients can visit in person? It seems extraneous, to put it mildly. A waste of overhead costs, too.

"I'm not even sure what I'm looking for," I tell the woman as she approaches. Her makeup was applied with a heavy hand and by the time she reaches her desk, her smile has become brittle. Like she's tired of wearing it already. Her gaze shifts to a closed door a little further back, the only door besides one with a sign for the restroom.

"You need cleaners?" she asks. When I nod, she nods back. "You've come to the right place. We just need you to fill out some forms, give us a basic idea of what you'll need and the size of your home. Once you're finished with that, we can talk about pricing and scheduling."

"Whatever you say." My laughter sounds a little awkward even to my ears, but it works. She doesn't seem to be suspicious of me, at least, instead she hands me a clipboard and directs me to one of the molded plastic chairs at my back. At least now I understand the reason for them.

"You're going to have to make something up," Daniel mutters in my ear. I'm glad he can't see my face, since I doubt I could keep from rolling my eyes at him if we were face to face. There are times he comes out with things like that, then takes a step back like he's waiting to be congratulated for it.

The fact is, I don't plan on finishing these forms. This is only a matter of getting an idea of the way things are done around here. I fill in lines at random. How many bedrooms does my house contain? Four. Why not? Bathrooms? Two-and-a-half sounds good. One for my nonexistent children, one for me and their nonexistent father, and a half bath for visitors.

A bell over the door chimes when it opens. I glance up more out of reflex than anything else. A bell rings, you look up. We're all sort of trained that way.

Instantly, my curiosity is piqued by the man who enters. He's in his mid-fifties, at least, wearing a black leather jacket over a t-shirt and a pair of jeans. There's nothing out of the ordinary about him, at least not on the surface. I do have to wonder what he's doing in a place like this, though. I doubt he's looking for a housecleaning service.

The girl behind the desk recognizes him at first glance, going stiff once his gaze lands on her. I chew my lip, tapping the form with my pen while watching them from under my lowered lashes. She shoots a look my way – when I don't react, she pushes her chair back from her desk and ducks through the door behind it, closing it with a soft click.

"Try to get this guy on camera," Daniel murmurs in my ear. "Let's see if we can get an ID on him. He sticks out like a sore thumb."

He's right about that. The man is not who I would expect to see somewhere like this. He jams his hands into his jacket pockets and looks my way. I sit up a little straighter, holding the clipboard in front of me rather than balancing it on my lap. This way, I can get a better image of the stranger for Daniel and Emma to analyze.

I'm still staring at the forms, pretending not to pay attention to him. "Look at him, sizing you up," Emma whispers. It's unnerving, but I force myself to feign ignorance. I can feel his gaze on me. Shrewd, calculating. It's enough to make me feel exposed – I have to resist the urge to cross my arms over myself, like he can see through my clothes or something.

One thing he doesn't know about me, I spent a very long time being observed like an animal in a zoo. I had no choice but to learn how to ignore it, or to at least pretend I was ignoring it. It's nothing to sit here and fake ignorance, humming softly to myself as I pretend to figure out my home's approximate square footage.

A squeak of hinges catches my attention, and I look up to find the receptionist stepping out from that room. After glancing my way, she nods to the man in the leather jacket, then ushers him through the swinging door in that waist-high wall. They don't exchange a word before she shows him through the door and quickly closes it behind him. There's no chance of getting a look inside. What could they be hiding in there? Or who?

"How's it going with that form?" she asks, cutting through the awkward tension left behind like the stranger's spicy cologne. Is it just me, or is she nervous?

Emma murmurs in my ear, "We've got an ID on this guy. Ran his face through the database and got a hit almost immediately."

"He's wanted in connection with a trafficking ring," Daniel announces, sounding grim.

"You want to get out of there," Emma urges. "This changes things. We need to regroup."

I've heard more than enough. "You know what?" I stand, pulling the form away from the clipboard. "I really need to discuss this with my husband before I make any commitments. But I'll be back."

"Uh, okay?" The woman laughs softly, like she's in disbelief, and the sound follows me out to the sidewalk.

"Are you all right? Talk to me," Emma implores. "Sorry. I didn't mean to spook you like that."

She didn't. I would tell her so, too, but I need to catch my breath. It's not fear that has me fighting to loosen the pinhole which my throat tightened into.

"I'm fine," I murmur, wanting to reassure her while thoughts and ideas and questions clang around in my head. "If I stayed any longer, I would've given us away."

I start down the sidewalk, taking a few sips of water from my cup in a vain attempt at cooling off the heat that's risen in me. Something is happening in that little office, something sinister. I have rarely been so sure of anything.

So sure, in fact, that it takes the blaring of a horn to snap me back into the present moment. I scramble for the curb after taking a step off, barely avoiding being struck by a dark blue truck with a string of beads hanging from the rearview mirror. A rosary? It could be.

"Are you okay?" Daniel asks, his voice sharp in my ear.

My heart is pounding and a sick, cold sensation

washes over me as I watch the truck's retreat. "I'm fine." I got a partial plate. Squeezing my eyes shut, I repeat the letters and numbers to myself three times, four, determined to commit them to memory. "And I just saw a familiar truck. Last four on the plate are D-8-H-K."

"The truck that almost hit you just now?" Emma asks. "Familiar how?"

I'm still fighting to catch my breath as another layer of questions and suspicions add what already had me struggling to hold myself together. "I noticed it parked across from Shenandoah Elementary yesterday, and I think I noticed it on surveillance footage before that."

There's more.

I caught a glimpse of the man behind the wheel. He must have left through a rear door after his meeting in that secret, closed-off room.

Why would he be parked across the street from an elementary school?

22

River

The next two days are spent setting up surveillance of the cleaning business which looks more and more like a front for something far less innocuous.

"I'll give them this much. They fly under the radar." Settling back in the driver's side seat of the late model easily forgettable van, I watch the building down the street the way I've done on and off ever since I went in pretending to be a potential client. Between the footage I gathered through the hidden camera and identification of the man in the leather jacket, it didn't take much to convince Special Agent Siwak what the next step needed to be.

Unfortunately, these guys are slick. Would it be too much to ask for a bunch of bumbling idiots? The most we've picked up so far is a handful of visits from men much like the one I encountered. Men who keep their heads on a swivel as they enter and leave the premises.

Men who would look more at home walking into a seedy bar than a cleaning service.

"At least Leslie hasn't set me up on any new dates lately." When Emma doesn't respond, staring out the window from the passenger side of the van, I gave her a gentle nudge. "You okay over there? Where did you go?"

"I'm right here." She sits up a little straighter, tightening her jaw, narrowing her eyes. "I guess I'm the only one who ever zoned out while spending hours sitting in the same place."

This isn't like her. Emma is one of the few people in my life who I would bother trying to understand. Most people are too much trouble. I don't have the time or the patience to figure out why they act like they do.

Emma is one of the good ones. That's why, instead of writing her off or rolling my eyes, I ask, "Are you all right? Did you have a late night with the baby?"

"They're all late nights," she whispers. There's something I don't like about the way she says it. She sounds lost. A million miles away. This is more than fatigue.

A few minutes pass while I search for something to say that won't upset her. I don't like being pushed to speak, and I doubt I'm alone in that. If I try too hard, she'll shut down. Then not only will she probably be angry with me, she'll be angry while we're sitting in the same van.

"I don't see why the whole world assumes I should want to find somebody." I'm taking a chance, hoping to learn a little more by making this about me for now. I've heard people say the first months of parenting can be the most difficult for a couple. I know that was true for Leslie

– I tried my best to be a shoulder for her to lean on in those days, though I don't know how much help I could've been.

Emma manages to muster a halfhearted smile, finally swiveling my way so I catch sight of her profile. How did I not notice those deep circles under her eyes? She's always understandably tired, but this is different. This is more than fatigue. She looks sick.

"Trust me," she murmurs with that same weak smile. "You don't know what it's like, having somebody in your corner all the time. I know not everybody is lucky enough to have that person, even if they are involved or married or whatnot. It's worth kissing a few frogs when it means eventually finding your prince."

"And you feel like you found yours?" I ask. Maybe it's not something marital, after all. Or maybe it is and she doesn't want to admit it. She'll loosen up and tell me what's on her mind if I keep her talking long enough. I don't know why it feels so important, getting to the bottom of her strange attitude today.

"Oh, of course I did. Don't get me wrong. Things aren't always perfect. But I know … " She trails off, almost like she loses her breath and can't continue.

"You know Steve will always be there for you?" I prompt, watching her.

Her head bobs, but she doesn't say anything until the door to the supposed head office of a supposed cleaning business opens and a tall, thin man steps outside. This is the second time I've spotted him, the dark-haired man with a crooked nose. It looks like it's been broken at least once. It's the sort of face that bears its owner's history in every strange angle, thin scar, the lines that seem to be permanently etched across his forehead and in between his eyebrows. There's always a sour set to his thin lips, too, like he just heard something that displeased him.

"What's he up to?" Emma murmurs, the two of us holding our breath as he lights a cigarette before pulling out his phone and holding it to his ear. We're too far away to hear anything he might say, but body language tells stories of its own. He's angry, jabbing his lit cigarette at some invisible adversary while he mutters into the phone and snarls.

"Somebody is keeping him waiting," I suggest. "Or they've disappointed him."

"How many different people have we seen come in and out?" Emma asks, going back through notes we've both kept. She runs a hand through her curls as she reads, and their condition catches my attention and holds it. It's one thing for her to be tired and maybe a little under the weather, but she never leaves her hair looking all messy and frizzy. I can't imagine how I would handle curly hair like hers and keep it looking half as good, so maybe I'm reading too much into it.

When she glances up from her notes, arching an eyebrow, I realize I'm the one zoning out this time. "If I remember correctly, there've been five different individuals, seven visits total."

"Your memory is unbeatable." Looking up and out toward where our unnamed man now paces the sidewalk, she snorts. "I wouldn't want to be whoever it is he's mad at right now."

"He walks like the sidewalk offended him somehow," I observe, making her snort again.

"Like he wants to punish it with every step." Her humor fades as quickly as it bubbled up. "This is a dangerous guy. I think we can call it like it is at this point. What is a guy like this doing with a cleaning business?"

"Simple. He isn't doing anything with the business itself. But it is a good front," I have to admit as we watch him continue to pace and take his anger out on whoever is on the other end of that call. "I never thought I'd feel bad for somebody who has to be a complete waste of air. I mean, if they're involved with him in any way, they have to be a cretin."

"I wouldn't feel sorry for them," Emma murmurs. "Anything he says or threatens them with is nothing compared to what they deserve, I'm sure."

It's unusual for her to sound this dark and bitter. That's usually my area of expertise. "Are you sure you're okay?" I have to ask before mimicking the way she groans. "What? You don't like somebody prying into your personal stuff? Guess what? Neither do I. But you make me deal with it all the time."

"Sometimes it's not that simple," she murmurs. She won't look at me. Why won't she look at me?

I open my mouth to ask, but she makes a strangled noise before nodding, staring down the street. "Look. Watch this."

I do, and I'm treated to the sight of a black sedan double parking close to where the angry, cigarette smoking man waits. A second guy – no older than a kid, probably barely out of his teens – jumps out of the passenger side of that car and darts over to where the angry man hurls what can only be insults at him. I don't need to hear him or even to read his lips to know he's delivering a scathing verbal assault. He even smacks the kid upside the head before shoving him back to the car, his mouth moving a mile a minute the entire time. The car peels away before the kid has the chance to close the door.

"I wouldn't waste any time getting away, either," I decide, snickering. "I wonder what that was all about. Do you think we should get closer? I need to be able to hear what's happening."

When Emma doesn't respond, I look her way – then forget everything else for a minute when I find a tear trickling down her cheek. She's shaking, pale, but worst of all is the way she recoils when I reach out to touch her arm.

"Sorry," she whispers, then covers her face with her hands. "I can't do this. I keep telling myself I'm wrong, but I don't think I am."

"Wrong about what?" I whisper while the sounds of her strangled sobs fill the van's interior. "You can tell me. It doesn't have to go any further than this van, I promise." It's the least I can do for her, after all.

"You don't understand. This isn't something I can just talk about. It's… complicated and maybe dangerous."

Dangerous? "Whatever it is, it's eating you up. I know how that feels, you know I do. And you know you can trust me. I mean, who would I tell? I barely talk to anyone." Now I know how desperate I am to make her feel better, since I made a lame attempt at a joke.

She takes a few deep, shuddering breaths, and enough time passes to make me wonder if she'll offer anything up. Finally she lowers her hands, letting them drop to her lap before staring at them. "I think ... somebody hurt me," she chokes out. "Somebody we both know."

23

River

I'm pretty sure I haven't breathed in the seconds since Emma broke down and admitted why she is the way she is today. Sometimes, you can hear something that is so entirely unexpected, it takes time to catch up.

Considering I was expecting this to be something domestic, it takes even longer for me to process what she admitted. "Okay," I whisper, grappling with the sense of being tossed out to sea without a lifejacket. I'm bobbing in open water, flailing around for something to grab a hold of. All she can do is stare at her hands, which are clenched into tight fists in her lap.

"But I'm not sure," she whispers, shaking her head. "I'm sorry. I shouldn't have said anything."

"Don't do that," I grunt. "That is the last thing you need to do. I asked you what was wrong, and you told me. There's nothing to apologize for here."

"But there is, because I'm telling you something I'm not sure of. This isn't something you just, you know … "

She waves a hand before tightening it again. "You can't go off half-cocked. It's a big deal."

My head is spinning, and that storefront could go up in flames this very second without my noticing it. The circles under her eyes. The frizzy hair. The way her knee keeps bouncing up and down, jittery. Whatever happened, she's suffering because of it. That's what matters more than anything.

"Do you think you can tell me what happened? Believe me," I add when she scoffs. "You won't get anywhere, holding it all inside. Ask me how I know." I've never told her any specifics, but she knows there was a trauma in my past. I'm pretty sure Special Agent Siwak is the only one who knows the details, and he's not the sort of person who would talk about it to outsiders.

"That's the thing. I'm not sure what happened, or whether anything happened at all. It's more like a feeling."

I'm more confused than ever. My impulse is to pepper her with questions, but I bite my tongue before any of them can come falling out of my mouth. There's nothing like feeling attacked to make a person shut down. How would I approach this if I was conducting an interview with a stranger? How would I make them feel comfortable opening up to me?

"You don't have to tell me anything you don't want to," I offer in a soft, calm voice. "Just know that I'm here, and I want to help if I can. Even if there's nothing I can do but listen. I want to do that if it means helping you. But there's no pressure."

Her lips twitch in a brief smile. "Thanks. I've been

sitting here for hours, asking myself if I should say anything, telling myself I made the whole thing up. But I don't think I did. I don't want to talk myself out of it." Her breath hitches, and she turns her face away from me, staring out the passenger side window. "I don't want him to do it to anybody else. If it really happened, I mean."

A sense of deep, burning dread has started to grow in my gut. With every word she speaks, she takes me a step closer to understanding if not the full situation, at least the general idea. More than ever, I want to press her for more details, to demand them. I need to know what happened and who did it. She said it's somebody we both know.

"It was totally innocent, I swear. That's another reason I didn't want to say anything." She knuckles away another tear that glistens on her skin when she lowers her hand. "I mean, how does that look? A married woman with a one-year-old kid goes out for drinks after work one night."

"It looks like a woman going out for drinks after work. It doesn't have to mean anything."

There's heavy bitterness in her laughter. "Easy for you to say. I believe you believe it, too," she adds. "But that's not how most people think. When you're a parent, especially a mother, every spare ounce of time and energy is supposed to be devoted to your child. Because of course, that's what a good parent does. You don't know how it is."

The back of her head touches the seat before she slowly turns it my way. "The second you have a baby it's like you stop being you. That's how people treat you. All of a sudden, you're not supposed to want anything for yourself anymore. Even if that something is as simple as an hour spent unwinding after a long day. I didn't want to go straight home and put on my Mom hat, you know? Just once."

"That is totally understandable," I murmur. I knew she was going through a lot after becoming a mom, but I didn't realize it was this complicated and emotional. And, frankly, bleak.

"I should've gone straight home. Maybe this is, I don't know, the universe's way of punishing me."

"Don't do that to yourself. It's not fair."

"Since when does fair matter?" she counters with a brittle, humorless laugh. "If life was fair, Tamara and Beth would be with their kids right now. Instead, they're still not home, and we could still be miles away from finding either of them. That's not fair, is it?" Before I have the chance to respond – besides, what would I say? – she groans. "I'm sorry. You don't deserve that. I just don't know what to do. I'm sick over this."

"Exactly what happened?" I finally have to ask. It seems the best way to get to the bottom of things, right?

She closes her eyes and groans again. "That's the thing. I'm not even sure. Everything is so fuzzy."

Fuzzy. Drinks. The overall image is getting clearer all the time, and the knot in my gut keeps tightening.

"I didn't drink very much. I swear. I mean, I can't." This time, there's wry humor in her soft laughter. "Oh, the days when I could get drunk after work and not care. I mean, even if it wasn't for the baby, I wouldn't want to deal with the hangover nowadays. I told myself to keep it at two glasses of wine, maximum."

Wrapping her arms around herself, she adds, "And the next thing I knew, I woke up in bed this morning. The baby was crying – I totally slept through it for much longer than I normally would. I was late coming in today. Did you notice?"

"Now that you mention it," I admit.

"And I was still so foggy when I got up. Even now, my brain feels like it's moving too slowly."

There's only one possibility I keep coming back to, based on her description. "You might have been drugged," I whisper.

"I think I was," she agrees. "That's why I can't remember anything after I started that second glass of wine. I think he must've drugged my glass when I wasn't looking."

There's more to it. There has to be. Nobody drugs a woman's drink only to drop them off at home afterward. Now, nausea threatens to take hold of me. "But you think something else happened?" It sounds pretty pitiful, not to mention like an understatement, but I'm trying to be delicate.

She squeezes her eyes shut before her chin starts to tremble. Her head bobs and her throat works, but she can't find the words right away. All I can do is sit here and watch and wait until she whispers, "There was blood in my underwear when I went to the bathroom this morning."

"Oh, Emma … " I whisper, emotion rising in my chest, tightening my throat.

"I think I was assaulted. I can't believe I'm saying it out loud." Her hands cover her face again and her shoulders shake, and this time when I reach out, she doesn't flinch. She lets me rub her shoulder while she cries and I begin fantasizing about stringing this guy up.

Finally, she goes still and quiet except for the occasional sniffle. I have to know. I have to ask. She's right – he can't be allowed to do this again. "Can you tell me who it was? How many people did you go out with? How many possibilities are there?"

"It was only him. Just the two of us. He asked … if I wanted to … he said it had been a long day and he thought we could both unwind."

"Who? Who offered?"

"I'm telling you, I'm not sure. Please –"

"And I am not going to say a word, at least not until we know for sure something happened to you. But you have to tell me, or else it could be someone else next time."

Her breathing quickens, color rising in her cheeks before she blurts it out. "Daniel. It was Daniel Brennon."

His name slams me back into my seat. I can't breathe. Daniel? But we work with Daniel. We know Daniel.

Do we ever really know anyone?

Her sharp gasp makes my head snap around, but she isn't looking at her lap or at me. "Look! What are they doing?"

As we watch, the man we saw smoking earlier emerges again from the front door of the building. A second guy emerges from the alley running between that building and the one next to it. He slides a hand under his jacket and withdraws a thick envelope which he hands to the man I'm beginning to believe is the business owner. The boss.

"I think we have enough to ask for a surveillance warrant," Emma concludes, but her voice is understandably flat, devoid of emotion. It isn't easy to celebrate at a time like this.

24

River

It's bizarre to the point of being ridiculous, sitting here at a diner two blocks down from the supposed cleaning service which is clearly a front for something more sinister. We're waiting on word of a warrant to place a microphone somewhere in that office. Once that's attained, there will be the matter of having the device installed so we can listen in.

But at the moment, all I care about is the woman sitting across from me in the booth, picking at a bowl of chicken soup and half a turkey club. I know better than most people what it's like to walk through the world while carrying an invisible burden. Knowing I'm broken, damaged beyond repair, but finding a way to function in spite of that. I can't count the number of times I've asked myself what people would think if they had the first idea who they were standing behind in line at the coffee shop. A woman who survived two years in captivity.

I know what it means to put on a brave face, and

that's what Emma is doing with every reluctant spoonful of broth that crosses her lips. "Like I said, there's not enough actual proof. I can't make an accusation based on a hunch."

I don't know why I bothered ordering a sandwich. I have to go through the motions of eating it simply because I know my body needs nourishment. As far as I'm concerned, I could take it or leave it since it tastes like sawdust anyway. "Let's look at the facts. The two of you went out for drinks after work. Your memory is blank starting with that second glass of wine, ending with you waking up in bed. You have no memory of getting home at all."

"That's right. Believe me, I've spent all morning trying to piece things together. When something like this happens, you don't want to believe it. You want to tell yourself anything, so long as there's a reasonable excuse."

"I understand."

"But no matter how hard I try, I can't come up with a single thing."

"I think it's safe to assume you were drugged," I whisper. This is not exactly the right place to be having a conversation like this, but there's the matter of getting the van outfitted with the equipment to record whatever goes on in the office. We needed to find someplace to wait while all of that is settled.

I can almost hear her teeth grinding together before she nods slowly. "Yes. I think we can assume that."

"And then, there's what you found in your underwear." I hate this. It's torture. The last thing I want is to hurt her, but I have to look at this from a law enforcement perspective, too. On top of that is the fact that this is a man with easy access to plenty of women in the office, not to mention a sterling reputation which would of course make it easier for him to get away unscathed.

Even now, I find it hard to believe, but then there's never any real way of knowing what goes on in a person's heart. There are monsters out there wearing disguises so convincing, they manage to fool even the people who spend a significant portion of their time with them. The way we do. If somebody put a gun to my head and demanded I tell them who at the field office would drug and rape a woman, Daniel would be pretty far down the list of possibilities.

My phone rings and I practically jump on it. It's Siwak, and he sounds downright jovial. "The warrant was approved. We have a couple of guys going in there momentarily."

"What's the cover story?" I ask, eyeing Emma. Is Daniel there, in his office? How is she supposed to face him every day after this?

"Possible gas leak in the area. They'll ask for fifteen or twenty minutes before letting anybody back in. We'll have a pair of devices – one in the front of the office, and one in that interior room." I won't bother asking how they'll get in if it's locked, since I doubt there's a lock in existence which can't be picked by one of our specialists.

"Good enough," I tell him. "What about the van?"

"You should have that back in a half hour or so, but we'll listen in on the feed here at the field office, too."

"Thank you for the update. Let me know if you hear

anything on that feed before we get the van back." He promises he will, then I end the call with a sigh.

"Well. We're making progress." Her eyes are overly bright with unshed tears when they meet mine.

With a heavy heart, I murmur, "By now, whatever he gave you will be out of your system."

"Of course. That's what they count on when they use these drugs. It wouldn't show up in a test now."

"What about your underwear?" I suggest, cringing when she winces. "I'm sorry to keep talking about it like this, but…"

"No. I get it. You're saying there could be DNA in my underwear." She runs a hand over the back of her neck, giving me something close to a guilty look. "To tell you the truth, my skin has been crawling all day… this is so gross… "

"I promise I won't gag."

She snorts, and for a second it's almost like everything is normal. Like we aren't sitting here discussing a sexual assault. "I was running late this morning, like I told you. So I never did take a shower. I wanted to, believe me, but there was no time."

"So there could still be evidence."

She nods, chewing her lip. "I can't believe I'm actually thinking about this. I can't believe this is me. But I guess that's what everybody thinks in a situation like this. How many women have I talked to after they've gone through a similar situation? A few years back, there was that one guy on the UVA campus, remember?"

"How could I forget?" He had torn his way through half the sorority houses on campus before somebody came forward to report him. After that, the floodgates opened and countless young women came forward to corroborate her story.

Her brow furrows. "I never thought it would happen to me. I'm a cliché."

Anger rises in me, hot and corrosive. "You are not. And I want to help you in any way I can. What can I do?"

"First, please don't look at me like you feel sorry for me. I don't think I could handle that."

"Done. You won't get any of that from me. Because I know how that feels, too."

"Otherwise ... " That bottom lip of hers is going to split open if she doesn't stop chewing it the way she is. "I guess ... I should have a rape kit processed."

She ducks her head, her eyes squeezed shut, and I want to cry for her. "It's the best thing you can do," I whisper, reaching across the table and taking hold of her hand. She grips mine so tight, squeezing hard, revealing the strain she's suffered under all day. There I was in the van, complaining about my insignificant dating problems. "You'll thank yourself later for not letting this go."

"I hope you're right." One more squeeze, then she releases me, running her hands over her hair. "I'm such a mess. I can't convince myself this is right."

"Emma..." I sigh.

"I'm not just accusing some random person I ran into at the bar," she whispers, looking straight into my eyes with an intensity that gives me goosebumps. "This is a man I work with every day. This is a man with friends in the Bureau. A reputation. A family. Those are the kind of things people throw in your face when you make accusations. How you would be destroying a good man. Breaking up his family. Costing him his job, his pension, his future."

"I know. It's terrible." A tear runs down her cheek, which she doesn't bother to brush away, too busy staring at me. "This is a big decision to make. But here's the thing, nobody is saying you have to accuse him. Wouldn't it at least grant you a little bit of relief to know for sure, rather than having to guess? If the kit comes back with evidence of trauma, at least then you'll know you aren't making it up in your head. After that, you can decide what to do. But this part can be just for you, just for your peace of mind. If that's what you want in the end," I conclude. Personally, I want to see the man hang for this, but that's easy for me to say. She makes a very strong point, too, as sick and depressing as it is.

Still, in spite of her protests, she tightens her jaw before nodding. "Fine. I'll have it done."

25

River

The next hour passes quickly, everything going by in a blur. Whoever is behind this operation is not sending their best people – I've barely begun digesting what I was able to eat for lunch before we get a warrant based on the information picked up by the microphones placed in the office. Normally, we would wait a while, get as much as we could, but too much time has already passed. We can't afford to wait any longer with lives hanging in the balance.

As it turns out, the man we've been observing is named Richard Grambs. He's in his late 30s and has a lengthy record. Vandalism, breaking and entering, assault and battery. He is, in other words, exactly the sort of gentleman I imagined he would be. Entering the interrogation room where he waits, I find him glaring at me like he's got a chip on his shoulder. If he thinks he has it bad now, he's in for quite a surprise.

Rather than waste time on pleasantries, I offer a

tight, professional smile. "My name is Agent River Collins, and I'm going to ask you some questions about your business and some of the activities it would appear involved in." He doesn't say a word, but the sweat that's begun to trickle down his temple tells a story. He's not so tough now, the way he was out on the street. He's not going to smack anybody around in here or shout to make himself heard. He's in my realm now.

And he knows it, the way an animal knows when they've been cornered.

"I'm not sure what you wanna know." He even shrugs his thin shoulders. "Unless you're thinking about opening your own cleaning business." Let him pretend all he wants that this is nothing more than an inconvenience, a blip in his day.

I take a seat across from him while he leans back in his chair and stretches his legs under the table, his foot brushing my ankle. It takes everything I have in me not to recoil in revulsion. Instinct tells me it's better not to give any reaction at all, so I don't, instead referring to the transcript of only some of what we picked up on audio this afternoon. "Do you understand it took all of an hour to gather enough evidence to secure a warrant to bring you in?"

"What do you mean?" Now he's interested, his eyes narrowing. If he was a dog, he would be sniffing the air, scenting danger.

"There was no gas leak in the area," I inform him with false sorrow, shrugging the way he did. "That was us, and we managed to get quite a bit of information about a shipment, money changing hands, the whole nine yards."

He sputters, his gaze landing on the folder in which the transcripts sit. The way he stares at it, it might as well be a ticking bomb. I suppose it is as far as he's concerned. "That ... That was ..."

"Please, don't waste my time telling me you were practicing lines from a play," I murmur. "Don't bother making up excuses. All you end up doing is irritating the people working on this case, and trust me when I tell you, we are not accommodating after we've been irritated by a suspect who wastes our time."

"You've got it all wrong. I don't know what you're talking about."

I'm glad he's stalling, refusing to cooperate with those big, fear-filled eyes darting around and what must be sweaty palms rubbing against his thighs. It gives me an excuse to drop the kid gloves and turn up the pressure. "Mr. Grambs, enough. You're trying to insult my intelligence. We have witnessed money changing hands. We already have recordings."

I lean forward, holding his gaze. "And I have two missing women, one of whom has made a bi-monthly payment to your sham operation for months. Now, I'll grant you, the work must have been done at some point, or else she wouldn't have kept paying. But now she's missing, and all signs point to you. So you better start talking."

It's incredible, really. The change that's come over him. Gone is the brash, arrogant, even threatening thug we observed earlier.

His tongue sweeps over his thin lips before his fingers begin tapping a frantic rhythm on the table. "What do you wanna know?" he asks, and now his voice is flat. Resigned.

I have to consciously conceal my glee. That took no time. "I want to know everything there is to know. About your operation, what you're really doing. What is this cleaning company a front for? And don't kid me," I add when his mouth opens. "We both know it's a front for something bigger. The more time you waste, the worse it gets for you."

"It's not just me." He wipes a hand over his forehead, which is now slick with sweat that shines under fluorescent lighting. "I'm not the one running things. You need to know that. You need to make sure everybody knows that."

"Sure, sure," I tell him, waving a hand. "That's what they all say. Tell me something I haven't heard before."

"Mayer Truby."

Interesting. "And who would that be?" I ask, glancing toward the camera in the corner of the room. Agent Siwak and Emma are both listening to this, watching us.

"He's the guy. The boss. I work for him."

"Can you spell that for me?"

"Don't you see?" he blurts out, his voice shaking almost as hard as the rest of him. "I'm trying to tell you he's the guy you want. Not me. I'll tell you whatever you wanna know, but this all comes from him. Understood? And you better protect me," he adds. "He is not gonna be happy when he hears about this. You're in for a whole world of trouble."

"Forgive me if I don't start shaking in fear," I murmur, offering a tight, brief smile. "What can you tell me about Mayer Truby?" Not that it matters very much. I have no doubt Emma is already searching the name, pulling together everything we have on him.

"Oh, come on." He slams back in his chair, sighing. "Tell me not to waste your time, but now you're wasting mine. This isn't his first day at the rodeo, if you get what I mean."

A soft knock against the door makes us both turn in that direction. I get up without excusing myself and open the door a crack to find Emma standing on the other side. "We looked up that name," she whispers. I knew she would, didn't I? "He's a known human trafficker."

My nerves are humming as I close the door and turn back to the man who is now about ready to jump out of his chair. "He's gonna kill me for this," he mutters, looking terrified as I take my seat. His already dark hair has gone a shade darker thanks to the sweat pouring off him. It fills the tiny room with an acrid odor that wrinkles my nose.

"He can't kill you if he's behind bars," I remind him, "and you can help us put him there."

His cynical laughter comes as no surprise. "Right. Because that's how this works. Bad guy goes to prison, there's no way for him to get his hands on the people who turned him over. Because he doesn't have connections on the inside or anything," he concludes, blowing out a frustrated sigh and shaking his head.

"To be honest with you, it's none of my business what he decides to do to you when this is all over," I admit, shrugging. "My business is getting to the bottom of what you've been doing. Now, you gave me the name of a man who is a known human trafficker. What are you trying to tell me? Is this a front for you to kidnap your clients and sell them? Some way to get into their houses, earn their trust?"

"I don't make any of those decisions!" he nearly wails like a scared, frustrated child.

"So you mean to tell me you don't have the first idea? Give me a break." Pushing back from the table, I release a disgusted laugh before gathering my files. "Forget it. Good luck finding your way out of this. If you manage to make bail, I hope this Truby guy doesn't track you down."

It's almost too easy. I haven't taken three steps away from the table before he blurts out, "Fine, fine! I'll tell you whatever it is you need to know." I turn back toward him but remain still except for my eyebrows, which I lift in silent invitation to continue. "But first thing is, you gotta understand, I'm just low level. The business attracts clients, I make money off of the ones Truby can use. He's got a place outside Charlottesville, an old restaurant that closed down years ago. That's where this whole thing runs. Not through me. Through him. I can tell you where it is," he babbles, as the words pour out faster with increased panic.

"You can tell us where we find his headquarters?" I confirm.

His head bobs. "Yeah! That's what I'm trying to tell you. He's the person you wanna talk to. He's the one making all the decisions, calling the shots. And he's the one with contacts to other guys like him."

"Fair enough," I murmur, returning to the table. "And let me tell you something. You're sweating now. I promise you, it will get much worse if you lead us on a wild goose chase with useless information. Do we understand each other?"

"Sure. Of course. I can give you the address and everything – I've been there before, once or twice." He's excited now, he sees a light at the end of the tunnel. His salvation, no doubt. What a shame I'm going to have to burst his bubble.

No, on second thought. It's not a shame at all.

Once he provides the location, I stand once again, walking to the door with my blood humming in anticipation of what's to come. "Hey!" he barks in a voice ringing with desperation. "I get immunity now, right?"

This is new. I'm barely able to stay neutral as I turn, staring at him. "Come again?"

"A deal. I gave you that info, you give me a deal. Right?"

If anything, he disappoints me. I don't know how many times I've ever met someone so thoroughly predictable. A big tough guy until his neck is on the line. Then, he becomes a sniffling, grasping rat. Just once, I would like to be surprised. "I never said anything about a deal," I remind him, heading for the door again. "You gave that information up freely. Next time, get some confirmation before you decide to spill your guts."

Harsh? Maybe. But maybe he deserves it. No, he

definitely does. Especially if he looks the other way while women like Beth and Tamara are kidnapped and sold to the highest bidder.

26

River

Chief Perkins manages to at least sound less argumentative than usual as we gather a couple of miles away from the location which Richard Grambs described in the interrogation room. "What we have seen so far is a handful of vehicles parked around the perimeter of the building," he explains, his voice ringing out with authority. He slides his hands into his pockets and looks around the group assembled in a park where nearby, a group of mothers and kids in strollers watch, too far away to hear what's being said but close enough that they're getting quite the show. I have no doubt word of this will spread – as it is, I see a couple of them on their phones, typing furiously.

"We're going in with three teams," the chief continues. "Team A will take the rear door, on the building's east side. There's a second door on the north side, along with a loading dock. That will be Team B. Team C will take the west side, the building's intended entrance. The drone we sent up to investigate the area showed us footage of men guarding the entrance, sometimes one or two at a time. The plan is to wait until nightfall, which should be another ten minutes or so, then surround the building from beyond the boundaries of the parking lot. At my signal, we move in."

I glance around, gauging the reactions of the men and women assembled. Like me and Emma, they're wearing their tactical gear in preparation of what we all have to know is going to be dangerous.

"Do we know how many are inside in total?" I ask, since it's been the local PD who have been on the scene in the hours since we got this address.

"We're looking at ten, maybe twelve," Chief Perkins reports. "We have the element of surprise on our side, and we have them numbered three to one. We're looking for the ringleader, Mayer Truby, so let's try to avoid lethal force when possible. We can't question a dead man."

He is loving this. There is not a doubt in my mind he sees himself as a heroic figure in his helmet and body armor. I'm sure there aren't many opportunities in an otherwise quiet area to conduct an exciting raid like this. Not that I would consider myself an expert, per se, but I've been through a handful and understand the realities. A couple of the younger cops look nervous, and they're right to look that way. One of the most dangerous things in a situation like this is a cocky, eager rookie looking to be a hero.

I turn to my team of assembled agents and split them

up into pairs, each of which will join one of the three groups of officers now double checking their weapons. The sun sank below the horizon minutes ago, and now the sky is faint purple and gray. We head out in our vehicles, following the routes already mapped out for us. Perkins was right about the element of surprise. We can't afford to give ourselves away.

"You okay?" I ask Emma once we are in the car following Chief Perkins.

"Fine," she replies in a soft, tight voice. "Looking forward to getting this over with." Is she talking about the raid, or about what we both know is coming after that?

"You don't have to be here," I remind her. "You can hang back. With everything you're going through –"

"Do me a favor and don't start getting all emotional and sentimental now," she warns, and she's only partly kidding. Her gaze is flat, unflinching when she turns my way. "There's a job to be done. I can always head over to the hospital after this. Once we are sure everything is locked down."

It's hard to imagine, carrying the burden currently on her shoulders while participating in something like this. Rather than rub salt in the wound, I clam up, pulling to a stop behind the Chief's prowler a block from the old restaurant. The parking lot is surrounded by what at one time must have been pretty shrubbery that's now wildly overgrown, and dead in spots. Cracks in the pavement allow tall weeds to poke through, while the building's darkened exterior bears all kinds of colorful graffiti. "I guess we don't have to wonder why this place isn't torn down," Emma muses, surveying the scene through a pair of binoculars.

Right, because one of the shell corporations owns this property. Truby must keep it as his base of operations, somewhere out of the way, somewhere there won't be a risk of people passing through. I wonder if anybody living around here has the first idea of what might be going on within these walls.

I don't have much time to reflect on that, since it's only another couple of minutes before Perkins gives the call to move in. We hurry in darkness, the parking lot lights dead and broken. Only a half-moon illuminates our progress as we close in, making bits of broken glass sparkle like diamonds. There's hardly so much as a footstep to alert anyone inside to our presence.

It happens fast, the way these things always do. It's Perkins who gives the call to ram the front door. Then there's the blur of movement, ear-splitting gunshots, confused shouts, and the much louder, authoritative shouts of the men and women now pouring into the building. "Everybody freeze! Show me your hands! Hands!"

"Drop your weapon!" I scream at a man who just finished fumbling through a drawer for a large gun which he very stupidly tried to turn on me. Even in these last moments, some people seem to think they can shoot their way out of it. Like this is a movie and they are the heroes.

It isn't long before the fight is up, with only one of their guys taking a hit in the bicep. Otherwise, everyone is alive and in one piece, lying flat on their stomach, zip ties around their wrists within five minutes of our arrival. The odor of gunpowder, blood and sweat fill the air.

Chief Perkins meets up with me in what used to be the waiting area just inside the front door which now hangs open, splintered by the battering ram. "It looks like there were makeshift rooms set up back in the kitchen," he tells me, crooking a finger before leading the way. "There're some cots back there. Everything's sort of sectioned off with those folding screens."

Yes, it looks as though this large room has been put to use in another way now that its original intent is no longer relevant. Officers move around, a couple of them taking photos to document what looks like barracks. Cots sit in a long row along one wall, separated by the adjustable screens which the chief described. There are thin pillows and even thinner blankets on each, though it doesn't look as though any of them have recently been in use. They're all neatly made, waiting. For whom?

A voice rings out over the others, coming from further back in the room. "Chief! We have some clothing over here."

I follow the sound of that voice, weaving around clusters of officers examining the scene until I reach a partly open door. The shelves lining the walls of the small room beyond it tell me this used to serve as a pantry. Now, it serves as something different.

"We need all of this cataloged," I murmur, scanning the interior. Pillows and blankets take up the top shelves running across three of the room's four walls. Beneath that are boxes, some stuffed with papers which I gingerly flip through with my gloved fingers. Some look like they might have been here since the restaurant was in operation, but others are dated recently.

What chills me is the stack of garments. Shoes. Purses. They represent the women who must have slept curled up on those cots, waiting for whatever came next. What happened to those women?

"Somebody get in here now," I bark, turning toward the open door. "I want all of this photographed immediately. We need to see if we can get an ID from the husbands."

It isn't easy, swallowing back the impulse to hurt somebody after seeing that pile of personal effects. Our perps are still waiting for transport while our team catalogs everything they're finding. I want to kick one of those slimeballs until he's unrecognizable. Somebody needs to pay for all of this.

"There's no Truby here." Emma doesn't sound surprised when we meet up in the dining room. There are only a few tables scattered around, littered with empty takeout containers and pizza boxes, beer bottles, playing cards. How many of those men out there sat here and played cards while terrified women shivered and wept only feet away?

She jerks a finger toward the rear of the room, where a door sits open and officers walk in and out. "It looks like his office is back here, but it's fairly clean. Like he pulled up stakes and fled."

I follow her into the room – it's more comfortable than any of what I've seen so far. There's actual furniture in here, including a pull-out bed with rumpled sheets and pillows. Maybe he decided to flee when he heard Richard

Grambs was brought in for questioning. There must be something we can use. Frustration floods my system and makes me grit my teeth in determination. "We have to search every inch of this room. I want it dusted for prints—who knows how many people we can link to this operation."

After the better part of an hour, it seems he only left behind one item which I find in the corner of the bottom desk drawer. "I need a bag for this!" I call out, holding the photo by its corner between my gloved thumb and forefinger.

Emma joins me, her head tipping to the side as she studies what I discovered. "That's the Blue Ridge Mountains, isn't it?" she asks. "We used to stay there sometimes when I was a kid. We had a cabin in the area."

"My parents were big on the outdoors," I reply, sliding the photo into a plastic bag to keep it safe. "We spent plenty of time out there, too." One problem, the chain spans from Maryland down to Georgia. There's no indication of exactly where this shot was taken.

The photo includes a cabin and a shot of a lake whose surface is as smooth as glass. It's idyllic, welcoming, yet somehow it holds a sense of foreboding. Turning it over, I discover writing along the back. "When the heat gets too hot..." I whisper, looking at Emma and finding the same confusion etched across her face.

"I mean, it is cooler in the mountains," she reasons, though she doesn't look convinced.

A lightbulb goes off in my head. "A hideout," I announce while adrenaline starts pumping again. This is it. I feel it in my bones. "It's where he goes when things get tense around here."

"Agent Collins?" One of Perkins' cops pokes his head into the room, looking grim. "I just got confirmation. Tamara Higgins' watch was mixed in with those items, and Dr. Clyburn identified one of the sweaters as belonging to his wife."

27

River

"Back in the day, this would have meant looking for a needle in a haystack." Agent Siwak looks grim but determined once we meet with him back at the field office. Incredible, the fact that it's barely eight o'clock, yet it feels like three days have passed since I sat in the van with Emma this morning, observing the office where Richard Gramb was doing Mayer Truby's dirty work. There must be some sort of pun in there, considering the addition of a cleaning service, but I'm too tired and wired to make the connection.

"How long do you think it will take the reverse image search to come up with a location?" I ask, sliding a glance Emma's way. She's nursing a cup of coffee, looking worn out, a little lost. When I clear my throat, she snaps to attention like she had zoned out for a second. I can't blame her.

"Who's to say? An hour or two," he predicts. "We'll be able to match that photo to satellite imagery, though.

Mark my words. There's no hiding anymore, not in this day and age."

"And then?" Emma asks. She keeps glancing through the window of his office and looking out toward the hall. I know why. It was harrowing enough, making the decision whether she should return to the office or not. There was a chance Daniel would be here. Luckily, he had some sort of family situation he needed to tend to tonight. His family. Do they know the kind of man he is? Does his wife?

"And then, we roll out there. I hope nobody was looking forward to an early night," he concludes with another grim smile.

With a glance at Emma, I ask, "Could we duck out for an hour or so? I know I could stand getting something to eat before we get on the road."

Emma's gaze locks on mine and I give her a tiny nod. "Yeah, that sounds like a good idea," she agrees. She sounds like she's reading lines from a script, but he doesn't seem to notice.

"Sure, sure," he urges. "Take care of yourselves. We have a drive ahead of us, and who knows what comes after that." Then he goes back to whatever grabbed his interest on his phone, and I incline my head toward the door. *Let's get out of here. Let's do this.*

Something tells me if I don't encourage her, she might not do it. I know all about second-guessing, questioning, even blaming myself. I've spent years perfecting my craft when it comes to that. I know deep down inside it was not my fault, everything that happened the day I was kidnapped and the two years that followed. I know I did nothing wrong. I did not invite that woman to interrupt my life the way she did, to stick a finger in my future and stir it around, destroying the childish plans I'd put in place, my hopes and dreams.

But in the absence of a real, breathing, physical person to blame, there was only one person to turn all those feelings and emotions toward. Emma, at least, has a living, breathing, physical person to blame. He just happens to be a highly respected FBI agent with a fine reputation, a family, the whole nine yards. So naturally, she feels like she has to turn the blame onto herself. I don't doubt she'll feel guilty raising charges against him. It's wrong, it's sad, but it's basic psychology.

"I'll drive," I offer, and she nods in mute agreement on our way to the parking garage.

She doesn't say a word until we're in the car, rolling down the ramp to the arm that lifts automatically at our approach. "I hope I'm not wrong about this."

"First things first." I have to consciously sweep aside the memories that won't stop bubbling to the surface and tainting every minute of our interaction. This isn't about me. It's about her. She's a good person, hard-working, honest. She truly wants to make a difference, to make the world a little safer for her family and the people around her. I have to support her.

"What happens if they find his DNA in me?" She wraps her arms around herself, shivering.

The thing is, she knows what happens. She's been through this before, only then she had the luxury of being on the other side of things. Acting as an observer, standing outside and looking in. "Then, you have the option of whether you want to press charges," I murmur. "And nobody but you can make that choice."

"Was that supposed to make me feel better?" she asks with a faint, shaky laugh.

"Honestly, no," I admit. "It's to remind you that nobody can push you into this, one way or another. You have to do what feels right for you, in your heart. I'll respect your decision either way."

"No, you won't," she predicts with another soft laugh. "Just like I wouldn't."

At a red light, I turn to her, surprised. "What do you mean?"

"I don't know what I mean." She rubs her hands over her face, groaning. "I guess I mean, if I was helping a victim who knew the name of her attacker and didn't press charges, I might look at her a little differently. Even if I understood why she was afraid, I would ask myself how she could betray other women by not getting this animal off the streets. Even if I understand up here." She taps the side of her head with her fingertips.

"I know what you mean," I admit. "It's always easy to stand back and judge and say what you would do in this situation. But when it's you ... " There's nothing else to say. We both know what I mean.

We pass the rest of the drive in silence, both of us lost in our own personal hell. Once we reach the hospital, she does the talking while I stand at a respectful distance. I know she's afraid, dreading the results, but she shows nothing but strength.

Though sometimes, checking out in your own head

looks a lot like strength. Shutting down, cutting off your emotions, can look like stoicism.

"You must be the bravest girl who ever lived." I still hear the nurse's soft, encouraging voice in my head as I follow Emma back to a curtained-off section of the emergency room. Emma looks back at me over her shoulder, her brows drawn together in a last minute surge of panic, and all I can do is offer a reassuring nod.

"You've got this," I mouth, only breathing again once the curtain is closed.

I didn't feel very brave when it was me on the other side of that curtain. Peeling off my filthy clothes, dropping them into plastic bags so they could be thoroughly examined for evidence. The light was so bright, I could barely keep my eyes open. Two years spent mostly in the dark will do that to a person. One of the cops who brought me to the hospital was smart enough and insightful enough to give me his sunglasses, which helped a lot. At least, they helped my eyes. The rest of me was still a filthy, stinking mess.

"You've been so brave so far," the nurse whispered. Her name was Donna—I remember that as clear as day, staring at her name badge after lying back on the gurney. I focused on it while the doctor placed my feet in the stirrups—dirty feet, feet that carried me through darkness, through the unknown.

"When can I get a shower?" I whispered, gripping the nurse's gloved hand as the doctor went to work.

"Once the examination is over," Donna assured me. She even stroked my hair, a gesture which both comforted and horrified me. It had been so long since I washed my hair, and I knew there were leaves and twigs in it after my run through the woods. She was wearing gloves, sure, but still. I was so ashamed. So dirty.

"You can stay in that shower as long as you want," she whispered, leaning down as I squeezed my eyes shut, trying to ignore what was going on under the cloth the doctor had draped over my spread knees. "You can wash up three, four times if you need to. Whatever it takes, sweetie. Okay? Once this part is over, you can start to get better."

Funny. I did shower after the rape kit was finished, along with a general examination to make sure everything was in working order. I showered until my skin pruned, and I still didn't feel clean. I unwrapped a brand new hairbrush from the nurse's station and worked on the knots that had developed over time until I could run the brush smoothly through from root to end. I ate until I felt like my stomach was going to burst—hospital cafeteria food never tasted so good.

Yet I never started getting better. Donna was wrong about that part. Physically, I healed. It wasn't long before there were no visible signs of what was done to me, of the horrors I was forced to live through.

It's the rest of me that's still a problem.

And as I wait, pacing the tiled floor, waiting for Emma's rape kit to be completed, I have to wonder when her healing will begin.

28

River

"Thank you so much for this." Emma looks and sounds a lot more like her normal self when she joins me in the passenger seat, now freshly showered and wearing clean clothes. It only took her around twenty minutes to dash into the house and clean up once we left the hospital and took the short drive to her house. I could almost taste her relief and still can. A weight has been lifted from her shoulders. At least now, she'll know for sure.

"Everything okay in there?" I ask, glancing toward the pretty little colonial she shares with her family before pulling away from the curb.

"That's the thing about being an agent," she reminds me, almost joking. "He's used to me being weird about things. I told him we have to track down this cabin and I'm not sure exactly how long it will take, so I wanted to freshen up before we head out to where we're going."

Seemingly out of nowhere, her voice cracks. "How am I supposed to tell him?" she whispers.

"One thing at a time." That's all I can say. That is all the comfort I can give her now. "We still don't know exactly what happened, but the rape kit results will give us a better idea."

"And then?" I know she doesn't mean to sound so antagonistic. Now I almost want to call Leslie and apologize for the way I acted out in the days and weeks and months after coming home. When everybody expected me to be happy and joyful now that the nightmare was over—their words. Never mine. The nightmare might have been over for them, but not for me.

That memory leaves me feeling like a hypocrite as I answer, "And then, you two will get through it together. Isn't that a big part of the reason why people get married in the first place?" I remind her as gently as I can. "To support each other when things like this happen. Terrible things. He's your support system, right?"

"Right. It's amazing, the things that go through a person's head." Is she being truthful with me? I can't tell. It seems like she's taken a pretty sudden left turn, which means she's decided to stop arguing. She probably thinks I can't relate, and in a way, I can't. The best I can do is think about the happy, supportive couples I've known and assume Emma and Steve would support each other the same way.

She combs her fingers through her damp curls before twisting them against the back of her head and securing them with a clip she pulls from her purse. "All right. Enough of this for now. We won't know until the kit comes back, so let's drop it for now."

What a relief to hear that.

We haven't made it back to the field office before Agent Siwak calls my cell. "We have a location," he confirms. The excitement in his voice carries to the inside of the car, where Emma and I sit bolt upright in preparation. "Around ninety minutes southwest. Satellite imagery confirms it."

We make plans to meet up at the office, then head out as a team. We take four vans and split up, with me and Emma in one van and Agent Siwak in another. "We'll meet at the rendezvous point two miles east from the cabin," he confirms before we set out in the dark.

Emma is driving this time, which I'm sure is for the best. It gives her something to focus her attention on. Unfortunately, that means there's nothing for me to do but sit in the passenger seat and try to find something decent on the radio while struggling with the memories that have popped up and bubbled away in my consciousness ever since we arrived at the hospital earlier.

"Do you think he would take anybody there?" Emma asks after a long stretch of silence. "The women, I mean. Do you think that's just his personal hideout?"

"Who knows?" I whisper, staring into the darkness, trying to shut down my thoughts, my memories. The sense of something watching from the trees. The way I felt that night, the night I escaped, running through the darkness and always feeling like something was watching me flee. Observing, maybe even judging, but not helping.

A shiver runs through me and I try to play it off, but I'm not successful. "Are you chilly?" she asks.

"A goose walked over my grave," I reply without thinking. "My grandmother used to say that."

"I never did understand that saying," she admits. "How many geese are randomly walking around on potential graves?"

We share a soft chuckle before falling silent again. I manage to find some soft rock on the radio and leave it there since the gentle, familiar sounds soothe the turmoil in my mind somewhat.

But not entirely.

By the time we reach the rendezvous point, gravel crunching beneath the tires before Emma pulls to a stop alongside two of the other three vans, my heart is about to burst out of my chest. It's comfortably warm in here, yet my skin feels icy cold. It's the sweat that's begun rolling down the back of my neck, running down my chest.

"River?" Emma asks once she's unbuckled her seatbelt and I haven't moved an inch. "What is it? Are you sick?"

Yes, I'm sick. I've carried the same sickness for almost twenty years. It was a night just like this one, wasn't it? A gentle, soft kind of night. A night my family would have spent around the fire pit outside our camper, roasting marshmallows, laughing, floating on the night breeze. When I ran blindly, panicked, my skin scratched and cut in a hundred places, but there was no stopping. I couldn't stop. I didn't know where I was going. I only knew I had to run.

Are Beth and Tamara going through that? What about the other women represented by that clothing, the purses, the shoes? Did they escape? How many were there? I can't breathe. I have to get away, to jump out of my skin and leave it and everything else behind.

"River."

The sudden sternness in Emma's voice snaps me out of it long enough for me to get a hold of myself. "I'm sorry," I whisper between gasps for breath. "It's just … sometimes … "

"Listen to me." Her hand closes over mine, sitting in my lap, and normally I would recoil and yank my hand back like her touch burned. Right now, I'm frozen, unable to break free of the paralyzing fear. *I'm safe. It was a long time ago.* Right now, it's not working.

Until she squeezes my hand the way I squeezed hers earlier. "I don't know the specifics," she whispers, "but I'm going to tell you that you are a strong person. The strongest person I ever knew. If anybody can push through and get justice for these women, it's you. I'm right here with you—we all are. You can do this."

Slowly, slowly, the message behind her words filters through the madness in my mind. I can do this. What happened to me happened a long time ago. I'm not helping Beth or Tamara or any of the other women by falling to pieces. I'm not helping myself, either.

A knock on my door takes us both by surprise. It's only Agent Siwak, who gestures for me to roll down the window. "What's happening?" he asks, his gaze bouncing back and forth between Emma and me. "You both look like you've seen a ghost."

I still can't find my voice, so Emma speaks up. "What's the latest? Have they sent out the drones?"

"Affirmative. We're getting a sense of the cabin and

its surroundings. There's a feed in the lead van." He jerks a thumb in that direction. "In the meantime, we're still waiting on clearance for the raid. All we can do right now is get as much information as possible."

I'm not ready to get out of the van just yet. As much as I want to analyze every second of the footage the drones are capturing, I can't make myself move. It's like waking up in the grip of a nightmare, when my body is frozen in cold fear, only I haven't been asleep.

"River? Agent Collins?" he prompts. Because of course he would be watching me closely. Unlike Emma, he knows the specifics of my history. "Are you all right? Is this ... can you ... "

Emma speaks up, sparing me. "Actually, Agent Siwak, River has spent this whole day comforting me through something."

As it turns out, I only needed a slight shock to snap me out of my fog. My head swings around, my eyes wide in shock. "What are you doing?" I whisper.

"Is there a problem? Is everything all right at home?" he asks. At the end of the day, he's tough as nails and sometimes frighteningly unpredictable when it comes to the way he expresses his frustration when a case isn't going anywhere, but he cares about his agents. I have firsthand knowledge of that.

"Not exactly," Emma tells him.

Without waiting to be prompted, he opens the sliding door on the side of the van and climbs in, then closes it behind him. Now it's just the three of us while the rest of the team works outside the bubble we're in. "Is it something you need to tell me? Can I trust you to handle what we need to do tonight?"

"Yes, you can trust me," she tells him firmly. "But it is something that might end up causing trouble, so I guess you should know about it."

"You don't have to tell him yet," I remind her in a whisper.

"Excuse me, Agent Collins, but I can speak for myself," he retorts. "If there's something Emma wants to share, she should do it. Especially if it might blow back on me at some point. What is it, Emma?"

I understand why she's doing this. I just don't quite understand why she's doing it now. Is she covering for me? I wish she wouldn't feel like she has to.

At the same time, he's going to find out if the rape kit points to Daniel. This tells me she plans on pressing charges, which fills me with pride.

And also fills me with apprehension, because although Siwak is a straight shooter who has never shown me anything but fairness and understanding, there's never any telling how a person will react to a situation like this. Especially a man, when another man is being accused.

I'm sure she's thinking of all of that as she takes a deep breath. "I have reason to suspect I was drugged and assaulted last night after work. River accompanied me to the hospital tonight, where a rape kit was processed. I'm still waiting on the results."

Before his jaw can fully drop open, she adds, "And I'm pretty sure it was Daniel Brennon who was responsible."

29

River

The silence that follows Emma's announcement is profound. There's a second where it feels like all the air got sucked out of the van. Siwak sits with his mouth hanging open for a beat before snapping it shut, then settles back against one of the two seats behind us.

What's he going to say? What will he think? I exchange a worried look with Emma, who most likely wishes she had never said anything. At least, that's what the wide-eyed stare she's wearing tells me. There's no putting the toothpaste back in the tube. She can't yell gotcha and laugh the whole thing off.

At the end of the day, it's his problem how he deals with this. Whether he chooses to be a standup guy—the sort of guy I believe he is—or if he'll urge her to keep the whole thing quiet for the sake of optics. I'm sure it wouldn't be the first time somebody has urged a woman to do that very thing.

After what feels like an eternity, he draws a deep breath which puffs out his chest, then releases it slowly. His jaw ticks, his nostrils flare, and it's clear her announcement has angered him. *Please, don't let her down*, I silently beg. *Don't let us both down.*

"Thank you for giving me a minute to process that," he mutters. I've heard him sound this serious before, and I've heard him angry, but somehow the deadly flat tone of his voice inspires fear. I've never heard him sound quite this way. Is he disconnecting, pulling back, already taking sides against her? *Please, don't let that be true.*

"I'm sorry," Emma whispers. My chest tightens when she runs a hand under her eyes. "Really. I'm sorry."

"Let's get one thing straight," he snaps, making me recoil. "You have nothing to apologize for. Do you understand? Don't let me hear you apologize again, not for this."

Oh, thank goodness. I can practically hear the tension drain from Emma while it drains from me.

"All I need to know is, what makes you think it was Daniel?" he asks. "That's it. I don't need to hear specifics. I'm not trying to grill you. I only want an idea of the situation." It's like he's shut down the emotional part of himself for the sake of dealing with this. I can relate to that, heaven knows.

"We went out for a drink after work last night. A casual sort of thing, a drink between friends. I woke up this morning completely disoriented, with a blank space where last night should be. I have no memory of what happened after I accepted a second glass of wine. There was … evidence left behind." She stares down at the floor and he clears his throat a little awkwardly. Certain things, you don't want to say out loud. At least not to a man, and especially not a man in a position of authority.

"Understood. That's all I need to know. To think, I wanted him on this tonight. What a relief he had to step back." He runs a hand over the back of his neck, growling. "What a mess. I'm gobsmacked, but I'm sure that's nothing compared to how you feel. I'm deeply sorry you're going through this."

"I know, and I'm—" Both of us give Emma a sharp look before her mouth snaps shut, cutting off the apologies she was about to deliver.

"What do you plan to do?" he asks. "You have my full support, either way."

I could cry for her. Relief radiates from her face when she breaks out in a grateful, tearful smile. The tears don't last long, I'm glad to see. "I'll wait for the results to come back, and if they point to him, I plan on holding him accountable."

"Thank you for giving me the heads up in advance," he replies. There's a note of gentleness in his voice. He pats her shoulder before giving it a tiny squeeze, his brows drawing together. "Whatever you need, you've got it."

"I'm just worried there won't be enough evidence to point to anyone in particular," she frets, her eyes meeting mine, her lip quivering again. I know how it feels, constantly swinging back and forth, my emotions all over the place. It's like she's never more than a second away from falling apart.

"What have we talked about already today? We'll deal with that when the time comes. One step at a time. Right?" I ask. "Either way, I'm with you. You're not alone."

"Thank you." She looks back at Siwak, who nods. "All right. I'm making this about me. Let's see what we've got out there, shall we?"

I'm feeling more focused now, able to step out of the van and into the cool night. The sounds of nature take me back to all of those camping trips when I was a kid. The rustling of leaves, the call of an owl in the distance, the skittering of tiny creatures. A bat zips by overhead, illuminated by the glow of the moon.

There's another glow coming from the lead van, which we now approach to watch the drone footage. "Easy does it," one of the agents murmurs, while another guides the drone which is examining the front of the cabin. Even with the addition of night vision making everything glow green, I recognize the cabin as the one in the photo.

I recognize something else, too, and my heart sinks. "Hold for a second," I bark, pointing to the screen. "See if you can get a little closer. Does that look like a security camera mounted above the front door?"

"I think you're right," Siwak agrees before muttering a curse under his breath. "That's probably not the only one."

He's right. It's not the only one. And it's not only security cameras we have to be aware of, either. Along with a trio of them—two pointed at the front door, mounted on the upper corners, and a third mounted on a tree several feet in front of the cabin – but what looks like a series of alarms set up around the perimeter. Floodlights, now darkened, are also positioned in the trees surrounding the cabin. If one of those alarms gets tripped, I have no doubt those lights will flip on and blind of all of us with the sudden light. In our disorientation, we would be easy to pick off by anyone inside.

The cabin itself, though, looks dark. Quiet. The drone flies slowly, keeping a short distance to avoid being noticed. But I'm starting to wonder if there's anyone inside to notice it. "There isn't so much as a glow from a candle," I whisper as we study one dark window after another. It's a single floor, with two windows on both the north and south end, a front door with a window beside it, and the same set-up around back. There's a small porch running along the front of the structure, where dead leaves and pine needles have gathered in drifts. A raccoon runs by, giving us all a start at the sudden flash of green, beady eyes.

I bark out a short laugh, holding a hand to my chest. "I guess if that's the worst we find here, we're in good shape," I point out. It's a weak joke, but then I don't feel much like joking.

"When was the last time anybody was here, do you think?" one of the agents asks nobody in particular.

"Recently," I decide. "Notice how there's no leaves or anything in front of the front door. Like somebody brushed them aside recently."

Yes, in fact, there's a larger pile beside the door, beneath the front window.

The agent controlling the second drone speaks up.

"And there's what looks like fresh tire tracks," he announces, drawing our attention to his feed, to the tracks he is now illuminating as he flies the drone away from the cabin.

That's enough for me. "All right. We know what we need to know. We have to take every precaution as we approach. Understand there could be booby traps set up with the intent of harming trespassers. I want all eyes trained for them. We'll split up in groups of three, with a point person and a pair behind them to sweep the area at all times."

"We'll drive down to the turn-off from the main road," Siwak decides. "After that, we go on foot. Like Agent Collins said, take caution with every step. It's only a quarter of a mile or so from the road to the cabin. it makes sense to follow the tracks," he adds. "That's the least likely area where there would be traps, as he would need to pass through in a vehicle."

"Let's remember what we're dealing with here," I add, fastening my body armor, pulling a helmet over my brown ponytail. "If this man is inside, he's desperate. This might not be as simple as getting the jump on him, the way it was back at his headquarters."

I look around me, faced with grim expressions that I know reflect my own.

There's a difference, though. As far as I know, none of my team members have ever been on the other side of a locked door, held in captivity, wondering if anyone was ever going to come and rescue them.

What if there are captives inside? "Let's not forget, he might have taken some of the women with him," I remind everyone as we split back up. "Keep them in mind. Let's not go off half-cocked."

After that, all we can do is get in the van and get moving.

There's nothing like walking into the unknown.

30

River

This isn't the same. This isn't the way it was with me. I'm safe. I am in no danger.

Well, that's not technically the truth. I'm in a lot of danger, at least potentially, as I tread softly and carefully with the rest of the team down the lane that has been carved out of the woods over years of driving back and forth. Fresh tracks indent the ground, softened by a few showers which passed through the area earlier. My feet sink into the dirt—it's a good thing we aren't looking to cover up this raid, because we could never manage it with all the footprints we're leaving behind.

The cabin sits dark and quiet just as it did when we observed it from afar. Goosebumps pebble the back of my neck and my breath comes in short gasps, but I can't afford to reveal my apprehension. I can't afford to give in to it, either. This is not the time for memories to cloud my actions.

Still, as I creep closer with so many behind me, I

can't ignore the questions brewing in the back of my mind. Is this the sort of place where they held me? I never did see for myself, did I? There wasn't exactly time to explore, and once I broke free, I wasn't about to turn around and mentally catalog everything I saw. Instinct told me to escape, and I did, but I ended up with no idea exactly where I was held or how to find it again. I was in shock – I know that now, with years of training under my belt, not to mention maturity. I had been through probably the most traumatic thing imaginable, had survived longer than anyone thought I could. It's no wonder I wasn't able to think clearly when surviving was all that mattered.

I only hope the rest of the team keeps any possible hostages in mind as we draw closer to the cabin.

I hold up a hand, bringing everyone behind me to a stop when I notice a thin wire running in front of the wooden steps leading up to the porch. After pointing two fingers to my eyes, then one finger down to the wire, I carefully and deliberately step over it. The rest of the team follows suit before we split up. Siwak takes half the team around the building's north side, intending to come in through the back while Emma and I will lead the rest of the team in through the front door. My heart is hammering and I can hear the blood rush in my ears. A deep breath doesn't do much to calm me, but I guess not much would at a moment like this.

Please, don't let us lose anybody. I'm not only thinking about the team when I send up that silent prayer to whoever or whatever might be listening. I lost faith in that nameless, faceless presence over the years of captivity—after all, if a higher power existed, why was I allowed to suffer for two years? Still, it can't hurt to ask for a little help when there might be innocent hostages whose lives are on the line behind a door which was painted red at one time, but is now chipped, weatherbeaten.

Through my earpiece, Siwak whispers, "Everybody in place. I'll give the count. Three … Two … One."

I raise my left foot and kick the door, which bursts open an instant before I drop to the side, looking for cover in case anyone in there decides to start firing. "FBI!" I bellow, while Siwak does the same from the back of the cabin.

All that greets us inside is silence. I exchange a look with the rest of the team before nodding, signaling us to head inside and fan out.

Within moments, my heart sinks. "It looks like nobody's been here in ages," Emma whispers. I hear her disappointment, not to mention the frustration running through it.

"I want every inch of this cabin scoured," Siwak orders, growling. "Those tracks were fresh. Don't let what you see right now fool you. That's what he would want us to believe."

Of course, he's right. If anything, what we've arrived at is the best case scenario. Sure, it would be nice if Mayer Truby was here, but then he could have unloaded an arsenal on us, not to mention anyone he brought along with him. We might not be able to take him into custody here and now, but we can gather more information. For all we know, he might have intended to return.

"Maybe somebody gave him the heads up," I mutter, then wave Emma over to the mantle positioned above a small fireplace before running my fingers over the surface. "It's been dusted. He only wants us to think the place has been empty all this time." That fuels us—at least, it fuels me. I'm more determined than ever to find this animal. He only thinks he's smarter than we are. Until now, he's gotten away with it, but that's only because we didn't know he was still in business. And there is nothing more satisfying than watching a criminal's pride disintegrate when they find out they aren't as smart as they thought they were.

The problem is, the longer we look, the more obvious it is how careful he's been. "He even took out the garbage," Emma observes, nudging an empty trash can with her toe. "He didn't want to leave anything behind."

Which tells me he had time before he got out of here. "If he left at the last second, he wouldn't have been able to do that," I point out. "Someone must've gotten word to him, somehow."

"It could be that one of those guys back at the headquarters heard us talking about the cabin and alerted their lawyer to raise a red flag." Emma shakes her head in disappointment.

"If that's true, we might be able to track down who did it … though that will take time," Agent Siwak admits.

I want to scream. Where is he? When is his luck going to run out?

My frustration takes me out through the rear door, so I can gulp in some fresh air and try to clear my head. With my hands on my hips, I tip my head back, closing my eyes, willing myself to pull it together. We're going to find him. And we are going to locate these women, no matter what it takes. They deserve that. I deserve that.

But this isn't about me. It's becoming more and more difficult all the time to separate myself from this.

Opening my eyes again, I turn in a slow circle, studying the area. It's heavily wooded, and the closest glow from another cabin has to be two or three miles away from where I'm standing. Granted, we're coming up on midnight now, so there could be cabins closer to this one whose inhabitants are sleeping with the lights out.

Still, it's very remote. I wonder if anyone would hear a scream from inside the cabin.

My heart skips a beat when I notice something that doesn't seem to fit in with everything else around me. At first glance, it could be nothing more than a pile of fallen sticks and branches twenty or thirty feet from the back door. But as I begin my approach, there's a glint from something metallic uncovered by the moon overhead.

Touching a finger to my earpiece, I announce, "I found something out back." I'm already moving in, my gun drawn, my head swinging from side to side just in case someone is watching. Waiting. This could be another trap, the biggest of them all.

Footsteps ring out behind me an instant before I reach what is obviously a padlock. After a quick examination to confirm there aren't any traps set up, we begin clearing the branches and sticks from around what is now obviously a storm cellar. It's unusual to find a cellar in an area like this, where the ground is so rocky. Maybe that was a selling point. Somewhere to stash things.

What has Mayer been stashing there lately? When I look to Agent Siwak, it's clear we're thinking along the same lines. He sweeps an arm, indicating for the rest of the group to stand back while I test the padlock, then examine the hinges on the windowless door. They're rusted, but not badly enough to give way.

It's clear what I have to do. Taking a step back, I train my weapon on the latch, looking to blow it open.

And then I fire.

31

River

The ear-spitting sound of metal hitting metal slices through the air, and now when I check out the latch on the storm cellar door, I find it hanging open. "Let's exercise caution," Agent Siwak urges, but I'm only half aware of him now. Instinct is screaming at me to open this door and find what's on the other side. The way I dreamed for so long when it was me in a dark, secluded place.

I'm opening the door for me just as much as I am for whoever is down there.

"FBI! Show your hands!" It could just as easily be Mayer waiting down there, weapon poised, prepared to mow down whoever comes storming in. So far, there's nothing but profound darkness down there. Inky black, capable of hiding anything. Or anyone.

A few heartbeats pass with no sound coming from the darkness, so I exchange a glance with Siwak before starting down the stairs with Emma at my back. The damp smell fills my nostrils and brings back too many things, memories as strong and vivid as any I have ever wrestled with. "Tamara Higgins?" I call out, moving deeper into the cellar, stooped slightly even though I'm not what anybody would consider tall. The wood beams overhead make exploring even more treacherous–I hear a thud behind me, followed by a groan as one of the taller agents hits their head. "Beth Clyburn? Is anyone down here?"

It's a relief when someone behind me finds a pull cord which lights a single bulb. There are shelves along the walls, mostly bare except for mouse droppings. Against the far wall opposite the stairs leading to the surface, a rusted cot sits.

The sight of it freezes me solid, makes my lungs go stiff until I can barely sip air. It's not the same. I escaped. I survived.

My shock passes once I realize there's a dark, immobile lump on the cot. Using my flashlight while holding my pistol in the other hand, I approach warily. "FBI. We're here to help you. You don't have to be afraid." Is it possible this is a trap? I know it is—my training tells me so.

There's something else at work, something that carries me forward. Maybe it's the memory of lying in a corner, curled in a ball, hoping wildly to be left alone so I wouldn't get hurt. Praying, though praying never did me any good.

All of that is enough to make me forget the potential danger, reaching out to nudge the lump with my foot.

The flashlight beam lands on long, stringy hair, and then on a delicate profile. I've studied the images long enough, thoroughly enough to recognize her on sight. "Beth? Beth! Beth Clyburn!" I drop to one knee, reaching for her, rolling her onto her back with my heart in my throat. *Don't let us be too late. Please, tell me we didn't get here too late.*

A pulse flutters weakly in her bruised throat and my heart swells, but she's unresponsive even when I shout in her face. "We need an ambulance out here now!" I bark while the rest of the team searches what little is left of the cellar. The thin blanket draped over Beth's half-naked body isn't worth much, so I remove my jacket and wrap it around her. "You're going to be fine," I whisper. "You're going to be just fine."

"Otherwise, the room was empty. For all we know, he left her there to hide her—which makes more sense, since all signs point to Truby making his escape today. He wasn't spending time at the cabin before that."

"So he stashed her there," Siwak muses, standing opposite me in the hospital hallway.

"It seems that way." I stare past him toward the room where doctors and nurses currently work on Beth behind a curtain drawn across the glass for privacy's sake. Her husband is on his way, and according to the staff who first assessed Beth when she arrived, there doesn't seem to be any serious physical damage. Bruising, a few lacerations which are on their way to healing, but dehydration and malnutrition seem to be the biggest issues. That, and the fact that she has yet to respond to anything going on around her.

"What's on your mind?" Siwak is watching me, keeping his thoughts to himself— something I am grateful for, to say the least.

Shrugging, I reply, "Oh, you know how it is. I'm standing here making up my grocery list for the week in my head."

He clicks his tongue, giving me a disapproving scowl. "Hiding behind sarcasm. I thought we were past that point by now."

"I wasn't being sarcastic." Tipping my head back to touch the cool wall behind me, I release a sigh I've held ever since we arrived at the hospital and the adrenaline began draining from my system. Once Beth was taken in for scans, there was nothing for me to do but stand back and let the aftermath of the situation roll over me in an enormous wave that almost knocked me off my feet.

"I froze up back there," I grudgingly admit. "When I saw her. The way she was. It reminded me a little too much … "

"You have to know there will always be situations that trigger you. To think, you practically rolled your eyes at me when I asked if you could handle this case."

When I don't retort, he finally gets the message. This is serious. "What do you need?" he asks, gentler now.

"I don't know. There have been so many times when the memories were fresh and overwhelming. But this was so real."

"Because you were thrust back into an environment not unlike the one in which you were held," he points out. "How could you not be overwhelmed? But what happened after that?"

"What do you mean?"

"What did you do with those feelings when they came up? Did you freeze up? Shut down? Leave the rest of us to handle things?"

My head drops, my eyes on the tiled floor between my feet. "No."

"I know. That's my point. I doubt you can control when those memories come up, but you controlled how you moved forward." He pulls his phone from his pocket and checks it, scowling. "Chief Perkins. Are you all right?"

"I'm fine. Thanks. I think I'll grab some coffee at the cafeteria." I'm sure they only offer the basics at this time of night, but I need a pick-me-up. Somehow, I'm capable of following the signs posted along the hallway, which lead me to a surprisingly busy cafeteria. Several of the food stations are dark and empty, but a handful are bustling, with people in scrubs grabbing sandwiches and salads, pizza and soup. I settle for pouring a cup of coffee from a tall dispenser and paying for it at the register.

I haven't yet reached for my wallet when a man's voice catches my attention from over my shoulder. "I can grab that for you, if you want."

"Excuse me?" Instinct compels me to move away from him—he's too close for comfort, practically on top of me in line. Considering there's no one behind him, it seems unnecessary.

He flashes an awkward smile that's almost endearing. But then Ted Bundy was good at luring women, making them feel safe. "Your coffee. Usually, you can get a sandwich, a bag of chips, and a beverage as a combo deal. I don't have a beverage, so I could pick up your coffee for you. It would actually end up saving me money," he continues. "A few cents, anyway."

"I think I can handle it," I murmur, aware of his scrubs and a name badge bearing an honorific. Doctor Aiden Watkins.

"It's just that you really look like you could use that coffee, and I'm in a position to help you out."

"How do I look like I need the coffee?" It shouldn't get under my skin, should it? The fact that he said that. I have no doubt I look like death warmed over after the day I've had.

"Considering the fact that this register is self-checkout and you've been standing here waiting for somebody to come and ring up your drink … " He swipes his badge, then scans a barcode on his wrapped sandwich and chip bag.

Sure enough, I chose the automated checkout and was standing in place like an idiot before he walked up. "Oh. All right, I guess I'm a little tired," I admit, blushing.

"This should help." Before I can stop him, he scans the barcode on my paper cup. "Wouldn't want you falling asleep on the road or anything. I'd hate to see you in the ER."

"Let me pay you back," I offer, pulling a couple of bills from my wallet. "Please."

"Do I look hard up to you? I can handle a cup of coffee, and I did offer."

There's something disarming about his attitude. The casual warmth. It makes me wonder how to make up for my abruptness. "Well, thank you, Dr. Watkins."

"You have me at a disadvantage," he counters. "I can't tell you you're welcome if I don't know your name."

Flirting? When was the last time someone flirted with me—without my sister throwing us together? "Aren't you on duty right now, doctor?"

"I'm on my break." His lopsided grin makes me believe there's nothing for me to do but grin back, which I do before catching myself. What am I doing?

"Well, thank you for the coffee. I really do need it." This is awkward, and that's coming from someone who has perfected awkwardness. It's who I am. How do I get out of this without coming off like some rude shrew?

"Walk with me," he offers, starting off before he knows for sure whether I'll follow. What's it like, having that kind of confidence? I don't get a sense of arrogance from him, though.

As we walk, I size him up. He's probably a little over six feet tall, with dark, curly hair. It's a little unruly, like he needs a haircut. "What brings you here?" he asks, looking me up and down with curiosity in his piercing blue eyes. "You're not dressed like a worried family member."

"Maybe I'm a worried family member who came straight from work," I suggest. Considering I didn't want to speak to this man in the first place, we're suddenly very chummy.

"Could be. Or you could have brought someone in for treatment."

"I did, in fact."

"Clyburn, right?" When my eyes pop open wide, he nods. "She's been through a lot."

"You're treating her?" Now, I'm glad we became friendly. I have to do the mental equivalent of sitting on my hands to keep from blurting out a question he might not want to answer.

"From the minute she was wheeled in. What made you decide to bring her back to Charlottesville rather than finding a hospital closer to where she was located?"

"She seemed stable enough when we found her," I explain. "We brought medical supplies along with us and were able to treat her before setting out."

"I see. And I guess that would make things easier for your investigation, and for her husband to come in to see her."

"How is she?" I have to ask.

"There's nothing physical we can't treat." I understand what he means all too well. They can fix her up, get her hydrated and fed, make sure none of her scrapes and cuts gets infected. In her head? That's an entirely different story.

"I guess we won't know what exactly she went through until she regains consciousness." His phone goes off, meaning he has to juggle what he's carrying to answer it. "Watkins," he murmurs. "All right. Be right there."

He's wearing a chagrined expression when he ends

the call. "So much for my break. It was nice to meet you, Miss…"

Right. I can only keep him hanging for so long. "Collins. River Collins."

"Now there's the kind of name I'm not going to forget." He leaves me at a loss for words before hurrying down the hall. I would say I don't follow his progress with a little more interest than normal … but that would make me a liar.

32

River

By late morning, I've managed to go home, catch some sleep, shower and dress. I only wish it was so simple to wash away everything that happened yesterday. From Emma's confession to locating Beth, it was easily the longest day in recent memory. Definitely since the weeks immediately following my escape.

I can't remember the last time I felt so completely sucked into the memories and emotions surrounding my trauma. Agent Siwak was kind and supportive last night, but I know myself best. I know it's unusual and downright morbid for me to wallow. It isn't like I'm trying to. I wish it was as easy as disciplining my thoughts.

Rather than go to the hospital and wait for Beth to wake up—something that could take days, at least—I meet with the team in a small conference room adjoining Agent Siwak's office. It takes a single look around the room to tell me I'm not the only one who could've used a little more rest.

Siwak runs a hand over his face, groaning. "I just checked in with the hospital. Beth's condition is unchanged."

"Any word from the forensics team?" I ask.

"They're still combing the cabin, trying to find anything to point us in a direction Truby ran in. It looks like he turned north after reaching the end of that driveway leading from the cabin, and we've contacted the nearest local businesses and residences to see whether any of them have security cameras pointed toward the road. We might be able to find him on someone's footage."

It's a thin possibility, the kind born from desperation. By all accounts, it doesn't look like Beth was in that room for long. It's like he stashed her there. He must've known there would be a chance he wouldn't return, but that didn't stop him. He left without knowing whether she would live or die.

None of this should come as a surprise, given what we already know about him—the sort of man he is, the way he makes his money. We know he doesn't think much of other people. Not beyond how he can profit from them.

"We got a description of a vehicle from one of the men we took in after the raid on their headquarters," he continues. "But no sign of it so far, though there is an APB out for it. There are plenty of places for him to hide in those mountains, if that was what he chose to do."

It would make sense for him to stay in that area, especially if he's familiar with it. If he plays his cards right, he could stay lost as long as he wants to. "But there are loose ends," I murmur, shaking my head.

"What's that?" Emma asks, barely stifling a yawn. Here I am, thinking about how a little extra sleep might've gone a long way, while she's going through hell.

"Loose ends," I repeat. "He won't be able to stay away for long. Why would he have left Beth behind and not Tamara? Either he's keeping her somewhere else, or he has her with him."

"You're ignoring another possibility," one of the agents mutters from elsewhere in the room. "She could be dead."

"We're all well aware of the possibilities." Agent Siwak's scowl renders the room silent. "The point is, he'll come out of hiding."

For right now, though, it seems like Mayer is more than happy to fly under the radar. My determination grows with every passing hour spent searching, checking in with the forensics team, following up with every business and resident within a five-mile radius of the cabin. If only we had an idea of what time he left. The fact is, we don't even have a solid window—it could have been anywhere from the time he found out his little flunky was brought in for questioning to mere minutes before we arrived. That's a solid seven or eight hour's worth of footage multiplied by countless potential cameras.

By the time my growling stomach can't be ignored anymore, my eyes are burning and my brain feels a lot like boiled oatmeal. "I'm going to stop by the hospital," I tell Emma as I push away from my desk, then throw my arms overhead to stretch once I've stood. It's easy to lose track of time when you're deep in the middle of a search.

I've spent more time poring over grainy video than I ever imagined possible, and I've barely scratched the surface.

"I'll come with you," she suggests. Habit is a funny thing. I have made a habit of living in solitude. Holding myself away from others because, let's face it, there are few trustworthy people in this world. Normally, I would come up with some excuse or other for why I want to be alone. I could make up a story about dinner at Leslie's house or another date that would put me under the gun, timewise.

Instinct tells me not to. She needs this. She might dread going home. Even though we asked that her results be rushed, there are still a heartbreaking number of rape kits pending processing. "I don't want to take anybody else's spot in line," Emma insisted at the hospital. The nurse promised to do what she could regardless.

"Let's go, then," I announce, grabbing my jacket. "I wouldn't mind picking up something to eat along the way."

"We could always grab something from the cafeteria," she suggests on our way to the elevator. "If memory serves, they have a nice selection down there."

I duck my head before she notices the smile that touched my lips with almost no warning. Thinking about the cafeteria brings to mind the doctor from last night. Aiden Watkins. The name is burned into my memory. For the first time in as long as I can remember, someone seemingly normal and nice chatted me up—and I didn't mind. On the contrary. I enjoyed it. There was something fun about bantering back and forth a little. Low stakes flirting, no pressure.

It was so nice, in fact, that I find myself looking for him everywhere we go once we reach the ICU. "You're awfully distracted," Emma observes as we had to Beth's room. "I should've asked how you were feeling. After last night, I mean."

"Oh, I'm okay." It feels wrong, letting her believe I'm distracted by dark, painful flashbacks. Not that they haven't visited at inopportune times throughout the day, but that's not what's on my mind now.

There's no chance to set the record straight before we round the doorway and enter Beth's room. I feel the way my cheeks heat up at the sight of a particular doctor standing at her bedside, typing something into the computer terminal.

He turns his head at the sound of our arrival—then does a double take when he recognizes me. "River Collins," he murmurs with a grin. "See? I told you I wouldn't forget your name."

Emma clears her throat, then offers a hand for the doctor to shake. "Agent Emma Bertinelli. I see you've already met Agent Collins. We wanted to check in on the patient."

His back straightens a little like he just remembered he's on the job. "There hasn't been any change, which isn't necessarily a bad thing," he explains. "She is responsive to external stimuli, so it's a matter of waiting until the shock passes. Whatever she went through, it was severe enough to lock her away."

"You can't lock yourself away." I hear my mother's voice like radio interference, overlapping with Aiden as he continues giving us a rundown of Beth's condition. *"You*

can't do that to yourself. You've been locked away for so long already. We love you. Please, let us help you."

"River?" Emma nudges me. "Did you have any questions?"

"No, not right now. Thank you for catching us up." I hear how stiff and awkward I sound, but don't have the first clue how to sound any other way. Of all the times for me to start wishing I had more experience talking to people.

Before we can leave, Aiden interjects, "Agent Collins, I was hoping to have a word with you." He washes his hands at the small sink in one corner, looking my way all the time. Like he's afraid I'm going to run away.

"I'll meet you down in the cafeteria." Emma shoots me a questioning look before ducking out.

"I'm sorry," Aiden offers, tossing wadded-up paper towels into the trash as he approaches. "We're both on duty at the moment, but I don't know any other way to reach you beyond catching you when we're face-to-face."

"What can I do for you?" I ask, then immediately want to slap a palm to my forehead.

"You can go to dinner with me," he replies, his mouth twitching. "Thanks. You made that easier than I thought it would be."

A date. This time, I have a choice whether or not I want to take him up on it. It's refreshing, really, having a choice.

Remembering the way my heart skipped a beat moments ago, when we came in, I smile. "Sure. Things are a little crazy right now with the investigation, but I would like that."

"Wow, a crazy schedule?" He chuckles wryly. "I have no idea what that's like."

"I'm just saying, you could have mentioned the cute doctor who flirted with you overnight." Emma takes a sip of her wine, shaking her head in disapproval. "He is very smitten with you."

"He is not. We met last night. He's the first nice man I've met in forever. If anything, we'll have a good time at dinner. He has a great personality."

"Yes, I was definitely admiring his personality in those scrubs." Her eyebrows move up and down, suggestive.

"Hey, I'm trying to act like a so-called normal person here." I pour a glass for myself, keenly aware of how much smaller my apartment is than her beautiful colonial home. It's not often I notice my sparse living conditions—at least, it's not often that the sparseness bothers me. At the moment, it does. This is why I don't bother inviting people over.

"I'm proud of you." When I'm unable to stifle a snort, she insists, "I mean it. Not to patronize you, but I know this is a big step. You don't have a trusting nature." Right away, she grimaces and sets the wine glass down though it's still half-full. "Sorry. It's not my business."

"No, you're right." Kicking off my shoes, I settle into the armchair which faces the sofa where Emma sits wedged in the corner, her head resting on the cushion behind her. "It's not easy for me to let people in. And lately, all these parallels ... "

That was too much. I shouldn't have said it. She doesn't know the specifics of my story.

Right away, she sits up straighter, unable to conceal her interest. "Parallels?"

It could be the wine. It could be the promise of a date with Aiden, who might be the first normal person to come into my life in years. The jury is still out, but I'm curious. That alone sets him apart.

It could be the fact that she is still wrestling with her own trauma. Whatever it is, it convinces me to open the vault I normally keep so carefully locked up. "I was kidnapped when I was twelve years old. It took two years before I was able to escape."

The color drains from her face and now I'm sorry I said it. "It's all right ... " I begin, but she cuts me off with a sharp slash of her hand in the air.

"Don't ever apologize. Ever," she almost snaps, like she's angry. That's how intense she is. "River, I am so sorry. Why didn't you tell me? No wonder this has been so hard on you! Why would Siwak—wait, does he know?"

I nod slowly. "He's the only one who does—until now, anyway. They kept me in a cellar like the one where we found Beth. It brought a lot back." That's as much as I feel safe saying without blubbering all over the place.

"Jeez, this explains so much. I've always wondered ... I mean, why you're so standoffish and ... no offense, but a little antisocial."

"No offense taken." I can even smile a little as I sip

my wine and let her process what I just laid on her with no warning. It shouldn't surprise me, the relief that comes with confessing. I didn't have to tell her everything for her to understand. And she is still here, sipping my wine, instead of running screaming from the apartment. Like an actual friend.

I wonder if my dinner with Aiden will also be pleasantly surprising. For the first time in recent memory, I have hope.

33

Tamara

Once Josh grows out of this year's clothes, I'm going to donate them to Goodwill. While I'm at it, I'll donate the baby clothes. They're only taking up space in the garage and all of those totes, anyway.

Footsteps overhead cut off my thoughts. My heart lodges in my throat, just like always, and I hold my breath as whoever it is passes by the door at the top of the stairs. They don't pause there, thank God. Nobody's coming down here to bother me. As much as I want fresh air and something to eat, I would rather sit here alone. Even if it means being tied up the way I am now, with my fingers going numb and the rope burns around my wrists getting worse all the time. I can almost ignore the pain. Almost.

Closing my eyes, I lean against the wall. For some reason, it always feels slightly damp. I shudder to think what kind of mold and bacteria I'm inhaling with every breath while I'm this close to the source, but I'm so tired. And there's really nothing I can do about it.

This can't last forever. I'm going to get out of here. Somebody's going to find me.

A tear rolls down my cheek and I curse it silently. I can't afford to give in to helplessness. I can't give up. If I give up, they've won, and they are not going to win. I'm going to make it through this.

Well, I was trying to lose those extra five pounds, wasn't I? My dry, weary laughter startles something in the far corner into skittering away. My only friends lately, the mice running around down here. I've never actually seen one, but I hear them. They give me plenty of space, and I do the same. None of us wants to be here.

One of the ever present male voices overhead gets louder, and I flinch at the sound. Whoever they are, they're in a bad mood. That's nothing new. All I ever hear is arguing, shouting, sometimes things crashing like they were thrown or kicked over.

Hope is dangerous. Hope can be a heartbreaker.

That doesn't stop it from blooming in my chest. If they're mad, maybe that's because somebody is closing in on them. I mean, they don't seem like the smartest bunch of guys. They're thugs who rely on hurting people, bullying them, tying them up and leaving them in a damp, moldy cellar.

And here I am, at their mercy.

All at once the hope I was so afraid to let loose turns to something dark and cold like the room I'm locked in. Before it can take root and grow into something awful, I turn my thoughts back to making lists of things I need to do when I get home. It's the only way I can get through this, by imagining everything I'm going to do when I'm free. I never could've imagined the sort of emotional labor I sometimes resented having to spend being the one thing keeping me sane through all of this. Thinking about everything I need to do to keep our family running.

Molly needs new shoes. Her feet will not stop growing. The old blender broke—I need to find a new one. I heard good things about the new Ninja model that just came out. I should ask around to see if it's worth buying.

More footsteps, heavier this time. I think I know which one that is. The one who first knocked me out after throwing an arm around me and pinning me from behind against his chest. He pressed a cloth against my face, and I smelled something sweet. That's the last thing I remember. Feeling his giant gorilla body behind me and that enormous catcher's mitt of a hand over my face. It only makes sense that he would be the one with those heavy, plodding footsteps.

Why is it taking so long for somebody to find me? A shiver runs through me and makes my teeth chatter. No matter how tightly I wrap my arms around myself, no matter how I fight to hold myself together, I can't keep from shivering in the cold and the damp and of course the fear. Fear of the unknown. Of what's happening next.

Of what they're going to do to me. Not like they haven't already given me a few ideas of what they have in mind, taunting me the way bullies taunt their prey. It's like they savor my fear, the way some people savor a fine wine or a great meal. It's not enough for them to destroy my life, take me from my children, from my home. They have to make sure I'm terrified every step of the way.

No. This isn't happening. I close my eyes and take a deep breath, forcing myself to imagine my kitchen. I can smell fresh coffee, can hear the quiet hum of the dishwasher. All the mundane things I used to take for granted just happen to be the things I miss the most.

One thing is for sure. When I get out of here, I'm never taking anything for granted again.

All I have to do now is get out.

34

River

"You know me." Emma pats her MacBook almost lovingly. "I can track down anything, so long as you give me enough breadcrumbs to follow."

Sitting on the edge of her desk, I sigh. "Well, I hope there are enough breadcrumbs, since we're running out of options when it comes to tracking this guy down." The only hope we have at this point is to research the accounts Truby uses to shift money around his shell companies. There has to be a connection somewhere that we can exploit.

"Leave it to me," she offers with confidence, cracking her knuckles. "You can spend your time at the hospital, flirting with your new boyfriend."

"Is it a complete waste of time to remind you he isn't my boyfriend?"

She taps her chin and pretends to think about it before nodding almost gleefully. "Could be."

The only thing keeping me from gritting my teeth is

remembering how much she needs a distraction. Granted, I wish I wasn't the distraction, but if it keeps her in one piece and functioning, I can deal with absorbing a little good-natured ribbing from a friend. Still, there are limits.

I have nothing to worry about, as it turns out, since she throws herself into researching, pinpointing the locations behind transactions like the ones between Tamara's bank account and the one used for the cleaning service. Now that we have access to those shell accounts, Emma will track down similar patterns. We might be able to locate other connections, other locations where Mayer hides out.

On my way to the break room for coffee, I catch Agent Siwak's eye. He's in his office, at his desk, and his brief nod answers the question I wanted to voice but haven't had a chance yet. He went out of his way to get Daniel out of the office over the past few days, assigning him to a case in Richmond to keep him away from Emma for the time being.

We still don't have definitive proof yet on whether he assaulted Emma—or whether anyone did at all. It isn't that I don't believe her. I happen to know it's not as easy as making assertions. There has to be proof an assault took place, and we don't have that as yet. Not until the kit is processed.

At least I can relax a little for Emma's sake, if not for Tamara's. It is possible Mayer has her with him, wherever he chose to hole up? It's possible, but is it probable? Could he have decided she wasn't worth the trouble and dumped her someplace, either alive or dead? He might have sold her off. He might have killed her. She could be out there right now in the wilderness, waiting to be discovered.

Either way, she's waiting for us. For justice.

I have to force myself to ignore the chill that runs through me thanks to the direction my thoughts have turned in. That's nothing new. Now that word has spread of Beth's discovery, David Higgins is more persistent than ever, calling the field office and the local police station every hour or two in hopes of hearing news. It doesn't matter how many times we've told him we will reach out to him the second anything changes. I can't pretend I wouldn't do the same thing in his shoes. I've never been the type of person who sits back and waits.

While Emma works her magic, I check in with the members of the team who are still trying to track down video footage of the truck described as Mayer's. "There's a good chance they were lying to us," Agent Greg Jenkins points out, pinching the bridge of his nose and wincing. I understand what he's going through, since I ended up with extreme eye fatigue after staring intently at my screen for hours yesterday.

"I know, but we have to keep trying." It's a pointless thing to say, something I know he understands, but I feel the need to say something to keep everyone encouraged. There's nothing worse than the feeling of killing time chasing down a dead-end lead.

"River! Look at this!" Emma's sudden outburst leaves me rushing to her desk where she is typing furiously, leaning in close to examine the information in front of her.

"What is it?" Standing beside her, I bend closer to the computer, trying to piece together what she's in the middle of working on.

"I've located a handful of accounts with the same payment history as Tamara's." Her voice is shaking with excitement which only heightens my own. "Monthly payments, small amounts, just like she did it."

The next step is tracking down those accounts, finding out their origins. I take down the routing numbers and start making phone calls while Emma continues digging through transactions. Agent Siwak catches wind of what's going on and joins us in time for me to confirm at least one name and location of an account holder.

"Lisa Nolan," I announce after ending the call to her bank. "That's the name of another woman who has been making payments to Truby for months."

"You said Lisa Nolan?" Siwak rubs his chin thoughtfully. "Location?"

"Northern Virginia, by the looks of it."

"There's a woman named Lisa Nolan who's been missing out of Northern Virginia." I follow him to his office, both of us almost jogging. There was always a possibility of this being much bigger than it looks on the surface, but having a possible connection in front of us gets my pulse racing.

He types the name into his keyboard and brings up the image of a pretty, smiling woman who reminds me a lot of Beth, Tamara, the other women in their circle. "Is she still missing?" I ask, though I know the answer before he nods.

"She disappeared six weeks ago," he tells me, still skimming an article. "I'm going to call up the local PD, get a rundown."

Meanwhile, when I return to Emma's side, she has already called up another two banks and come up with names and locations of Mayer's customers. A quick search on my phone leaves my stomach in knots. It's one thing to feel a sense of accomplishment, tracking down the bad guys, linking names, uncovering an entire web of activity that is illegal at best.

But these are real people represented by each and every bank routing number. People who went missing from their otherwise happy, comfortable lives. Blake Danvers, 28, mother of two-year-old twins. They've been missing their mommy for the better part of two months. Polly Klein, 26, mother of a four-year-old. She went missing while out on a run a few months back.

Something tells me there are so many more. That we've barely scratched the surface.

And every one of these women is connected to that man.

"It might be easier and more efficient to look at any missing person cases where the victim fits our general profile," I decide.

"Good idea," Agent Siwak agrees when he rejoins us, looking grim but determined. "I'll have anyone combing through surveillance footage switch tracks and search for missing women in the area. That could be a better use of their time."

"Have them get me that list as soon as possible. We can start cross-referencing as soon as we get our hands on their financials." It's incredible, the change in energy, the fresh determination that comes over all of us. I feel it in the air as we get down to work, uncovering more names, all of us both encouraged and saddened by each discovery. How long has he been at this? And how has he gotten away with it?

By the time a couple of hours have passed, we've located another half-dozen women who've been missing for weeks and months after doing business with one of Mayer Truby's shell companies. "They're all classified as service providers," Emma concludes, rubbing her sore neck after spending so long bent over her machine. "It looks like he figured out what works for him and decided to stick with it."

"Why would he change?" I point out, bitter to say the least. "He's had so much success until now. This means he might have other centers of operation across the state, rather than calling Charlottesville his homebase."

We have essentially widened our search, but we've also connected the dots. Now, we're dealing with a statewide ring … and there's no guarantee he hasn't branched out of Virginia.

I'm in the middle of mulling over our next steps when my cell buzzes in my pocket. I programmed Aiden's number in yesterday after accepting his offer of a date—and though my mind is definitely on my work, I can't ignore the quickening of my pulse when I find his name on my screen.

That doesn't mean I can or should take random phone calls in the middle of the day. I step away from Emma's desk before answering, since I don't feel very much like hearing her reaction when she finds out who called. "Dr. Watkins," I murmur after answering. "I'm a little—"

"I knew you would want to hear right away, so I called you myself rather than reaching out to the main number for the field office." The tension in his voice makes my heart lurch, leaving me hanging in suspense until he continues. "Beth Clyburn is awake. She said she wants to talk to you."

35

River

The hospital is mere minutes from the field office, but it feels like hours of fighting through traffic, then navigating the parking garage in search of an empty space. By the time I'm out of the car and running for the door with Emma at my side, I'm ready to scream out my frustration. In reality, not much time has passed since Aiden's call. It only feels that way.

He meets us in the hall just outside Beth's room. "She's still very fragile," he murmurs after we exchange a brief smile that soon hardens into something more professional. "But she's determined to tell you everything she knows while it's still fresh."

"And she's fully alert and everything?" Emma asks.

He nods. "It seems that way. She came around roughly a half hour ago, asking for her husband and kids, but then immediately asking for a cop so she can give a statement. She was determined to do that. I explained it was the FBI who found her, and she insisted on talking to you before she sees her family."

I have to give her credit for her determination. From where I'm standing she is partly visible, sitting up in bed, looking very small while surrounded by machines. She's staring out the window, arms wrapped around herself, and I have to ask myself how to approach this in a way that won't leave her feeling threatened or pushed too hard. I can't afford to have her shut down, not now, and especially not while she's so eager to tell us everything she can remember.

Emma and I approach slowly, almost inching our way through the open door. "Beth?" I murmur, thinking back to how I wanted to be treated after my escape. The last thing I wanted was to be coddled, but then I don't know where Beth is right now. Yes, she's eager to speak with us, but that doesn't mean she feels strong.

She slowly turns her head, squinting a little, eyeing us warily until she sees the badges hanging from around our necks. She softens as her eyes fill with tears and even manages a brief smile which winds up looking more like a pained grimace when her chin quivers.

"Thank you so much for rescuing me." She's soft spoken, choosing her words carefully while her breath hitches with every stifled sob.

"You're so welcome." My emotions are running high, too, tightening my chest. "How are you feeling?"

"I'm dying to see my kids, but I don't want to forget anything that might be helpful."

"We are so grateful you're choosing to speak to us." Emma stands at the foot of the bed while I position myself at Beth's left side, so she can continue looking out the window if she feels overwhelmed.

"I guess it was kind of silly, asking how you feel," I venture with a grimace that makes her smile again.

"I'm just glad to be here, and not where I was." She shudders slightly and shakes her head. "The whole time, I kept telling myself it was a dream. I mean, it was so surreal. The kind of thing that happens to other people, not to me. Do you know what I mean?"

"I understand exactly what you mean," I assure her. "I went through a kidnapping when I was a kid."

Why did I tell her that? To loosen her up, I guess. The words came out before I could weigh them and decide if it was a good idea to open up. I'm normally careful, but a situation like this is worth more than self-preservation. I have to be willing to be vulnerable if I'm asking a victim to also be vulnerable, to open up and share the details of her greatest nightmare.

Her eyes widen a fraction, and her already sallow complexion goes paler. "Oh, wow. I'm sorry. That's terrible."

"I only want you to know that I do understand. I'm not speaking as an agent, you know?" When I gesture toward the bed, eyebrows raised, she nods quickly. I take a seat, careful to give her space so she doesn't feel crowded.

The pain in her eyes is striking, heartbreaking. "What do you want to know? I'll try to remember everything I can."

Emma pulls out a notepad and I start to ask questions, almost tiptoeing in hopes of keeping Beth from becoming overwhelmed. "We found you in a storm cellar. Is that where you were held all this time?"

She shakes her head. "No, he took me there."

"He?" Emma prompts.

"I think his name was ... " She closes her eyes, squeezing them tight, and I can almost hear her teeth grind as she tries to recall. "Mayer. That's what the guys called him. They were afraid of him," she adds. "He was a pretty scary guy."

"How so?" I ask.

"Well, for starters, he kept me blindfolded and tied up all the time." Right away, it's clear she regrets that retort. "I'm sorry. The last thing you need is my attitude at a time like this."

"There's no need to apologize."

She draws herself together and takes a deep breath. "He was intimidating. The other guys, they would raise their voices almost like they were trying to get his attention. The way kids do sometimes, you know? Hey, look at me, pay attention to me. That was how it felt, anyway. And there were times ... "

She swallows hard but pushes her way through it. "There were times when they would hurt me just to get a reaction out of him. I sensed it, you know? So I would get a slap, or I would get pushed to the floor with my hands tied, so I couldn't catch myself. And they all found it hilarious," she concludes, sounding disgusted. I don't blame her.

"Were you alone all the time?" Emma asks. "Was there anyone with you?" Like Tamara. I don't want to lead her in any one direction, though. It's better to hear the story coming organically from her than to feed her names.

"I was held on my own," she explains. "At first, I was in a ... almost like an old kitchen? I was blindfolded a lot of the time, but the few times I could see, it was pretty obvious that was what the space was used as. I was in a curtained-off section. I heard movement nearby but... I knew better than to try to catch anybody's attention."

"Why is that?"

"I was afraid I would get in trouble—or that I would get someone else in trouble. I didn't want to risk putting anybody else in danger. A couple of times, I heard someone cry out like they were in pain after it sounded like they were slapped. I didn't want it to get any worse than that."

"Were any other names ever mentioned?" Emma asks. "Beyond Mayer's?"

"Lou, Jimmy, Bryan. No last names, though. There were always people around, like they worked in shifts. Armed, for the most part. When I couldn't see them, I could still smell them—cigarette smoke, liquor on their breath, that kind of thing. Otherwise, I was literally flying blind."

"What about locations? Any idea of what their next moves were?"

Something sparks behind those pain-filled eyes, and it's enough to give me hope. "They did do a lot of talking about shipments, moving things from one place to the other."

Emma writes rapidly while I ask, "Can you remember any specifics?"

"Somebody kept talking about a payment that was overdue out of Virginia Beach," she replies, sounding distant as she dives deeper into her memory. "And there was one time Mayer was angry about a pick-up in Charlottesville that didn't go how it was supposed to. Something about someone being called in for questioning?"

"That was us," I tell her. "So he knew about that?"

"Before I knew it, I was thrown over somebody's shoulder with the blindfold over my eyes, and I ended up in the back of a car or a truck or something. To be honest with you, I was pretty out of it at the time. I think they might have drugged my food."

It makes sense that they would want to keep the women under their control. Drugging them is probably the easiest way to make sure of that. I make a mental note to ask Aiden about anything that might have lingered in her system when she first came in.

"I do remember one of the guys," she muses. "When I wasn't blindfolded. He was one of the guys guarding us. A big man, huge, like a linebacker. Gigantic hands, thick neck. I think his name was Bruno, which seemed to fit. That's why I remember it."

"Did you ever get a look at anyone else?" I don't remember a man like the one she described being part of the raid. It could be he was out doing his master's bidding at the time.

"Not really. A flash here or there. They only ever let me take the blindfold off when I had to use the bathroom, but they put it right back on as soon as they opened the door. Sometimes I would pretend I had to go just to be left alone for a few minutes. Isn't that amazing?" she asks me.

"Isn't what amazing?"

"The things that become important at a time like that. I mean, going to the bathroom became something I looked forward to."

Now I'm glad I told her the basics of my past, since it's clear she feels connected to me. "All I remember is craving a milkshake like you cannot possibly imagine."

Her gaze softens before she sighs. "For me, it was an ice cream float. Root beer, vanilla ice cream. I can't wait to have one. I can't even remember the last time I did," she adds, chuckling before wiping away a tear that suddenly rolled down her cheek.

I make another mental note, this time to order her exactly what she wants. If I have to go to the store and buy a bottle of root beer and a carton of ice cream, I'll do it.

There's slight commotion in the hall, which Emma goes to investigate. She turns our way with a smile. "You have visitors."

I stand and step aside in time for Dr. Clyburn to rush into the room with a child gripping each hand. "Mommy!" Beth's son runs for the bed and scrambles to climb up and be with her. Beth's loving, cheerful laughter rings out over the joyful shouts of her children as Emma and I silently excuse ourselves from the room so they can have private time together.

"She didn't say anything about Tamara," Emma murmurs, echoing what has already been on my mind.

"We still don't know for sure whether there's any

connection between them in the first place," I point out, glancing toward the room to find Beth in her husband's arms while the kids cuddle close to her. "And she did say she was kept alone."

"I guess that works for them, just like the drugs do." Emma taps her pen against the notepad where she has scrawled notes I'm sure only she could read. "If you keep them together, there's more of a chance of them concocting a plan. These guys are idiots, obviously. I doubt it would take too much to outsmart them."

Again, something that's been on my mind all this time.

One thing is certain as the Clyburn family celebrates being together again, I was already bound and determined to locate Tamara Higgins and put an end to this trafficking ring, but now that I'm faced with the aftermath of locating one of the victims, I'll stop at nothing to reunite the others. Tamara … and heaven knows how many more.

36

River

"Don't worry about anything." Keeping my voice low, I glance around, gauging the atmosphere while Emma sits frozen at her desk. Her chair is vibrating thanks to the way she can't stop shaking. "Just stay where you are. I'm here with you."

"What if he –" She cuts herself off, shaking her head. "Tell me it's going to be okay."

"Is absolutely going to be okay." And it is, I know it is, though I'm more than a little worried about how Daniel's going to take Agent Siwak's announcement. This is the first day Daniel has been in the office since Emma told me what happened, and I can't pretend the idea of seeing him this morning didn't make me sick when I first opened my eyes. This isn't about me, though. I have to swallow back my disgust while waiting for the news to break.

And break it does.

Out of the corner of my eye, I watch Daniel

approach Siwak's office. I don't want to make it obvious there's something wrong, so I don't want to stare at him openly. "He's going in," I whisper, since Emma is too terrified to look.

"What if I'm wrong?" she whispers back, staring at her screen.

"What did we already talk about? He is not losing his job. He's only being placed on leave until this is all settled. And there is absolutely nothing wrong with you saying hey, I don't think I can work with this person anywhere near me. You are perfectly within your rights, and Siwak has your back."

"Right." She draws a deep breath, nodding firmly but remaining in place. "Thank you. It's so easy to question myself."

"You're what?" My head snaps up at the sound of a raised voice. "You can't be serious! What are you talking about? Is this a joke?"

I can't help but look over toward the office, where glass walls make it possible for me to see what's happening inside. I'm treated to the sight of Daniel Brennon—someone I thought I knew, someone I thought I respected and used to enjoy working with—losing his mind. "Who said I did that? Who? Who accused me?" he shouts. Even the closed door is not enough to muffle his rage.

Siwak's voice is more measured, but I can still hear him when he replies, "It doesn't matter who came forward. The fact is, until we are sure after conducting an internal investigation, I'm going to need your badge and your service weapon. You're being placed on administrative leave."

"What?" Daniel shrieks, making Emma flinch. "I didn't do anything! This is all some misunderstanding, it must be. You can't take my job! What the hell is wrong with you?"

I know that was a mistake before Siwak rises. By now, I'm not the only one watching, and unlike me, they don't bother hiding their interest. It isn't every day you see somebody flipping out the way Daniel is now, throwing his hands in the air, pounding his fist on the desk as he demands answers that are not coming.

"Have you lost your mind?" he bellows. "This is me you're talking to! You know me, Eric! Never in my life have I— "

"You might want to be careful what you say next," Siwak warns, holding up a hand. "And for the record, you refer to me as Agent Siwak, not Eric. Let's not lose sight of protocol in the middle of all of this."

"You care about protocol now?" Daniel laughs wildly, unhinged, before throwing his badge onto the desk. "You're the one telling me I need to go on leave because some bitch is accusing me of going too far, and I'm the one who doesn't care about protocol?" Emma flinches again. I cover her shoulder with one hand and give it a squeeze.

Siwak is unimpressed. "Are you finished?"

Daniel yanks his pistol from its holster and leaves it on the desk along with his badge. "You're going to be sorry for this. You are all going to be sorry. When I decide to sue your ass "

"Spare me," Agent Siwak snaps. "Security is on the way up here to escort you out if you aren't willing to go quietly. Take your choice. It doesn't matter to me."

"You are going to be so sorry for this. All of you are going to regret this."

I watch Daniel storm out of the office, marching down the hall without looking my way. I'm honestly grateful to him for that, because making eye contact might be too much.

Something interesting tugs at the back of my mind as I rub Emma's shoulder, hoping to calm her down in the aftermath. I would think he'd know instantly who would accuse him of this, considering he did go out for drinks with Emma that night. Yet there he is, asking who accused him. Is it a tactic to prove his innocence?

Or is it possible there's more than one woman who has a reason to accuse him? The thought makes me sick to my stomach, and I breathe slowly to fight off a wave of nausea that threatens to pull me under.

Siwak gives us both a few minutes before catching my eye and waving me into the office. He's still slightly flushed, revealing how worked up he actually became even if he hid it well. "Are you okay to go in and talk to the boss?" I ask Emma, who nods firmly before standing. I don't want to hover too closely, to smother her, so I choose to accept her determination at face value as she follows me down the hall.

I appreciate the fact that he doesn't mention what happened with Daniel. Obviously, we are aware of everything. I'm pretty sure the entire floor heard every word, and by now gossip must be spreading.

He settles for giving me an inquisitive look. I nod the way he nodded to let me know Daniel was on his way in, and he accepts this before launching into something more closely related to our case. "Tell me we have some positive updates."

"Actually, we do." Nobody would ever know what Emma's going through based on the way she takes control of the situation, stepping up before I have the chance to. "We have identified another potential hideout in a more remote part of town. It's one of a handful of similar properties that were purchased for cash all within the same one-month timeframe a couple of years back. They were purchased at the same time as the restaurant we raided," she explains.

"That's a strong lead," he agrees. "Good work. We need eyes on those locations, as soon as possible."

"We were waiting on your say-so," I tell him with much more positivity than I'm feeling at the moment. Yes, things are moving on the case, but I can't brush aside the way Emma trembled as Daniel threw his fit. Is she the only one? Are there more women like her with a similar story to tell about an innocent night that turned into something much worse?

"Consider my say-so granted," Siwak announces. "Let's get eyes at each property as soon as possible. Anything else about Beth Clyburn?"

"I took the liberty of calling the direct number to her room," I admit. "She still doesn't have anything else to offer beyond what she shared with us yesterday."

"I'm sure right now, she wants nothing more than to forget about it," he muses.

"I don't know," Emma replies in a soft voice. "It seemed to me she was pretty determined to remember everything she could. She wanted to help."

Is she thinking about herself now? I wouldn't blame her if she was. "You're right," he agrees, giving her a concerned look I recognize all too well. He's looked at me that way so many times. "I'm sure she's doing her best. Now, both of you get out there and organize surveillance."

If I had to describe in one word the smile that crosses Emma's face, I would choose *grateful*.

37

River

Sitting on surveillance isn't exactly my favorite way to pass the time, mostly because it involves so much passivity. Watching. Waiting.

After splitting up the team and spending a day observing the various properties which Emma located during her analysis, three of them stuck out as being the most heavily visited. The others were sort of empty, with only a car or two parked outside. It seems the bulk of business is done from a small handful of locations.

I sit several dozen yards away from one of them, behind the tinted windows of a van with Emma at my side. There's no chance of either of us working without the other right now, considering how close this case has brought us together. There must be something about me that leaves her feeling more secure, like she's protected. I can't imagine what it is—I've never exactly had a talent for making people feel relaxed and at ease.

She seems to be glad we're together now, almost

cheerful as she takes notes, making sure to carefully study each person passing in and out through a set of double doors to what is supposed to be a small appliance repair shop.

"I can't even tell you the last time I saw a place like this," Emma muses, unclipping her hair and shaking out her curls before letting her head touch the back of her seat. "The little Mom and Pop shops, you know?"

"Yeah, most of them got eaten up by big box stores—and the fact that today's small appliances are practically disposable doesn't help either. Built cheaply, sold cheaply, quickly replaced and tossed in a landfill."

She snorts, turning her head my way and grinning. "Normally, I would question your cynical viewpoint, but that's something we can agree on."

"I'm flattered." At least she's feeling well enough to joke, even if the joke is at my expense.

"Wow." She turns her attention back to the action in front of the store, pulling out her binoculars to zoom in on a man who's stepped outside. "That's a big boy right there. What must he weigh? At least three hundred pounds, from the looks of it."

I watch, too, and something about the man tickles a memory in the back of my mind. At first, I can't place it, not until I recall Beth's description. "Didn't Beth Clyburn talk about a man that size? She said he was the one who grabbed her and was in charge of watching her, right?"

"That's right." There's excitement in her voice, much like the excitement running through my veins. Like another piece has slid into the puzzle, locking with the other pieces, helping complete the picture. "I mean, guys in this line of work probably hire monsters like him if only to scare the women into compliance, but I'd be willing to bet he's the one she described. He's the only one so far that comes close to her description."

I make a note of his appearance, then glance at the clock on the dash. It's five minutes later than it was the last time I looked. My knee jogs up and down and goes dry. Tonight is my date with Aiden. What was I thinking, agreeing to have dinner at a time like this?

When I voice that question, she shakes her head. "You and I both know if you waited for a time when everything lined up perfectly and you had room in your schedule, you would never go on another date as long as you live. And don't even try to tell me that's a good idea," she adds before I have the chance to say exactly what she predicted.

"How am I supposed to think about getting to know somebody new when I have all of this hanging in the balance?"

"You can remind yourself you are not the only person working this case," she suggests. "And you can remember we all know what we're doing. Nobody is asking you to sacrifice your entire life for a case. You're allowed to go to dinner with a nice man."

"The jury is still out on whether or not he's so nice," I reminded her.

She only rolls her eyes. "Right. and that's why you blushed as hard as you did when you saw him in Beth's room. I swear, the temperature went up."

"Don't even say that," I grumbled, which only made her laugh.

"Fine, have it your way. I'm just saying, I'm going to start looking for dresses to wear to your wedding." Her wicked giggle leaves me grumbling to myself, though I don't mean it. Not entirely.

"Can I be honest with you?"

Aiden's eyes widen a fraction from across the table. Outside of a set of scrubs, he looks almost as good as any of the food we've seen pass by on trays, which is saying something. Every dish looks better than the last.

But he also stands out from every other man in the room. Why? I can't put my finger on it. It could be the easygoing nature that first made me curious about him. His effortless charm.

Charm that translates into a pair of dimples when he grins. "I'm not going to ask you to lie to me," he jokes. "What's on your mind?"

"It is very difficult for me to turn my full attention to anything other than a case when I'm knee-deep in it, which I am right now. I'm sorry if I'm terrible company." Now that I got that out, I can take a sip of my wine and blow out a sigh of relief.

"You don't give yourself enough credit," he murmurs after taking a moment to absorb my words. I appreciate that. How thoughtful he is. It helps me relax, though I can't quite understand why. I guess it's the sense of being listened to and taken seriously, something I certainly didn't experience during either of the dates my sister set me up on.

"I think you're too kind," I retort.

"I don't think so." He cuts off a hunk of his porterhouse steak, but stares at me rather than at the meat on his fork. For once, I don't experience the wave of resentment I usually do when someone is staring at me, studying me. I don't feel like I have to guard myself.

There's no judgment to it, I realize. That must be the difference. "If anyone can understand the complications brought about by a high-pressure, high-stakes job, you're looking at him." He points to himself with the tip of his steak knife. "I can't tell you how many women decided I wasn't worth the effort after the first two or three times I had to cancel plans or postpone them because I was running late after a last-minute emergency. Suffice to say there aren't many people with endless patience. It wears thin after a while."

"At the same time," I counter while flaking off a bite of my buttery grilled salmon, "that can become a comfortable excuse. A reason to not devote enough time or energy to a relationship."

"Have you ever been guilty of that?" His eyes twinkle and I know it's not a serious question, but it still makes the back of my neck prickle. We're stepping into personal territory here, also known as someplace I try to avoid as much as possible.

Yet somehow, none of the old reflexes come into play. There's no invisible wall between us. Nothing tying my tongue.

"Honestly? I've never … I mean, it's complicated."

And I've already said too much. Now I know what happens next. He's going to look at me like I sprouted a second head, ask himself what is so wrong with me that I've never been in anything resembling a relationship, and decide I'm not worth the trouble.

He chews slowly, thoughtfully, while I wish I could crawl under the table and disappear. What was I thinking? That this incredibly kind, charming, handsome man would look at me and consider me a project worth working on?

"Well, to be honest with you, I went through a long period where I decided not to pursue relationships." Setting down his knife and fork, he dabs the corners of his mouth with his napkin before leaving it on his lap again. "In fact, that's becoming increasingly common nowadays. People are becoming more independent in ways they weren't before. Women no longer have to find a man to marry if there's any hope of a future. Men no longer consider it a sign of weakness if they head into the kitchen to fry an egg or wash a dish."

"I don't know about that," I murmur with a grin, thinking about my brother-in-law. I'll never forget my sister describing the one and only time she left him home to take care of the kids on his own. It's amazing the house was standing by the time she got back.

"But you see my general idea," he insists gently. "People are understanding more and more that a relationship is something you should want because it's what you want, not because you've reached a certain age or a certain point in your life. And certainly, no relationship should be entered into out of necessity. All that does is breed contempt. I think you were playing it smart by taking your time and being choosy," he concludes.

It's kind of him to assume the reason why I haven't been able to strike up a relationship. He's kind in general. "You're very empathetic," I observe. "I'm sure your patients rave about your bedside manner."

"I sort of backed into becoming a physician," he explains with a shrug. "My original plan was to become a therapist. I probably would have been able to set my own schedule and build an actual life."

"It seems like that would be a perfect fit for you. What made you change your mind?"

"I guess I've always been a sucker for a challenge." He winks, and to my surprise, the gesture sets off fluttering in my belly.

"Are you saying I'm a challenge?" I ask.

I can't help but laugh when he does. "The jury is still out on that, but you definitely started us off on the right foot when you wouldn't let me buy you that coffee." The memory makes me laugh again, and it's nice to realize this is the most fun I've had on a date in … well, ever. All it takes is sitting across from a kind, genuinely interesting person.

It's no surprise, really, when we end up getting dirty looks from the staff long after our plates have been cleared. "How is it so late?" Aiden asks, checking his watch. "No wonder the place emptied out. I hope we haven't kept anybody here longer than they should've been." I pretend not to notice when he adds a few more bills to the already hefty tip which he tucks under a salt shaker before we leave. Anyone can be generous when they think someone is watching. I'm much more interested in people like Aiden, who waited until he thought I wasn't paying attention.

I'm interested in him in general, it seems. So interested, I'm almost sorry when it comes time to part ways in the mostly empty parking lot. "Thank you so much for tonight," I tell him in complete sincerity when we reach my car door. "I like talking to you. I only hope you weren't bored to death."

"Are you kidding? You're the first woman I've met in years who didn't ask within the first five minutes whether I ever pulled something out of rectum that shouldn't have been there."

"What?" My laughter rings out in the empty lot. "You can't be serious." But then I remember my disastrous dates, and how they pumped me for information about my job.

"Scout's honor," he insists, stepping closer and making my heart skip a beat. "I was sort of hoping you would wait until at least the second date before asking any questions like that."

I don't have time to ask, who said anything about a second date, before his light, sweet kiss makes me forget just about everything I ever thought I knew. By the time he backs away, the pounding in my chest paired with the heat in my core tells me a second date is inevitable. Maybe even necessary.

38

River

My heart drops like a rock the morning after my date with Aiden, when I enter the office and reach my desk to find Emma's computer off, her chair empty. She never reached out to tell me she was running late. Dread leaks into my veins and I reach for my phone while a hundred ugly possibilities swirl around in my head. She seemed fine yesterday, but something might've happened while I was out last night.

It's Agent Siwak who notices me, tapping on the glass wall between me and the inside of his office. "It was a late night. She'll be in a little late."

I touch a hand to my chest before releasing a shaky breath. There I was, thinking something happened with Daniel, or maybe that she decided she couldn't handle being here right now.

As it turns out, Siwak's announcement was unneeded, since Emma calls me not a minute later. I've barely hung up my jacket when my phone buzzes, and

I'm quick to pick it up and find out why last night ran so late. Her voice is still a little sleepy when she greets me. "Sorry, I meant to send you a text to let you know. I needed a little extra sleep this morning. I was up half the night." Her explanation ends on a loud yawn.

"Did something go wrong?"

"No, just the opposite. I think I found something, and I couldn't stop pursuing it."

My skin is tingling as I sit down at my desk, all of my attention focused on whatever she's about to say. I'm sorry I missed it, whatever it was, but that kiss with Aiden was special, too. I would hate to have missed that.

"After everything seemed to get quiet last night, I reviewed all the notes from the other surveillance teams. Everything pretty much seems the same across the board—these guys are creatures of habit. They have to be, right? They can't afford to be sloppy."

"True, or otherwise we would have wrapped this up by now."

"Exactly. It stood to reason they have a means of communicating that would fly under the radar, so to speak. I started looking at those transactions again, after I came back from the stakeout. I focused on comparing the dates to messages the computer forensics guys accessed once we got the warrant for the cleaning service. I don't know what I was looking for, but I found a pretty clear pattern of activity."

"Don't keep me hanging," I begged when she paused to catch her breath.

"They use a lot of code. Have you noticed that? Not,

like, complicated code. We're not talking genius-level stuff."

"Like that line about things getting hot, written on the back of the cabin photo."

"Right! Nothing complicated, but they use the same words and phrases. And every six weeks or so, there was always the mention of a shipment coming in or going out. Around that time, there's more money changing hands, moving through those shell accounts Truby set up."

"A pattern," I conclude, as the hair on the back of my neck stands straight up. "They're gearing up for something."

"Wouldn't you know it, it's happening again. Almost like earthquakes before volcanic eruptions." There's pride in her voice. I'm glad to hear it. "That would explain why reports from the other surveillance teams note increased activity. A lot of people going in and out, a lot of phone calls made from cell phones out on the sidewalk. One of the teams even witnessed a guy ending a call, then smashing the phone on the ground when he was finished."

"Using burners," I mutter, gritting my teeth. Of course they are. They know we're onto them, they have to know we're watching, so they're not going to take a chance of using a landline or a number that could be traced through a phone carrier.

"Exactly. And since they know we're onto them, I have to wonder if Tamara will be part of that so-called shipment. They would want to get her out of here before we can discover her."

My hand tightens around the phone while my heart starts to pound hard enough that it almost drowns out Emma's voice. "Were there any dates used?"

"I tried to break through the encryption in the message where the shipment was mentioned, and I found coordinates hidden there, but no date or time."

"Where is the location?"

"It's another one of Truby's properties in the mountains, closer to Charlottesville this time. I found it in the list of properties we haven't yet surveyed. I already talked to Siwak about it," she concludes. "So he's caught up."

"I'll go in and talk to him about it now. You've more than earned a late morning." I'm already on my way to his office, ignoring the coffee I wanted to pour for myself before I settled in to any tasks this morning.

"I won't be much longer," she promises before ending the call. Siwak is waiting, hands folded across his flat stomach, eyes trained on me.

"Where do we go from here?" I ask, tucking the phone into my pocket as I come to a stop in front of his desk.

"Good morning to you, too, Agent Collins."

"Now is not the time to lecture me on my manners. What do we do now?"

At least he drops the joke, getting serious before sitting up straighter. "I was going to ask you the same thing. What is your gut telling you?"

"It's telling me we need to park at that location and stay there until it's time to go in and clear it out."

"And we'll do that. I've already submitted a request for search warrants."

I shouldn't feel so taken back, but I do, sputtering a little as I process this. "Oh. Okay, good."

"You know, I am capable of doing these things when you aren't here," he reminds me, gentle but stern. "You can't carry everything on your shoulders. You can't expect yourself to be everywhere all at once."

My mouth falls open as I prepare to defend myself, but he shakes his head and gives me the sort of look that tells me anything coming out of my mouth right now would be ignored. "It's especially important in cases like this for you to know when to take a step back and take care of yourself. I understand you went out last night."

I could get whiplash from the sudden change of topic. "How do you know about that?"

"Emma let it slip. We weren't talking behind your back," he insists when I fold my arms. "It doesn't have to be a secret. People have personal lives. You're entitled. And you are especially entitled to do everything you can to find balance when a case strikes as close to home as this one does for you."

"I'm handling it."

"Tell me another good one," he retorts as his mouth settles in a thin, disbelieving sort of line. It's the look Dad used to wear when I was a kid, trying to talk my way around his rules.

"I am. And let's face it. The sooner we get this over with, the sooner I can move on and ... you know, heal."

"You practically made quotes around that word."

"But I didn't, did I?"

There's a tiny smile tugging at the corners of his mouth when he shakes his head. "I'm trusting you to do what's best for you right now. I wish I had the bandwidth to follow you around and look after you. I need you to be honest with me, and I need to know you'll come to me if you need help."

"Of course." I don't mean to sound so dismissive, but there are more important things at stake than my mental emotional well-being. I can deal with that later.

He sighs, shaking his head at me again. "I wanted to give you the heads up, too, that Internal affairs is advancing with the investigation. The rape kit came back. It was Daniel's DNA."

I knew it, didn't I? Of course, I believe Emma, I did from the moment she opened up and shared. Still, getting that sort of confirmation Leaves me reeling. "Is he aware of this?"

"Oh, he certainly is." There's a growl under his words, which pairs nicely with the way his brows draw together over eyes that are suddenly hard and darker than before. "He's furious. Insists there's a side of the story that hasn't been heard yet. I told him to take it up with the investigators. I'm not interested in hearing his excuse."

"I know that means a lot to Emma." Really, as much as I already respected Agent Siwak, the feeling has deepened thanks to the way he's handling this. "And once word gets out, if it hasn't already, I know it will make every woman working with you feel a little more secure. Like she'll be listened to."

"I hate the fact that any agent working in this building would ever have to worry about that in the first place." Scrubbing his hands through his hair, he groans.

"How could something like this happen here? When I first entered the Bureau, there was this ... I don't know, unspoken code. There are certain lines you never cross."

Rising from his desk, he raps his knuckles against the surface before going to the window and looking out onto a bright, beautiful day. "Call me naïve, but even at my advanced age, I imagined my agents having the sort of character and principles that would make an attack like that impossible. It never occurred to me that one of them could do something so heinous to another, especially when it's someone they've worked with closely. I can't wrap my head around it."

For once, I can comfort him a little. "That's because you're a decent person who can't imagine hurting someone else like that. It doesn't make you naïve. I'm the last person I would ever describe as naïve, and I was shocked, too. This isn't a reflection on you," I conclude.

After all, if there's anybody who knows the depth of depravity which seemingly normal people can sink to, it's me.

39

River

Let her be in there. Let her be alive. My throat is so tight. I can barely swallow my saliva. My stomach is in knots. I have to wonder if a heart can literally beat out of a chest.

Chief Benjamin Miller chats with Agent Siwak, going over last-minute details of the raid that's about to be conducted by our teams and local law enforcement combined. Instead of a cabin in the woods, this is an old warehouse that according to records hasn't been in use in ten years, but was kept and maintained under private ownership.

I can see it in the distance, lights burning behind windows, glowing in the darkness. We're barely half a mile away, and the energy that's built between our team and the uniformed officers called in for backup is palpable. We all understand the stakes.

Still, deep down inside, I know there's no one who understands them as well as I do. If Tamara is in there, and if she's conscious and aware of the situation, this will be the scariest part of her entire ordeal. Those last few minutes before freedom, when literally anything can go wrong. I know that terror. I fought my way through it when I escaped, when the fear wanted me to stay where I was because at least there, I knew what I was in for. It was the unknown beyond my darkened room that was truly terrifying.

I know something else, too. Her situation has never been more dangerous. No doubt she's being guarded, as any of these women would be, and we have already received confirmation that a man fitting the description of Mayer Truby was seen entering the premises two hours ago. Since no one has left, it's safe to assume he's still there. He's ruthless, no doubt, and there's not a question in my mind he would eliminate Tamara if it meant one fewer person to testify against him.

Which means there's no time to waste. We have to locate her immediately, or else risk going through all of this only to lose her.

"We move in at seven hundred," Chief Miller announces, with Siwak nodding in agreement. "It's ten minutes, people. Remember your team assignments and the route you're taking to the warehouse. We shoot to wound, not to kill. Locating and securing the hostage is the primary objective, but we are looking to capture the man behind this."

Siwak adds, "I can't get information from a dead man."

Emma glances my way. "You all right?" she whispers.

Am I? I feel the cool night air on my skin, even cooler thanks to the perspiration that's begun to form as the clock ticks down. "I'm fine," I whisper back. "It's just that I imagined this sort of thing happening so many times, only I was the one trapped inside, waiting to be rescued."

"I'm sure you could never imagine something as big as this," she points out, looking over the two dozen bodies now assembled. There's also an ambulance waiting, with a pair of medics on hand in case Tamara needs medical treatment.

"I don't know. I imagined some pretty big things. There was a tank involved at one point." I can laugh at myself now, though there's no humor in it. "Like they would ever mount a rescue operation that size for a single girl."

"Look what we're doing for a single woman," she points out. "It's just a shame there was nobody with your skills and tenacity working your case. I am so sorry."

It's funny. Normally, when someone says something like that, I dismiss it as empty words, meaningless platitudes. It doesn't feel that way now. I hear her sincerity. I feel it.

At the top of the hour, we set out on foot to avoid being spotted for as long as possible. Nothing like a half mile jog through dark woods, though the night vision goggles I'm wearing go a long way toward helping me find my footing. The warehouse looms larger the closer we get. We're about fifty yards away before I can identify vehicles parked outside the structure, and the single guard smoking a cigarette while carrying a semi-automatic weapon in his free hand.

I hold my breath, my body tensed, poised for a fight. Agent Siwak holds up a hand to signal our silence, then picks up a rock and throws it in a wide overhead ark. The rest of us watch as the rock sails through the air before dropping near a trio of garbage cans. It hits the ground and rebounds into one of those cans, making it rattle, startling the guard. With his weapon poised, he walks over to where the rock struck, his head swinging back and forth as he searches the darkness for whatever might have caused the noise.

Siwak's voice rings out in my earpiece. "Let's move."

It all happens so fast. Out of the corner of my eye, I see a pair of agents in body armor quickly and silently subdue the guard, disarming him, pulling him away from the building before he can send up an alarm. We're on the move, cutting as silently as we can through the darkness before rushing the warehouse through the front and rear.

"Hands in the air!"

"Drop your weapons!"

"This is a raid! Federal officers!"

It's a frenzy, countless voices overlapping, the deafening cracks of gunfire. One of the local PD wounds, then disarms a gunman, clearing my way. I jog past one room after another, all of them positioned along the building's exterior walls. Probably offices at one time. Now, they look like empty cells.

A pair of officers follow close behind me, the three of us heading for the stairwell at the far corner of the floor. I barely register the half-hidden figure at the bottom of the stairs before the glint of gunmetal makes me recoil and take cover. It isn't a half second before a chunk is taken out of the cinderblock wall when the man opens fire. One of the officers shouts for backup while the other waits a heartbeat, then fires down the stairs.

"Careful!" I warn, letting him cover me while the others follow. We can't risk hitting Tamara or any other innocent people who might be down there.

"Hands! Let me see hands!" The officer in front of me takes aim at the man who looks like he stopped to reload his pistol. He now holds his hands up, cursing and snarling.

Over the chaos, I hear what sounds like a strangled scream from deeper in the shadowy basement. The officer flinches, turning his head like he heard it, too. The man he's holding in place takes the opportunity to lunge, and all at once he drops back thanks to the bullet wound in his chest.

I keep moving, following that scream, walking past more rooms like the ones upstairs. There's a bare lightbulb glowing in one of them, the light spilling weakly on the concrete floor. "FBI!" I bellow before rounding the open doorway.

"Please—!" The arm around Tamara's throat tightens and cuts off her air while her bulging eyes look toward the gun pressed against her temple. She's sweating, filthy, her hair greasy and matted, her cheeks sunken.

"Here's how this is going to go." The man holding her looks as frantic as she does, just as sweaty and wild-eyed. "You're going to back up and get that gun off me, or her brains are going to paint the walls. She's not worth the trouble, anyway."

I can't get a good shot. Maybe if this was the big guy, Bruno, there would be a chance. Trying to get a shot off on a big guy like that would be like shooting the side of a barn. But this man is smaller. Compact. There isn't so much surface area.

The officers fall in place behind me, and now it's three to one. Sweat rolls down his temples as his gaze bounces back and forth. "Drop the weapon," I urge. "You're not getting out of here on your own. We have the place surrounded. It would be a waste of time to try."

He looks at me.

I look at him.

And he fires. Not at Tamara, though. At me.

A volley of shots pierce the air before I can react, making my ears ring by the time he drops to the floor thanks to a headshot from one of my two backups.

If only he was the single casualty.

Tamara sways, staring down at herself in time for the first bloom of red to begin seeping into her shirt.

There's no time to think. I can only react.

Tamara has barely hit the floor before I throw my body on top of hers while feet pound all around us. I cover her head with my arms, shouting to be heard over the cacophony. " Hostage injured!" I scream. "She's been shot! I need that stretcher in here!"

The problem is, I'm not sure anyone hears me, with the *pop, pop, pop* of gunfire, interrupting overhead and outside this little room. As soon as it's safe, I raise myself up on my palms and scan Tamara's trembling body. A bright patch of red is blooming across her stomach, soaking into the thin tank top she wears.

"You're going to be fine," I tell her, pressing a hand

against the wound. Blood seeps between my fingers, and I press harder, desperate to stop the flow.

"I ... please ..." That's all she says before her eyelids begin to flutter and her voice trails off.

"Tamara. I need you to keep your eyes open." I can barely hear myself over the chaos still unfolding around me. The roaring in my ears doesn't help as my heart races out of control. Adrenaline is still pumping through my system, leaving me laser focused on the task at hand.

Her eyelids flutter weakly and her chapped lips move, but no sound comes out. She's so pale. So thin. And there's so much blood. "Open your eyes!" I bark, and it's a relief when they open wide, like she's startled. That's fine. So long as I can get a reaction.

Maintaining pressure on the wound with one hand, I look around. My backup is gone, probably taking care of the situation elsewhere in the basement. We're alone in here with the dead man. I touch the fingers on my free hand to my earpiece. "Hostage has been shot! I need a stretcher down here now! We have an abdominal wound!"

It's a relief when EMTs reach us. Still, I hesitate before letting them take over—I don't want to let go of her, I don't want to see the blood pouring from the hole the bullet left. "We've got her," one of the men tells me, finally giving me a gentle nudge to get me out of the way so he can work.

A hand appears beside my face, and an upward glance reveals Siwak standing by my side. He helps me to my feet before looking down at Tamara in obvious concern. "They know what they're doing," he tells me, though I have to wonder which one of us he's trying to convince.

"I was so close to getting her out," I tell him, my eyes searching his lined face for understanding. I need him to know how close I came to freeing her before getting her shot.

"None of this is your fault, and you know it." He's sharp, a little harsh, but it gets through to me the way I got through to Tamara when I raised my voice. He's right, of course.

The problem is, it's not as easy to remember that when a woman's blood is all over me. "How's the rest of the team?" I ask, stepping out of the room, noting the restrained men now sitting in a row along one of the walls. They're battered, bloody, but not nearly enough.

"Everybody's in one piece. There's at least ten guys up there ready to spill their guts. Tough guys when they're terrorizing women, but now?" He chuckles darkly and shakes his head, leading the way up the stairs to the main level.

"No surprise there."

"There's somebody up here you're going to want to meet." He leads the way through several darkened rooms, most of which have been blasted by gunfire. The acrid smell of gunpowder hangs heavy in the air to mix with the smell of blood, and the combination is almost enough to choke me.

None of that matters once I set eyes on two men seated side-by-side on a small sofa in an office. The desk was turned on its side, almost like somebody was using it as a shield. There are bullet holes in the oak surface, wood splinters scattered around the floor.

Agent Siwak gestures toward the men. One of them I recognize right away from surveillance. He takes up two-thirds of the sofa, and is so enormous I have to wonder how something that looks so cheap can hold his weight.

But it's the man next to him who Agent Siwak addresses. The man with the shaved head that now gleams in the only working light in the room, positioned directly above him. His deep-set eyes practically burn holes into my head as he glares up at me. There's something unspeakably cold and calculated about him, like even at a moment like this, he's sizing up the situation and weighing his options for escape. Unlike the rest of them, who I hear protesting their innocence or cursing the agents currently placing them under arrest. His whole demeanor is unnerving, like the touch of a reptile's scales.

Siwak clears his throat before gesturing toward the man with one hand. "Mayer Truby, this is Agent River Collins. I know she's been anxious to meet you."

40

River

I need to be alone for a minute. I need my thoughts to stop racing. My heart is about to beat out of my chest by the time I pause to catch my breath outside the emergency room, where Tamara was just wheeled in. This time around, there was no closer hospital to where we located our victim. There was nothing to do but follow the ambulance as it tore through the night.

Emma steps outside and finds me standing with my back to the wall. My eyes open and close slowly as I drink in one deep breath after another. "That girl is a fighter," she concludes. "She made it through all of this already, so she's not going to give up easily." She is kind enough to keep her distance, her posture like mine, leaning against the wall for support. "Wow. Once the adrenaline leaves your system, it's a whole other story, isn't it?"

"You don't have to keep me engaged in conversation." Do I come off rude or ignorant? Do I care? The truth is, my social meter is at an all-time low. I have been more open and honest and forthcoming lately than I have as long as I can remember, sharing parts of myself I would rather keep locked up tight.

My therapist's voice rings out in my memory, echoing through the years. *The worst thing you can do is shut people out, close yourself off. No matter how much you feel like you should. It's a defense mechanism, yes, but from what? You have nothing left to defend yourself from. It's time to heal.*

"Have you seen—"

My eyes snap open at the sound of a familiar male voice. Aiden must've come out looking for me. Emma ducks back inside without a word, leaving the two of us alone. I wish she didn't feel like she had to do that. I doubt he came out here for anything romantic.

"How is she?" I ask, grateful to be able to look into a pair of friendly, understanding eyes. I wonder how friendly or understanding they would be if he knew exactly what's going through my head right now. The monsters that still live there, the ones who only come out at night.

"You saved her life," he announces point blank. There's fatigue touching the corners of his eyes and lacing its way through his words, but he's smiling. "Nothing less. She would've bled to death if it weren't for your quick thinking."

"Have you been able to repair the damage?"

"It's a little more extensive than that, I'm afraid. They're prepping an OR right now. We have her stable, until we get in there and see exactly what sort of damage was caused by that bullet, we don't know for sure. We do know she's bleeding internally, so there's no time to waste."

"Is she conscious?"

"in and out. She asked to see you—the woman who helped her."

Funny. I didn't think she would even remember me, seeing as how spotty her consciousness was at the time. "Can I see her for a minute?" I ask, already on my way inside before he has the chance to answer.

"Has to be very, very fast," he tells me, hot on my heels. "Don't make me regret this. We can't have her getting upset. She's under a lot of stress."

This is not the first time I've ever spoken to a victim in distress, though she might be in the worst shape of anyone I can remember. There are still staff running in all directions like chickens with their heads cut off, asking questions, barking orders. I have to sort of elbow my way through, albeit as gently as possible.

She is awake, her eyes blinking slowly as she stares at the ceiling. In the bright, glaring ER light, I now see the bruises running along one side of her face.

"Tamara?" I lower my voice, speaking softly, hoping to give her a moment of respite in the middle of so much chaos. Something for her to focus on, to hold onto. "Tamara, it's me. The doctor said you wanted to see me. My name is River." *And I'm still wearing your dried blood on my jacket.*

She turns her head as much as she can with her neck in a brace. "Thank you," she whispers, her eyes filling with tears. "Thank you, thank you."

"I'm just glad you got out of there. Is there anything you can tell me?" Because why not? I'm sure I'm pressing my luck, but we have this man in custody now. This monster. I have no doubt in my mind he's already spinning a defense with whatever slimy lawyer he has on retainer. It's never been more crucial that we nail this guy, now, while we have our chance.

"It was so stupid. It was all stupid. How is Beth?" Her eyes search my face almost desperately.

A chill runs down my spine. "Beth Clyburn?"

"Yeah. Is she okay?"

"We found her," I murmur, confused. "She's recovering. But she'll be all right."

"Thank God." Her eyes close and a pair of tears roll down her cheeks. "So stupid."

I can barely hear her over the beeping of monitors all around. I have to lean in close, hoping it doesn't upset her too much after what she's been through. The last thing she needs is to feel crowded at a time like this. "What happened? Are the two of you friends?"

"Yes." Her head bobs ever so slightly.

I glance up to find Aiden running interference for me, barring one of the nurses from kicking me out. I have to do this quickly. "How did you end up there? How did they get you?"

"We were gambling … " She winces in pain, and while my heart seizes in sympathy, I can't let up now. Not when we're so close. "Owed a lot of money."

"You were gambling? Both of you?"

"For fun. At first. Lost a lot of money." She takes a deep breath like she's trying to center herself before adding, "We found where the company was run. Went in. Asked for more time to pay."

That, I can imagine. Two pretty young women throwing themselves on the mercy of a heartless monster like the one we're dealing with. Gambling is not one of the businesses we managed to connect him to so far, but I have no doubt we would've gotten there eventually, given the time. And if there weren't a matter of two missing women to contend with.

"Told us we could … work off our debt." She opens her eyes and hits me with a knowing look that speaks a thousand words. "We said no. Tried to leave. They wouldn't let us. Next thing I knew, somebody grabbed me." Her eyes flutter shut and her face goes slack. She's unconscious.

"Excuse me, we really have to get her out of here." A pair of nurses look at me like I'm in their way, which I am. I have no choice but to step back and let them do their job, wheeling Tamara out of the room, while others follow behind, wheeling the machines she is still hooked up to. Aiden lingers for a moment, just long enough for us to exchange a meaningful glance before he follows the group.

The finished puzzle doesn't look exactly how I expected, but it's not surprising, either. They weren't using Truby's cleaning service. They were spending money every month on their gambling habits. Probably trying to hide it from their husbands, unable to squeeze enough money out of the monthly budget to pay back the full debt.

Emma is waiting for me along with a handful of agents out in the family lounge. "We need to go out to talk to Beth," I tell her, grim but determined. "Maybe this time, she'll tell us the truth."

41

River

Emma decides to wait out in the hall so Beth won't feel too overwhelmed. "Good luck," she whispers, taking my jacket for me so I don't present too ugly a picture for a woman who is still recovering from trauma.

"Is it true?" Hope rings out in Beth's voice the second she recognizes me in the doorway. She was transferred out of the ICU earlier in the day and is now in a regular, smaller room on the fourth floor. Down below us, Tamara is about to undergo surgery. And miles away, Mayer Truby is being questioned and booked. But I still don't have the full story, and I won't until the woman sitting up in bed with a book in her lap opens up and gives me the full rundown of what she and Tamara went through.

I enter the room and take a seat in a chair next to the bed. "They told you?" I ask. "About Tamara?"

"It must have been on the news, I guess. My husband

called to tell me. How is she? Did you find her yourself? What did she say? Is she—"

I have to hold up a hand to stop her. As it is, she's getting overly excited, almost hyperventilating. "One thing at a time," I murmur. "I did find her myself, along with a lot of others. She's having surgery right now. There was a little bit of a struggle once we found the place, but we took everyone there in custody. Including the ringleader," I conclude, watching her carefully.

It's like a veil drops in front of her face, dimming the light in her eyes. "Good. Thank you. Thank you so much. I was afraid … for my family … " Bowing her head, she trembles, and a tear drips from her chin onto the flowered hospital gown.

"She was conscious for a little while, once we brought her here. Beth, I need you to be honest with me now."

"What do you mean?" She sniffles, glancing my way before running a hand under her eyes.

"It wasn't a coincidence, you and Tamara being kidnapped at the same time was it?" I prompt. Somehow, I can still manage to sound gentle. I have to remember she's a victim. She didn't ask to be kidnapped, and I'm sure whatever she got into, she got into it with no idea how serious the consequences could be. The sort of thing people do all the time.

"What do you mean?" she asks again.

"Beth, I'm not here to judge you. I only need the truth, so we can build a proper case against this man. How were you involved with him? How are you involved with Tamara?"

"We're friendly," she admits with a shrug. "We see each other around, sometimes meet up at Starbucks or the nail salon. Not planned, you know. Just the sort of thing that happens when you live in the same community."

"And which one of you started gambling first?"

Her soft gasp is all the confirmation I need. Not that I thought Tamara was making something up, but I didn't want to give Beth a chance to talk her way out of it or sidestep the truth. "How ... I mean, what ... ?"

"I understand wanting to keep something like that a secret, but withholding information is only going to hurt our case. How much money did you owe?"

It's clear when she comes to the realization there's no point in keeping up the act. Her shoulders sink along with the energy in her voice. "A lot. Thousands. I kept telling myself I could get a handle on things, but it only got worse and worse. I was trapped. It was a nightmare."

"I'm sure it was overwhelming." That's what a predator like Truby counts on. Waiting until a situation snowballs, until a person can't possibly dig their way out of the debt they've amassed.

"We didn't know what to do. And we're not the only ones who dabble a little," she insists. "I'm not trying to get anybody in trouble or anything like that. It's just something some of the moms do for fun online. A diversion. I know one or two who won enough to treat themselves to things, to take their kids on vacation even. I was hoping I could make a little extra money to put into my business."

She stares down at her folded hands, her breathing shaky. Like she's trying to control her emotions. "But it just got worse and worse. I started getting phone calls, asking for money. I would block the numbers, but they would just call back from different numbers every time. I told myself I should come clean with my husband, but I'm too embarrassed. And I was afraid ... I was afraid he wouldn't be able to forgive me. For getting us into debt, I mean. Like he would never trust me again."

"So you decided ... "

"To find out where the guy who ran things worked. I heard something about a house cleaning service he runs and got the address of the business."

She barks out a sharp laugh. "It's so stupid, looking back. How could we be so stupid? What, was he going to be like, sure, your debts are forgiven, you're free to go? Who did we think we were kidding? We were only kidding ourselves. But ... I don't know," she concludes with a weak shrug. "I guess I never imagined there were really people like that in the world. You see it on TV, these cruel, heartless monsters who only see people as dollar signs. I figured he would be willing to work with us so long as it meant getting his money."

"But he wasn't willing to work with you?"

Her short laughter is cold. Brutal. "When we got there and said we wanted to speak to the guy who runs things, we had to wait a little while. He didn't work out of that office all the time. But he eventually showed up, and we were taken to a little office in the back. And that was when he gave us an ultimatum."

I have a pretty strong feeling what that ultimatum involved, but I wait rather than filling in the blanks for her.

"Either we were going to sleep with his clients to pay off our debt, or he was going to hurt our kids. He knew their names," she whispers in a voice tight with desperation, edged with panic. "Don't you see? He already knew about us. Where we live, what our husbands do, what we do—our habits, that kind of thing. It's like he had eyes everywhere."

"There's a good chance he did," I point out. "He has an extensive network."

"Anyway, we said no, of course. I wasn't going to let him use us like that. I think we were too shocked to even believe he was serious at first. But then ... when we went to leave ... "

"You found out how serious he was," I conclude. She nods slowly, sniffling again. "What did he do?"

"Told us we weren't going anywhere. The next thing I knew, that big guy grabbed me from behind."

She looks at me, eyes wild, her chin quivering. "I'm sorry. Really, I am. I wasn't trying to hurt your investigation, I swear. I just didn't want my family to know. I didn't want anybody to know. I knew Tam would feel the same way, too. We promised to keep it a secret, just between the two of us."

I understand where she's coming from, even if I don't agree. Some situations are too important, too fraught with danger to worry about saving face. Did she think the truth would never come out?

"I hope she's okay," she breathes, her eyes drifting shut as her head touches the pillow behind it. "Please, let her be okay."

"She's in good hands." I stand, unsure what to say

now. It's none of my business what anyone does with their money and their free time, but she withheld information we might have been able to use. Rather than chasing our tails, we could have asked around about this gambling operation Mayer has been running. I doubt Beth and Tamara are the only ones who got sucked in – and I wouldn't doubt the missing women from across the state were also involved in similar traps. Telling themselves they were only having a little fun, that they could handle the repercussions, that they'd stop before it became a problem. There isn't a gambler alive who hasn't told themselves the same thing.

With a promise to keep Beth posted, I leave the room, getting as far as the door before she asks, "You're not going to tell my husband, are you? Please, Agent Collins. Let me do that on my own."

"It's none of my business," I remind her, turning my head to look back over my shoulder. "That's up to you. But he is going to find out, either way, as the investigation and the trial come up. You should figure out what you're going to say to him now, before he finds out some other way."

"You're right. Thank you," she whispers as fresh tears fill her eyes. I feel awkward leaving her like this, but there's still more work to be done. I doubt a man as connected as Truby will throw up his hands and admit defeat easily. He'll have a trick up his sleeve, no doubt.

The real trick is going to be outsmarting him.

42

River

I'm used to having nightmares. They're one thing about my life that never changes. But sitting in front of my boss and being told the man we've hunted night and day is about to be released on bail not twelve hours after we brought him in is the sort of nightmare I can't wake up from.

"You can't be serious," I blurt out.

"This isn't so surprising." Agent Siwak drains what's left in his coffee cup and immediately looks regretful when he stares into it, like he's double checking to make sure there's nothing left. To call it a late night would be a vast understatement.

"They can't do this. They can't!" I can say it all I want, I can insist until I'm blue in the face, but I know it doesn't make a difference. Our so-called justice system happens to benefit most the people with the money to buy their way out of anything. In his case, he can afford a slimeball lawyer who will get him out of trouble.

"You're tilting at windmills," Siwak informs me with a weary sigh. "We both know this is going to end badly."

"The man has the financial means to skip the country! Why don't they take that into account?" I'm too upset to sit still, almost jumping out of the chair when I can't literally jump out of my own skin. I'm that worked up, frustrated and disappointed, and very much wishing I could throw something through a window. All this work, all this effort. All the pain this man has caused. "There has to be something we can do."

Siwak perches on one corner of his desk, rubbing the back of his neck with one hand. "Short of convincing the DA he's making a mistake, there's not much else within our power. We've done everything we can, River. You have to believe that."

"No way." It's unthinkable. I can't believe I heard that come out of his mouth, honestly. "We're not giving up like this. If the DA isn't going to demand they take a bail agreement off the table, it only means nobody has convinced him yet."

"Yet?" He sighs, shaking his head. "Please, don't start a fight we can't win. I don't need one of my agents alienating the district attorney."

Rather than calling the office and arranging a meeting—there's no time for that—I head straight for the DA's office. Siwak has only one condition, that he go along with me. "I'll do the talking," he warns as he drives us into town. "Understood?"

"This is my case."

"You are my agent," he reminds me, and I hear the irritation that has leaked into his voice. We're all tired, on edge right now, especially after our late night. It's better not to fight with him—besides, I barely have the energy. I can hardly keep my eyes open, adrenaline or no adrenaline. I need to save my energy for the DA when we arrive.

As it turns out, Siwak was thinking along the right lines when he insisted on leading the way. His name and position earn a little more courtesy than mine. "We're here to see the DA," he announces once we reach the courthouse, where Truby's preliminary hearing is due to be held any minute. The energy around here is almost frantic. Bodies moving all directions, voices overlapping, phones ringing. It's enough to make me practically vibrate with apprehension – I can't stand the sense of being so closed in, surrounded.

Some situations are worth putting up with discomfort, and this one qualifies. I stand straight and tall next to Agent Siwak as he gives the clerk behind the desk his most withering stare. "Immediately," he adds. "It's extremely urgent."

"Mr. Harrison is prepping for a hearing at the moment."

"That's why we're here," I blurt out. Siwak can take the lead while we're talking to DA Harrison. He never said anything about a clerk. "It's crucial we see him before the hearing."

Her phone rings and she picks it up, her brows pulling together like she's worried. I'm fairly sure I can guess who's on the other end of the line. "Yes, sir," she murmurs, glancing at us before adding, "All right. I will."

Replacing the receiver in its cradle and standing, she

announces, "Follow me. He says he can give you three minutes."

Three minutes. How can so much ride on three short minutes? With my heart in my throat, I follow Siwak past the desk and through the door behind it. On the other side waits District Attorney Harrison, a handsome, middle-aged man whose face I recognize from various news reports. "I don't have a lot of time," he reminds us, dispensing with pleasantries. "What is it you have to say?"

I was supposed to stay silent. To let the boss do the talking. Yet as soon as the question is asked, my mouth opens and words come tumbling out almost on top of each other. "You cannot allow bail for Truby."

Agent Siwak clicks his tongue and shakes his head slightly while the DA tips his head, studying me. "And you are … "

"Agent River Collins. I've led the investigation into Truby and his businesses. And I am telling you, this man cannot be allowed bail."

"Agent, with respect, certain procedures—"

"Don't give me that," I fire back before anybody can tell me to rethink my approach. There's no time for that now. The clock is ticking faster than it ever has. "This man has shell accounts set up all over the world. Endless resources. The second he is out, he is gone. The case we are building against him involves human trafficking. Illegal gambling operations. Kidnapping. Extortion. We are currently in the process of linking him to a number of missing person's cases across the state of Virginia. At this point, there is no telling how far his influence stretches – and we will never find out if he is granted bail and flees. He will. I know it."

"You can't know that."

"And yet somehow, I do—and I would bet you know it, too," I add. His eyes widen slightly, but he doesn't say a word. I might have gone too far, but it's too late to care.

"All we're asking is that Truby be kept where he is, not a threat to anyone, and can be monitored," Agent Siwak concludes. "This is a very dangerous man. He has the resources to disappear and stay gone as long as he wants. There is no telling just yet how many lives he has destroyed and how many more he could destroy if he is allowed to continue operating the way he has. He does not deserve freedom and is most definitely a threat to the public."

"Just try," I beg softly, barely stopping short of wringing my hands and falling to my knees. "Please. If you saw the condition those women were in when we found them, you would know there is no way he should see the light of day. This is the first step to making sure he won't anymore."

There's a brief knock at the door before it squeaks open behind me. "Sir, they're calling for you in the courtroom."

I can't breathe. I'm not even sure I can blink. All I can do is stare at the man in front of me, willing him to speak the words we need to hear.

With a soft sigh, he nods. "All right. No bail. I'll recommend he be held until trial."

"Thank you. Thank you so much." I could kiss him, honestly. There's no guarantee the judge will agree with the DA's recommendation, but at least now we have a chance of making this man pay for everything he's done. For right now, it's a win.

"Come on." Siwak's jaw tightens while he lowers his brow. "We're already here. Might as well get a front row seat for the show."

I happily take one of the rolls from the bread basket when Aiden offers it. "We still have a long way to go," I point out before tearing off a piece of bread and using it to sop up some of the flavorful sauce on my plate. I will never turn down a nice steak or piece of seafood, but a hole in the wall Italian restaurant is much more my speed. Somewhere I can hide in a booth in the back corner and drown my sorrows in a bowl full of carbs.

"But at least you know that guy isn't going anywhere."

"You should've seen his face when the judge decided to hold him without bail." The memory makes me grin in grim satisfaction. "For a second there, it looked like he was going to punch his lawyer."

His mouth twitches like he's trying to hold back a laugh. "Would it sound weird if I say I'm proud of you?"

"Not weird," I tell him, shaking my head gently. "It's nice. Thank you. But honestly, it was pretty risky. I might've ended up talking myself out of a job."

"But you didn't, and those women have you to thank. Not just them, either. Anyone else that monster has preyed upon or would prey upon if given the chance. This is a win for you." It's unusual for me to spend time with someone so relentlessly positive. Even Emma has her dark moments, no matter how hard she fights to brighten up my mood– usually at the worst possible time, when I want anything but to be brightened up.

It doesn't seem like he has to try hard, either. He's that skilled looking at the bright side. What would it mean, having someone like that in my life?

I can't believe I'm thinking along those lines, but there's no denying it. When he asked me to dinner during my post-hearing visit to the hospital, I didn't have to think about my reply. In fact, I didn't realize until the question came out of his mouth how hard I was hoping he would ask. I can see myself getting to know him.

More surprising, I can see myself wanting him to know me. Maybe it's time to let down some of my walls, since it feels pretty nice to be seen and heard.

When my phone buzzes, I jump and reach for it purely out of reflex. Our eyes meet and we exchange a knowing grin. "Go ahead," he murmurs, twirling pasta on his fork. I still feel a little guilty as I answer Emma's call.

"We have a missing ten-year-old girl," she reports, tension in her voice. "Siwak just called for all hands on deck. You know what that means."

Ten years old. My hands are shaking and my body goes cold, but somehow I manage to croak, "I'll be there."

"A new emergency?" Aiden asks, wearing a chagrined expression.

"I'm so sorry. Please, understand the last thing I want to do right now is to leave." And that is so true. I can't find the words to make him understand this is more than lip service. For the first time in as long as I can remember, I have found peace in the presence of another person. I don't want to lose it.

"I get it. Remember, I'm pretty much on call all the time, too. And I would be the world's biggest hypocrite if I gave you a hard time over the sort of thing that happens to me at least twice a week." He slides out of the booth and refuses my offer to split the check. "Go ahead. Do your job, Agent Collins."

His hand finds mine, holding me in place as we stand face to face beside the table. "One thing. You have a little bit of sauce at the corner of your mouth."

He leans down, pressing a soft, lingering kiss against my lips. He tastes like tomatoes and garlic, a combination I already enjoyed but could learn to love.

"There you go. Got it." His smile sends a shiver down my spine before he squeezes my hand, then releases it. "Go ahead, River Collins. Go off and be a hero. You know where to find me when you get back."

I do. And I will.

Thank you for reading River's Edge. I hope you enjoyed the book. Can't wait to find out what happens to River next? **Get River's Shadow Now!**

In the sleepy town of Charlottesville, Virginia, ten-year-old Sarah Truby vanishes without a trace, shaking the community to its core. FBI agent River Collins is tasked with unraveling the mystery of the missing girl, but the shadows of her own traumatic past loom large over her. Twenty years have passed since River escaped her abductor, yet the scars of her harrowing past linger—her captor has never been caught.

While River's sister embraces the perfect life of marriage and motherhood—a life that River feels perpetually distant from—River immerses herself in the case, driven by the desire to prevent another family from suffering as she once did.

As she digs deeper, River uncovers a horrifying reality: Sarah has been engaged in conversations with an adult man in an online game, who masqueraded as her friend. This seemingly charming youth pastor hides a sinister agenda.

As River races against the clock to rescue Sarah, her investigation unveils a chilling network of child predators, revealing that Sarah's abduction is merely the tip of the iceberg. Each lead forces River to confront her own buried fears and the pervasive dangers that technology poses to children.

Can she save Sarah and other kids before it's too late? Or will her relentless pursuit endanger her own life? In *River's Shadow*, River Collins faces her greatest challenge yet, where the line between protector and prey blurs, and the darkness threatens to consume them all.

Suspenseful and full of thrills, River's Edge is the second book in a new addicting FBI mystery series from bestselling and 3-time Silver Falchion award winning author Kate Gable.

Get River's Shadow Now!

If you enjoyed this book, please don't forget to leave a review on Amazon and Goodreads! Reviews help me find new readers.

If you have any issues with anything in the book or find any typos, please email me at Kate@kategable.com. Thank you so much for reading!

Also by Kate Gable

FBI Agent River Collins Mystery Thriller
River's Edge (Book 1)
River's Shadow (Book 2)

Detective Kaitlyn Carr Psychological Mystery series
Girl Missing (Book 1)
Girl Lost (Book 2)
Girl Found (Book 3)
Girl Taken (Book 4)
Girl Forgotten (Book 5)
Gone Too Soon (Book 6)
Gone Forever (Book 7)
Whispers in the Sand (Book 8)

Girl Hidden (FREE Novella)

FBI Agent Alexis Forest Mystery Thriller

Forest of Silence
Forest of Shadows
Forest of Secrets
Forest of Lies
Forest of Obsession
Forest of Regrets
Forest of Deception

Detective Charlotte Pierce Psychological Mystery series
Last Breath
Nameless Girl
Missing Lives
Girl in the Lake

About Kate Gable

Kate Gable loves a good mystery that is full of suspense. She grew up devouring psychological thrillers and crime novels as well as movies, tv shows and true crime.

Her favorite stories are the ones that are centered on families with lots of secrets and lies as well as many twists and turns. Her novels have elements of psychological suspense, thriller, mystery and romance.

Kate Gable lives near Palm Springs, CA with her husband, son, a dog and a cat. She has spent more than twenty years in Southern California and finds inspiration from its cities, canyons, deserts, and small mountain towns.

She graduated from University of Southern California with a Bachelor's degree in Mathematics. After pursuing graduate studies in mathematics, she switched gears and got her MA in Creative Writing and English from Western New Mexico University and her PhD in Education from Old Dominion University.

Writing has always been her passion and obsession. Kate is also a USA Today Bestselling author of romantic suspense under another pen name.

Write her here:
Kate@kategable.com

Check out her books here:
www.kategable.com

Sign up for my newsletter:
https://www.subscribepage.com/kategableviplist

Join my Facebook Group:
https://www.facebook.com/groups/833851020557518

Bonus Points: Follow me on BookBub and Goodreads!

https://www.bookbub.com/authors/kate-gable

https://www.goodreads.com/author/show/21534224.Kate_Gable

amazon.com/Kate-Gable/e/B095XFCLL7

facebook.com/KateGableAuthor

bookbub.com/authors/kate-gable

instagram.com/kategablebooks

tiktok.com/@kategablebooks

Printed in Great Britain
by Amazon